IN PRAISE OF

The Big Bad

"*The Big Bad* is both thought-provoking and thrilling. Readers will discover an unflinching look at the moral complexities of combat, gender on the battlefield, and justice. Sometimes in war, the law falls silent."

—Aramis Calderon, author of *Fugitive Son* and USMC veteran

"Brad Huestis portrays in *The Big Bad* that military unit loyalties can remain for a lifetime, depending on how firmly a cult of personality is imprinted on the group by its leader. The three-star commanding the war zone of Iraq in 2006 sees his mission as transitioning to defensive force protection, which is at complete odds with Colonel Wolfe and his brigade. The young Army JAG major agonizes over the heartbreakingly stark realities she discovers. They will be operative in every conflict we engage in today and in the future, where combatants blend with civilians. A compelling and suspenseful read about details that challenge trigger-pullers and their leadership every day on our behalf. Freedom is not free, and these struggles to implement consistent rules of engagement are part of the cost."

—Richard K. Perkins, author of *The Tide Waits for No Woman* and captain (US Navy, Ret.),

"As an Air Force flyboy, I appreciate the difference between dropping bombs from thousands of feet versus being eye to eye with potential enemy combatants. *The Big Bad* opened my eyes to the challenges faced by our young soldiers as I followed Major Jessica Gilbert as she investigates an explosive war-crime allegation, explores the confusion in making split-second life-and-death battlefield decisions, and struggles to reconcile her commitment to justice with the military's desire to protect its reputation. A thrilling story that raises important issues—I highly recommend it."

—Richard Hess, author of *High Flight: A Pilot's Journey Through Life* and *Night of the Bear*, and colonel (US Air Force, Ret.),

"Brad Huestis focuses *The Big Bad* on the harsh reality that wars are won and lost accompanied by the deaths of combatants on both sides of the conflict. The drama surrounding the actions of Colonel Mike 'The Big Bad' Wolfe forcing his troops to commit extreme cruelty is enhanced by telling the story from the perspective of Jessica Gilbert, a US Army JAG Corps major, deployed to Iraq in 2006."

—Ray Collins, author of *The General's Briefcase*, *Motive for Murder*, and *Setup*, and Korean War combat infantry NCO

"A great story that raises important questions, *The Big Bad* is a five-star novel. The tension escalates from page one as the story's gutsy protagonist, Major Jessica Gilbert, faces down a revered Army commander accused of committing war crimes in Iraq. As Gilbert fearlessly pursues military justice, she confronts sharp questions about rules of engagement, laws of war, and command responsibility—all questions urgent in America today."

—Carolyn Warmbold, author of *Peripheral Vision*

"Huestis writes with the voice of experience, weaving together an exciting tale that keeps the pages turning through use of brisk pacing, exceptional character work, and high-tension stakes. This one is a winner!"

> —Justin Herzog, author of the Blue Moon Investigations Boston series

"Brad Huestis does it again! Another great military thriller, this time set in the sand and palaces of Iraq, with the main characters in a battle of wits complicated by the difference in ranks, age, and sex. Major Jessica Gilbert investigates the wily, charismatic infantry colonel, and the resulting investigation, trial prep, and courtroom battle is a master class on legal ethics and the military loyalty. I'm already wondering who will play them in the movie!"

> —Genie Hughes, author of *Frauline Zen: The Art and Zen of Retirement*

"Powerful read. Like reading or watching *Apocalypse Now* and *Platoon*, but with a current war scenario that Global War on Terror veterans can relate to. My wife and I could not put this book down!"

> —Nathan Aguinaga, author of *Lifer: My Epic Journey as a US Army Paratrooper* and master sergeant (US Army, Ret.)

"This searing legal thriller authentically exposes the moral and legal chaos of today's asymmetrical battlefield. Through the eyes of an idealistic young attorney, the fog of war is laid bare—where right, wrong, and duty blur. Writing with authority, Huestis's story cuts to the bone. In a time when leaders ignore the human cost, this story demands: What does justice look like in war? Who decides—and who pays the price?"

> —Mickey Miller, colonel (US Army, Ret.)

"*The Big Bad* brought me straight back to my time serving as a judge advocate in Iraq. Its authenticity put a lump in my throat and took my breath away. It doesn't pull any punches and lays bare the complex legal and ethical issues military attorneys face during combat. Brad Huestis also gives his idealistic protagonist, Major Jessica Gilbert, a pitch-perfect voice. This highly engaging and thought-provoking read has something for everyone: mystery, military justice, thrills. It offers no simple answers and forces you to ponder the ethical and legal issues in a life or death environment. I highly recommend it!"

—Monica Lynch, former US Army judge advocate

"Brad Huestis was the U.S. Army's top prosecutor in Iraq, and his second novel shows why. *The Big Bad* exposes the limitations of command, the ambiguity of ROE, and the injustice that can arise when the warrior's code of honor collides with explosive allegations and criminal investigations. In this gritty and far-too-real story, the fog of war extends from the battlefield to the courtroom and the questions it raises will most certainly stick with you."

—Bill Delehunt, lieutenant colonel (US Air Force, Ret.)

"A superbly written and authentic account. Through vividly rendered characters, Brad Huestis places readers in the middle of complex and competing interests. Entertaining and thought-provoking, *The Big Bad* provides an honest glimpse into the emotional, physical, and human toll of combat, command, and the pursuit of objective truths under the most trying circumstances."

—Randolph Swansiger, colonel (US Army, Ret.)

"Brad Huestis has done it again, following his terrific first novel *Ahab* with a true page-turner. *The Big Bad* superbly captures the nuances and challenges faced by soldiers on today's battlefield and in the legal arena. When you finish the last page of the story, I am confident that you will say to yourself that this tale is on par with, or even better than *A Few Good Men*."

>—Scott Black, lieutenant general (US Army, Ret.), 37th judge advocate general of the US Army

"Brad Huestis masterfully captures the raw, unvarnished realities of the battlefield in *The Big Bad*. Through stark dialogue and unflinching narrative, he transports the reader back to the most difficult moments of the Iraq conflict—viewed through the eyes of those directly involved. The book lays bare not only the operational and moral challenges of counterinsurgency warfare, but also the deep cultural misunderstandings, gender dynamics, and the harrowing psychological toll of decisions made in the fog of war. Huestis does not shy away from the complexities of war crimes and command responsibility, making this a gripping, important contribution to the literature on military justice and modern armed conflict."

>—Dr. Gurgen Petrossian, LLM, International Criminal Law Research Unit, Friedrich-Alexander-Universität

The Big Bad
by Brad Huestis

© Copyright 2025 Brad Huestis

ISBN 979-8-88824-777-8

All rights reserved. No part of this publication may be reproduced, stored in a retrieval system, or transmitted in any form or by any means—electronic, mechanical, photocopy, recording, or any other—except for brief quotations in printed reviews, without the prior written permission of the author.

This is a work of fiction. All the characters in this book are fictitious, and any resemblance to actual persons, living or dead, is purely coincidental. The names, incidents, dialogue, and opinions expressed are products of the author's imagination and are not to be construed as real.

Published by

3705 Shore Drive
Virginia Beach, VA 23455
800–435–4811
www.koehlerbooks.com

THE BIG BAD

BRAD HUESTIS

VIRGINIA BEACH
CAPE CHARLES

For those who fight for justice one case at a time,
and for Maya, because sometimes fairytale monsters are real.

THE AUTHOR'S DISCLAIMER

The Big Bad is a work of fiction. While it refers to material from the real world, including references to real places and events, Jessica Gilbert and her fellow characters are fictional. They and their dialogue are figments of my imagination.

Defense Office of Prepublication and Security Review Disclaimer

The views expressed in this publication are those of the author and do not necessarily reflect the official policy or position of the Department of Defense or the US government. The public release clearance of this publication by the Department of Defense does not imply Department of Defense endorsement or factual accuracy of the material.

PROLOGUE

Jess
Heidelberg, Germany
19 October 2005

The comforting hum of Heidelberg's Römer Strasse doesn't work its usual magic on me this crisp fall afternoon. I shift restlessly, close one thick file, and grab another one. *Damn, another drug case*, I think. How many shroom-heads do I need to put away before they get the message? Stop bringing your psychedelic souvenirs back from Amsterdam. On the plus side, the drug cases do guarantee full employment for me as the Army's chief of military justice.

My work used to satisfy me. Looking back, the whirlwind of entry-level JAG jobs at Fort Carson—legal assistance, administrative and operational law, and military justice—were a blur. Then, on to a year of legal studies at the JAG school, promotion to major, and selection to lead the military justice team here at V Corps. But now, I feel stuck in Germany while my friends and colleagues are deployed to either Afghanistan or Iraq.

I shake my head and smile at my improbable discontent. Nobody was shocked when I followed my father into the law. But following my grandfather into the Army? No one saw that coming. And now, I long to deploy. My mom and dad would take out a restraining order to prevent it.

My first memory of my dad was when I asked my mom why he was never home in time for dinner. "He's a very important man," she had explained. "A partner in a big law firm." I was too young to grasp the meaning of "law firm" or "partner," but I could hear the pride in my mother's voice. That was enough. It inspired my early and outsized desire to practice law. So, when most of my sorority sisters graduated, married, and started families, I eagerly set off for law school. Then, when my brainy, learned classmates pursued clerkships and accepted lucrative job offers, I surprised everyone by joining the Army.

Why? I really don't know. Maybe it was the September 11th attacks. Maybe it was an unquenched thirst for adventure. Maybe I just didn't want to join my dad's firm right away. Anyway, I don't regret it . . . not really. The duty in Heidelberg is good and tonight, I'll head to my favorite beer garden for a cold *Hefeweizen* and a crispy schnitzel. The rub is that I know I'll be too distracted to savor it. I guess that's just how my brain is wired. I like to be in the middle of things.

My office door swings open. Colonel Denise Miller strides in, snapping me out of my melancholy thoughts. She's a head-turning officer whose quiet confidence shines through. This means she's often the center of attention—whether she wants to be or not. I don't have that problem. I am pretty in a way that never gets in the way of commanders taking my legal advice seriously. My Southern European complexion hints of the Mediterranean, and I keep myself lean (and sane) with my early morning runs. I always try to project energy and confidence because that is especially important in my chosen line of work.

"Jess," Miller says, "we've got a meeting with the general in thirty minutes."

It's not often that I'm summoned to the general's office. So, I raise an eyebrow, straighten my files, and follow Colonel Miller across the street to the commanding general's office in his historic headquarters. Truth be told, we are both star-struck by Lieutenant General Theodore J. Benetti. He is a big, broad-shouldered tanker, but not your stereotypical combat arms knuckle-dragger. A former West Point political science professor, he holds master's degrees from Harvard in public administration and national security. He's been the driving force for reconstruction efforts in Iraq since 2004, when he commanded the 1st Cavalry Division in Baghdad.

We arrive to a buzz of activity in Benetti's oversized conference room. Officers bustle around, preparing for a no-notice, all-hands meeting. Benetti enters. His presence draws every eye, and a hush falls over the room. He's wearing his dress uniform decked out with an impressive array of medals.

"At ease," he says, taking his place at the head of the oak conference table where General Eisenhower once presided.

Benetti scans the room as we all sit. "Colonel," he greets my boss with a nod, "thank you for joining us."

"Sir, I've brought my chief of justice, Major Jessica Gilbert," she says, looking over at me. Her use of my full name surprises me. My parents did name me Jessica, but I've been known as Jess ever since I joined the Army. Over the years, I've grown to prefer it.

I nod from my seat in a row of chairs lined up along the back wall. It's my first time attending a Corps staff meeting, and I can't help feeling both excited and nervous.

"Please, everyone, let's get started," General Benetti says. He begins by telling us that we will deploy. His words are deliberate, painting a picture of the situation currently unfolding in Iraq. He stresses the challenges, the opportunities, and the need for capable minds and steady hands to guide the way.

Everyone in the room is aware that Benetti recently deployed to Iraq with the Texas-based 1st Cavalry Division. Their mission was to subdue the Baghdad militias controlled by Moqtada al-Sadr. Benetti and his planners studied maps showing access to electricity and running water against those showing insurgent activity. The correlation between a lack of services and terrorist incidents was obvious, and Benetti concluded that the only way to win Baghdad was through outreach and reconstruction. He shifted his unit's focus from combat operations to improving life for the locals. While some troopers fought bloody urban battles, only a few blocks away others assisted contractors with power grid repairs. His tactics were hailed as a success and used as an example for follow-on units to emulate.

"Early next year," Benetti continues, "we will deploy to implement outreach and reconstruction efforts across Iraq. The 1st Cav made great progress in Baghdad, and now it's time to extend those efforts to the whole country. The people of Iraq need to view us as partners working together for a better future."

I'm drawn in by Benetti's vision. I take a deep breath. This is it, the call to serve in a time and place that really matters.

"As for you, Colonel Miller," Benetti turns his gaze toward my boss. "Your leadership will be essential in guiding the legal, fiscal, and administrative complexities of our mission."

Colonel Miller also nods. I sense an unspoken understanding between them. She could retire, move on to a quieter chapter of her life. But, she won't. Something about this mission calls to her, and I respect her for it.

"Major Gilbert," Benetti says, addressing me directly, "your work as a prosecutor is impressive, and I believe your skills will be critical in our efforts to build up the rule of law in Iraq."

His remark catches me by surprise. I smile and nod. The prospect of deploying to a war zone, a place I've only read about and seen on news reports, is exhilarating. I am flat-out thrilled I will be given the chance to deploy with Benetti. The man is a legend.

General Benetti takes a few seconds to make deliberate eye contact with each person in the room. Then he says, "Welcome to the team. We've got about ten months to prepare for deployment and educate ourselves on how to get a country back on its feet. Let's make sure we get it right."

As we leave the meeting, I feel the tug of something that will challenge, test, and define me. This is the challenge I've been hoping for, one that will allow me to walk in my grandfather's boots and define my career. Still, it is daunting.

I turn to Colonel Miller. "Get ready, Jess," she says, giving me a big smile and a thumbs-up. "This is going to be the adventure of a lifetime."

CHAPTER 1

Wolfe
Fort Campbell, Kentucky
16 January 2006

Colonel Mike "the Big Bad" Wolfe wakes. He tries to go back to sleep, but his brain races. There is nothing in the world like preparing soldiers for combat. If twenty-five years of leading soldiers has taught him anything, it's that training is fun. Training is important. But preparing for a specific deployment pulls every goddamn thing together in a way that's impossible to replicate. He grins to himself. This gift of supreme focus has fallen onto him and his unit. And goddamn, the Big Bad is burning to get started.

He is too jacked-up to stay in bed. So, he rises at 04:30 instead of his customary 05:30. He races through his morning lifts—shoulders and back today—and jogs from his house on Colonels' Row over to the barracks for 06:30 physical training with his men—the Raiders of the 7th Brigade Combat Team. With an extra hour to kill, he heads into his spotless office to fire up the computer and make some coffee. Down the hall, he sees a light on in the brigade operations shop.

"Jackson!" he bellows.

"Moving, sir!" the husky brigade S-3 answers, making his way to Wolfe's office at double-time. "Sir?" Jackson asks, pausing in Wolfe's doorway to wait for permission to enter.

"Come in, Ernie," Wolfe says, grinning. "Have a seat. We've got some news."

Major Ernie Jackson sits in one of the padded leather chairs facing Wolfe's broad, faux-oak desk. He waits silently while Wolfe pours himself a coffee and takes a big swig. "Uncle Sugar has given us a belated Christmas gift, Ernie-boy," Wolfe announces with a broad grin, raising his mug in a celebratory salute. "He's sending us on an all-expense paid trip to the desert."

"When?" Jackson asks, leaning forward.

And that's exactly why Wolfe loves him. Ernie is always thinking. He's always planning. He's a goddamn wizard of war.

"We got three months, Ernie. Going to Iraq with the Division. They'll be in Tikrit, and our battlespace will be the Sunni Triangle."

"The triangle of death?"

"You got it, Bubba. We're going to take control of that godforsaken shit hole and rid it of insurgents."

"Jesus, three months," Jackson whistles.

"You're right." Wolfe grins. "It'll be tight, and every second is precious."

Fort Campbell, Kentucky
21 January 2006

Colonel Wolfe immediately shifted his staff from their normal weekly staff call to daily staff calls after the call came in to prepare to deploy. One week in, he's already concluded that his staff isn't embracing their new reality quickly enough. They aren't moving quickly enough. They aren't aggressive enough. They aren't embracing their opportunity to get things right. And it's making him angry. Very angry.

Wolfe enters the brigade conference room at 09:00 sharp for Friday's meeting.

Jackson shouts, "Room, attention!"

Wolfe slowly makes his way to the head of the table, takes a seat in his padded leather swivel chair, and pauses for a ten count before calling out a gruff, "At ease."

After everyone takes their seats, he says, "I lost twelve men in Panama due to lack of preparation. It will not happen again." He lets his words hang in the air. "None of you will let that happen. Not for lack of goddamn preparation. Understood?"

"Yes, sir!" they answer in unison.

Back when Wolfe took command of the Raiders, he planned to jump into the driver's seat and drive the brigade like he'd stolen it. He intended to use his two years in command to burn rubber, drive as hard and fast as humanly possible, and turn his Raiders into a lean, mean warfighting machine. Now, instead of working to prep for some vague, imaginary foe, he suddenly possesses a concrete mission to deploy.

Wolfe leans back in his chair and grins, excited by what fate has thrown his way. The key to getting everyone home safe, he knows, will be tough and realistic training. That's the only way to ensure everyone knows what the hell they're doing, and his staff needs to embrace that fact now. They have a once-in-a-career opportunity to concentrate their efforts on fighting a specific enemy, on a specific terrain, in a specific climate. Wolfe relishes it and will jolt his punk-ass staff into action. To motivate them and to prep his beautiful brigade for ugly combat.

"S-1, where are we at on backfills? Are we staffed at one hundred percent across the brigade?" Wolfe asks.

"Yes, sir, sort of—"

"Sort of?" Wolfe growls. "What the hell do you mean by sort of?"

"Technically we're fully staffed, but our nondeployables will take us below ninety percent once we go wheels up."

"Unacceptable," Wolfe hollers. "We're going to war at one hundred percent. Either get them deployable or get them off our goddamn books. Do you read me?"

"Yes, sir."

"S-2, what you got? Anything new in the intel world?"

"No change, sir. The Sunni Triangle remains the most active battlespace in Iraq."

"Why?"

"Sir, Saddam's hometown is right there. When we kicked all the Ba'ath party members out of their government jobs, they went home and became insurgents. Tikrit is full of them."

Wolfe nods and turns to Jackson. "S-3, go ahead. Impress me."

"Sir, per your guidance, we've revamped physical training to focus on combatives. We'll start with individual fights, move up to squad-on-squad fights, and climax with platoon-on-platoon fights next month."

"Good. I don't want any Raider being punched in the face for the first time in Iraq."

"Yes, sir, and we're working up a similar range plan. We'll qualify everyone on their service weapon this month and move on to crew-served weapons next."

Wolfe scowls. "Everyone needs to zero and qualify on a long gun. Even if they carry a pistol, they must qualify on both. And while we're on firearms, Doc, have you gotten our medics into the local emergency rooms?"

"Sir, ah, there are some legal hurdles—"

"Bullshit!" Wolfe snaps. "You're a smart guy. A doctor, for Christ's sake. Figure it out, because none of our medics will treat their first gunshot wound down range!"

"Yes, sir, but—"

Wolfe pushes his chair back and rises to his full height. He makes his way around the table to the back wall where Dr. Gomez sits with the special staff pukes. Wolfe towers over him and locks eyeballs with the terrified doctor. Sure, it's pure theatrics, but if that's what it takes to properly motivate the little creep, so be it. "No buts, Doctor," Wolfe growls.

From the front of the room, the brigade executive officer stands and says, "Sir, it's really not his fault—"

Wolfe spins. "I didn't say it was his fault, Frankie-boy. I said I'm blaming him. But goddamn it, Frank, maybe I should be blaming you!"

"Excuse me?" Lieutenant Colonel Frank Zimmerman asks.

"Don't play innocent with me, you pencil-necked little fucker," Wolfe says, making his way back to the head of the table. "You are supposed to be running my goddamn staff, and my staff doesn't get that we're prepping to go to war. And if they don't get it," Wolfe booms, stabbing his finger in Zimmerman's face, "that's your goddamn fault!"

Zimmerman's face turns bright red as he sits stoically absorbing Wolfe's wrath.

"You know what, you're fired!" Wolfe snaps.

"You don't have the authority—"

"Shut your goddamn pie hole," Wolfe bellows. Wolfe scans the shocked faces in the conference room and likes what he sees. He looks back at Zimmerman. "Okay, you just became my rear detachment commander."

"And you," Wolfe turns to Jackson and says, "just became my XO and S-3."

Jackson nods and wisely says silent.

Wolfe turns back to Zimmerman. "Get the fuck out of my meeting."

"What?" Zimmerman stammers.

"You heard me!" Wolfe growls. "I'll let you know when I need to talk to you about the wives' club bake sale."

Zimmerman fumbles as he gathers his things and exits the silent room.

Wolfe sits, taking the time to make eye contact with his scared-shitless gaggle of staff officers. *Good*, he thinks. *Now they are finally waking up to smell the goddamn coffee.*

Fort Campbell, Kentucky
20 February 2006

One month in, and the Raiders are using their precious time to prep from before sunup until long after sundown. They do make measurable progress, but not nearly as quickly as the Big Bad demands. Wolfe didn't have the luxury to prep his guys for their fatal mission in Panama. This time around, not a second of their predeployment window will be wasted.

Wolfe abandons the Army's bullshit physical training, with its arbitrary fixation on push-ups, sit-ups, and running. Instead, he switches to combatives based on his grueling wrestling practices at Oklahoma State. The focus is building strength, speed, and ruthlessness. That's the only way to rapidly build the warriors Wolfe will need to choke the life out of Al Qaeda.

Wolfe stands at the edge of a sand volleyball court that Captain Hart and First Sergeant Durham have converted into Delta Company's combatives pit. Hart was a first captain at West Point, and Durham is a two-time combat vet. Wolfe smiles in approval. These hard chargers get it.

Staff Sergeant Ray Fleury's squad goes into the pit first, while the company looks on. Fleury stands in a loose circle with the ten men under his command. The men are barefoot and clad in desert camo uniforms. Fleury is a former drill sergeant, who probably made rank too quickly. He thinks he knows it all, but the young NCO hasn't yet stared death in the face.

"Get going, Fleury," Durham yells.

Fleury steps into the middle of the circle and calls out, "Willowby."

A nervous young trooper shuffles forward to join Fleury. They bow, karate style, and begin to circle each other. Fleury finally lunges forward, pulls Willowby's legs out from under him, and drops him like a sack of flour. He backs off and allows Willowby to get to his feet.

"Gruber!" Fleury calls, summoning his next opponent.

"No, hold on!" Wolfe barks. "Get your sorry ass back in."

Willowby timidly shuffles back in. Wolfe strides over to Fleury's side. Loud enough for the whole company to hear, Wolfe says to Fleury, "You give him your best here, so that he's ready over there. You read me?"

"Yes, sir!" Fleury answers, flushing bright red.

Willowby visibly shakes as he bows to Fleury. The two circle each other again, and Fleury easily takes Willowby to the ground just like the first time.

"Goddamn it!" Wolfe yells. "If he's going to keep going down quicker than a two-dollar whore, I want you to pop him in the nose and wake him up!"

"Sir?"

"Don't *sir* me! Friggin' do it again!"

This time when Willowby falls, Fleury slaps him across the face with a loud crack.

Wolfe turns to First Sergeant Durham, "Was I clear about what I wanted?"

"Yes, sir, extremely clear."

"This ain't Sunday School, stud," Wolfe yells at Fleury. "Stop pulling your punches and toughen that little motherfucker up!"

Fleury circles Willowby. Instead of going for his legs a third time, he lunges and punches him square in the face. Willowby drops to his knees as both hands go up to hold his bleeding nose.

"That's it, boys. That's the good stuff!" Wolfe hollers and claps, everyone joining in the Big Bad's enthusiastic applause.

Fort Campbell, Kentucky
12 March 2006

The sun casts a warm, golden glow across Fort Campbell's expansive airfield as the Raiders prepare to pack out. *It's unseasonably warm for early spring*, Wolfe thinks as he steps up onto a wooden riser to address the troops. Looking out over his Raiders and the rows of Apache and Blackhawk helicopters, Humvees, and lightly armored gun trucks lined up for deployment, Wolfe feels a surge of pride.

He scans the faces of his troops, and he sees anticipation, excitement, and determination. *It's a fine mix of emotions*, he thinks. Ones he'll savor as they embark on their journey to Tikrit, where it will be a hell of a lot hotter than Kentucky. Memories of previous deployments flicker through Wolfe's mind—the camaraderie, the sacrifices, and the warrior spirit that carries soldiers through their darkest moments.

"Brigade, attention!" the adjutant calls out, his voice carrying through speakers set up across the front of the tarmac. Instantly, six thousand soldiers snap to attention, their faces locked forward.

Wolfe steps to the microphone, the heavy step of his boots on the wooden platform echoing through the air. He calls out, "At ease!" and his Raiders' eyes meet his admiring gaze. "We are heading into a volatile region, a place where danger will test us, but we're ready. We're ready to meet the enemy head on. We're locked and loaded and ready to crush any son of a bitch that gets in our goddamn way. Got it?"

"Yes, sir!" they answer.

"We've trained, we've prepared, and we will succeed in bringing order to a lawless, godforsaken corner of the world," Wolfe declares, his voice steady and resolute. "Our mission is clear. Bring order. Bring stability. Bring everyone home." Wolfe pauses. He sees the fire in their eyes. Their manifest confidence causes him to swell with pride. He knows that his Raiders are true warriors who will put their lives on the line for each other.

"We are brothers and sisters in arms, bound by shared commitment," he continues. "Always remember that we carry the pride of our nation with us. Let's go over there, kick some insurgent ass, and make America proud." Wolfe pauses again, allowing the weight of his words to linger. Then, with a firm nod, he dismisses his Raiders.

The sun sits higher in the sky and casts a brilliant light that seems to illuminate the path before them. Wolfe's Raiders move with purpose, completing hundreds of different tasks in their final preparations for going wheels up. Wolfe steps down to join them and relish their bone-deep determination. They are alpha predators. They will ship their equipment to Kuwait. They will prep and up-armor their vehicles and flight test their helicopters. They will move north and take control of the Sunni Triangle with decisive action, overwhelming firepower, and unwavering courage. And this goddamn time, Wolfe will bring everyone home.

CHAPTER 2

Wolfe
Kuwait City, Kuwait
14 March 2006

Wolfe lands in Kuwait with the main body. His advance party is already there preparing the unit's helicopters and wheeled vehicles for movement into Iraq. Wolfe is beyond furious when he learns that his motor officer has failed to up armor the brigade's hummers and gun trucks. "I don't give a flying fuck!" he says, interrupting his motor officer's explanation that the supply system is out of steel plates. "Find the goddamn metal and we'll make the plates ourselves!"

Within hours, some top-notch NCO scrounging leads to the discovery that the US Navy has millions of dollars' worth of metal stored in Kuwaiti warehouses for routine repairs and maintenance.

"The Navy isn't asking their sailors to drive over IED-infested roads," Wolfe says, cutting off his staff's explanation as to why they can't legally acquire the Navy's plating.

Turning to Jackson, he says, "Ernie, this is must-have stuff. Can you make it happen?"

"I'm on it, sir," he says.

The very next night, Wolfe is in a giant warehouse with his welders and grease monkeys. They spend all night cutting and fitting metal plates into the floorboards and doors of the soft-skinned vehicles. It is damned hard work under normal circumstances, but with one-hundred-degree temperatures and an extremely short timeline to get it all done, it is hellish.

"Nothing rolls north until it's up armored," Wolfe orders.

At midnight on their fourth day of around-the-clock twelve-hour shifts, all the Raiders' gun trucks and Humvees are plated.

"And the goddamn Navy will never know the difference," Wolfe says, putting his beefy arm affectionately around Jackson's broad shoulders.

Tikrit, Iraq
21 March 2006

After a week of meticulously planned and flawlessly executed flights and convoys, Wolfe is finally in Iraq with his Raiders. As he steps off his command helicopter, the sauna-hot air hits him like a wall. The scorching sun beats down, its rays bouncing off the flat desert floor in shimmering waves. His boots crunch against the gritty concrete as he makes his way down the makeshift, open-air helicopter bays lined up along the old Soviet-built runway. He looks out across their dusty new home, an abandoned airbase near Tikrit. It is an expanse of faded buildings that once housed Saddam's Air Force Academy. Now it houses Wolfe's brigade headquarters, two attack helicopter battalions, and four lift battalions. The echoes of distant gunfire and the hum of diesel generators fill the air, an audible reminder that he and his Raiders are now in the heart of an active war zone. Wolfe has been through deployments before, but this one is different. The stakes are higher, the environment is harsher, and the challenges are more complex. And this time, he carries the weight of responsibility for the lives of the six thousand troops under his command.

Wolfe approaches the low-slung building that will serve as the nerve center for brigade operations. He steps inside, the dim coolness a welcome change from the oppressive heat outside. His men move with purpose, setting up computer equipment, coordinating logistics, and establishing a working command center to support the troops patrolling the deadly battlespace in and around Tikrit.

The largest room, roughly the size of a basketball court, serves as the brigade's operations center. Oversized flat-screen monitors mounted high on the far wall display maps marking troop movements and suspected enemy positions. The two wall-mounted AC units puff out pitiful streams of air smelling of dust and sweat.

The soldiers working to bring order to the chaos are a healthy mix of seasoned veterans and fresh faces. Each displays resolve that stokes Wolfe's pride. They've trained hard, prepared well, and in short order it will be time for them to seek and destroy the enemy.

"Sir," Jackson says, interrupting Wolfe's thoughts, "we're coordinating with our remote units and establishing communication lines with our sister brigades."

Wolfe nods, acknowledging the progress. "Make sure our lines of communication are solid, especially to our air and ground troops. We don't want them out there operating in radio silence."

"Higher wants to know the status of our progress with assuming responsibility for the Bulldogs' outreach programs—rebuilding a couple of schools and some spot repairs on Tikrit's power grid," Jackson says.

The Big Bad's face contorts with contempt. "Winning hearts and minds is a deeply flawed counterinsurgency concept, Ernie. It failed in Vietnam, and it will fail here. Benetti can wax poetic all he wants, but the truth is he's wasting a lot of time, money, and American lives. We can build roads, schools, and hospitals. But at its very best, it's just government sanctioned bribery. And what happens when the money stops? The rented hearts and minds stop being loyal, that's what. It's a fucking disgrace!"

Wolfe turns and stomps back to his spartan office to immerse himself in reports, briefings, and the constant flow of information. It's all part of the burden of command. His mind races considering how to best combat the insurgency. Forget about Benetti's naive desire to win Iraqi hearts and minds! They have to be vigilant about force protection and find a way to take the fight to an enemy who hides in the shadows.

Tikrit, Iraq
23 March 2006

Wolfe gets up from his desk, walks fifty feet down the hall, and steps into Jackson's command center. The harsh fluorescent lights wash out the maps and monitors that line the walls. Wolfe makes a mental note to get those damn lights changed out. Jackson stands at the center of it all, his gaze fixed on the map of the Sunni Triangle. The brigade's tall and willowy intelligence officer, Major Ingram, flanks him, their faces etched with weariness, anger, and frustration.

"Jackson, Ingram." Wolfe's voice cuts through the electronic hum. "Update me."

Wolfe's men exchange a quick glance before Jackson goes to the heart of the matter. "Sir, another midnight mortar attack and three early morning roadside bombs."

Wolfe listens, his jaw set in a hard line.

Jackson continues. "The Sunni Triangle security mission is one hell of an ass-kicker. Attacks have been on the rise throughout the battle handoff with the Bulldog Brigade."

Wolfe's lips thin and he cracks his knuckles.

Jackson continues, his brow furrowing. "Sir, we've been trying to coordinate it all with them, but communication has been spotty. It's been a challenge to maintain a smooth transition."

"Their focus is on departing," Ingram adds.

"I hate battle handoffs," Wolfe mutters, mostly to himself. "Just give me the mission and get the hell out of my way. Right, boys?" he asks rhetorically. "We didn't need to shadow the Bulldogs for a week and we sure as hell don't need them following us around for another goddamn week."

Major Ingram clears his throat and speaks up. "Colonel, the Bulldogs are experienced, but they're also itching to wrap things up. Maybe it's high time for us to cut them loose and take the reins?"

Wolfe's gaze narrows, his eyes locked on Major Ingram. "You might be onto something," he says. "We're ready. We know the lay of the land. Let's cut the cord and let them fly."

Major Jackson nods in agreement, his posture relaxing.

"They can continue to provide my team support and intel, but we don't need them micromanaging our ops every step of the way," Ingram adds.

Wolfe loves these two, especially Jackson. A rare hint of a smile tugs at the corners of his mouth. "Exactly, men. Let's give them the green light to pack their shit, get on their planes, and go home. That's what they want anyway, so good goddamn riddance."

Jackson and Ingram nod in agreement.

Wolfe likes it. They are adapting, pivoting, and making the tough calls necessary to ensure success. "All right, gentlemen," he declares, his voice ringing with authority. "We've got a plan. Let's execute it." And with that, all the counterproductive frustration in the room is replaced by a focused energy.

Tikrit, Iraq
24 March 2006

"Jackson," Wolfe hollers to start his first Bulldog-free battle staff meeting. "Please give me some good news."

"We're on our own, sir. No lines at the shower trailers or chow hall. No more double bunking. It's all ours now," he says grinning and spreading his arms like P. T. Barnum in the center ring.

"What about attacks, Mr. Smiley?"

Jackson drops his arms and gets serious. "Three last night, sir. Mortars at twenty-three fifteen and zero two hundred, and an IED early this morning."

"Casualties?"

"The mortars didn't hit anything, and our counter-fire put them out of business. Reports on the IED are still coming in, but it seems the bomb went off too early to do any real damage."

"Keep me posted."

"Yes, sir," he says, sitting down.

"All right, heroes," Wolfe says to the twenty officers assembled in the brigade conference room, "keep these morning dumps short and sweet. Jackson just set a pretty good example. If you've got nothing for the group, say that and sit. If you've got no change or no significant activity, say that. Got it?"

"Yes, sir!" they answer in unison.

Wolfe makes his way from his headquarters to the chow hall as the sun rises above the rim of the pitch-black horizon. The rays of light burst forth, casting a warm, red glow over the desert. The air is still and quiet. As he walks in silence, he thinks about how fortunate he is, because he now has complete command and control over the battle space—his battle space. The weight of it is heavy, but he and his team are ready. God help the poor bastards who dare to stand in their way!

Tikrit, Iraq
03 June 2006

Wolfe's first ninety days in theater have not been easy. Three months into the grind of daily 06:00 and 18:00 changeover briefs are peppered with the relentless onslaught of insurgent attacks every goddamn day, with no signs of abating. Snipers hide in shadows, mortars erupt in darkness, and those goddamn roadside bombs lie in wait around every blind corner. It's a nerve-jarring symphony of violence that has become the twisted national anthem of this broken land.

Wolfe paces the command center, the harsh light of the fluorescent bulbs causing him to clench and unclench his fists. His patience is threadbare, frayed by the hidden dangers that lurk outside. The artillery guys do their damned best with counter-fire, their rounds ripping through the night air to quiet the harassing nightly mortar attacks. But even their deadly prowess doesn't bring solace. It doesn't still the angry pounding in Wolfe's skull that comes with each explosion. He knows that much like counterpunchers, counterfirers rarely win.

"When are you going to fix those goddamn lights?" Wolfe yells, entering the ops center.

"Today, sir," Major Jackson answers.

Wolfe continues pacing. Angry thoughts fog his mind. *Air superiority, they said. A potent advantage,* they claimed. But here, in this godforsaken corner of the world, it amounts to nothing. A big goddamn zero! Raider helicopters streak across the sky like avenging angels, but the enemy hunkers down, hides, and waits. They hide among civilians and slip through the gaps in our worthless technology. Hiding just outside our grasp, they snipe at us from the shadows.

Ingram gives Wolfe a copy of the latest intelligence report. It's a testament to the enemy's ingenuity.

"Al Qaeda," Wolfe whispers, the name carrying the weight of a curse. A name that has become synonymous with torment. The elusive enemy. The cowardly phantoms who haunt Wolfe's nightmares. He knows their handiwork, recognizes their signature, but pinning them down is like trying to catch shadows with his bare hands.

Wolfe's fingers trace the contours of the billboard-sized map, his mind a tempest of anger and frustration. The solution seems simple, so goddamn obvious. Hunt them. Find them. Crush them. Crush them beneath the might of the Raiders' overwhelming firepower. It should be a straightforward matter of calculation and execution.

"Goddamn it," Wolfe mutters through gritted teeth. "We have to take the fight to them."

The room falls silent, Wolfe's words hanging in the air like a storm cloud. Everyone recognizes it—the need to rip the initiative from the hands of the gutless savages who hide behind women and children and skulk in the shadows.

"I'll coordinate with Special Forces," Major Ingram speaks up. "Pinpoint the enemy's positions, so we can unleash our air power."

A moment of quiet solidarity passes between them. It's a decision born of frustration and the cold resolve that comes with the fact that Wolfe simply cannot endure this torment any longer. "Get it done, Major," he growls, his voice a low, menacing rumble. "Let's make sure these ugly bastards know who they're fucking with."

Tikrit, Iraq
07 June 2006

Major Ingram briefs Colonel Wolfe, his exhaustion mitigated by guarded optimism. "It appears that Al Qaeda has set up a training base at an isolated bend in the Euphrates River."

Wolfe's gaze fixes on the area on the oversized map that Ingram highlights with a laser pointer. "It's an out-of-the-way peninsula; the perfect place to hide."

Wolfe nods, signaling Ingram to continue.

"The area consists of an abandoned school, a petroleum processing plant, a cluster of houses, and some small farms near the village of Ahradin," he says. "Our informant indicates that Al Qaeda has been using this location to recruit and train new fighters."

Wolfe exhales slowly. The enemy has rooted itself in the heart of the land, using terrain and the local population to camouflage their activities. The thought of them appropriating a school and turning it into a training ground for terror fuels an anger deep within him.

"Special operators went to check it out and drew fire. They engaged in a firefight, killing sixteen and detaining three suspected terrorists."

Wolfe acknowledges it with a tight-lipped smile. The kills are an indicator of a larger nest of terrorists. They're like cockroaches: breeding and multiplying in the dark until the light exposes their true numbers.

Major Ingram's voice grows firm. "Sir, we believe that these kills are just the tip of the iceberg."

It is enough for Wolfe. The time for hesitation is over. His Raiders need to strike and need to strike hard. "Get with Jackson and start planning a brigade-sized operation. We'll call it Operation Judgment Day."

The name resonates. It is a declaration of intent that reverberates through Wolfe's core—Judgment Day—a day of reckoning for those who sow chaos and despair. A promise to those who have suffered, a vow to bring an end to the terror that plagues this land. The pieces are finally falling into place, and Wolfe feels a growing optimism. Operation Judgment Day will be a declaration that his Raiders will not stand by while darkness seeks to engulf everything. His team will rise, they will fight, and they will bring about a reckoning that will be etched into the annals of goddamn history.

Tikrit, Iraq
15 June 2006

Wolfe's eyes trace the high-definition satellite photo spread out before him. The contours of the peninsula stand out, with the river and man-made canals weaving intricate patterns around it. The canals are flanked by reeds standing like silent sentinels guarding deadly secrets. It's the goddamn marsh reeds, those unassuming tufts of vegetation, that provide the insurgents a leafy sanctuary. The pieces of the puzzle are scattered before Wolfe and Jackson, and it's now their responsibility to assemble them into a coherent plan, a strategy that will allow the Raiders to fix and destroy the enemy.

"We need to neutralize them in their main stronghold," Wolfe says. "The abandoned Al Fanni chemical complex. This is most likely where they gather and train. And I'll bet this is where they plot their attacks."

Major Ingram leans in, his eyes locked on the peninsula. "Our sources have confirmed it, sir. Informants have pointed to Al Fanni as the epicenter of their operations."

Wolfe nods, his mind whirring with possibilities. *Damn.* The complex extends almost a mile along the horseshoe bend in the river. It's a massive chunk of land, littered with scores of potential hiding spots.

"We've been working closely with the Defense Intelligence Agency and Special Forces to understand it," Major Ingram adds. "The reeds along the irrigation canals offer cover, which allows them to hide and defend the strips of land in between."

"We'll start with a targeted artillery barrage," Wolfe declares. "We'll soften them up, create chaos, and expose them."

Jackson nods, his expression a mirror of Wolfe's determination. "We should add a blocking ground convoy here," he says, pointing to the narrow opening to the peninsula, "to prevent any reinforcements from coming to their aid."

"But the heart of our assault," Wolfe continues, his voice taking on a steely edge, "will be an overwhelming brigade air assault. Following the artillery barrage, we'll land and hit them with everything we've got. We'll unleash hell on them."

"Intelligence reports indicate that they've gathered there before," Ingram adds. "Zarqawi himself has been spotted at Al Fanni. He was allegedly disguised and armed with a laptop we believe was filled with attack plans."

Jackson raises an eyebrow. "Zarqawi? The very top of their leadership?"

Ingram nods. "He's been there to train them, to guide them."

"Then, gentlemen," Wolfe says, "we have a chance to take out the very top of their command structure."

Jackson's lips curl into a determined grin. "It will be a day they will not soon forget."

"Indeed, Ernie," Wolfe agrees. "Let's finalize the details, gather our forces, and let loose a shitstorm they won't see coming."

Jackson and Ingram dive into the detailed planning with purpose and resolve. They will break Al Qaeda's grip on the Sunni Triangle. They will shatter their forces, and end their reign of terror with one decisive blow.

CHAPTER 3

Jess
Baghdad, Iraq
30 June 2006

The Al Faw Palace's marble atrium with its ornate architecture and grand chandelier lend a sense of history to General Benetti's assumption of command ceremony. Thankfully, we're inside, because the June desert heat is unbearable for those of us used to Heidelberg's gentler climate. The hushed hiss of air conditioning and the murmurs of uniformed officers and Iraqi dignitaries create a subdued hum. Hope underpins it all.

The departing commanding general addresses the room first, his voice carrying the heavy weight of his tenure and the sacrifices of those who died under his command. His words are a poignant reminder of the dangers that lurk in this war-torn land. He concludes his remarks and formally passes the Multinational Corps Iraq flag known as a guidon to General Benetti. The guidon represents the mantle of command, and its passing symbolizes the Corps' leadership changing hands.

Lieutenant General Benetti plants the guidon back in its stand and steps forward to address us. His uniform and bearing are impeccable. As he begins to speak, his voice resonates through the airy atrium, each word carrying authority and conviction. He expresses gratitude to the departing team, acknowledges their sacrifices, and congratulates them for a job well done. He pauses, allowing for a moment of reflection. He wishes them a safe passage back home to Fort Bragg and his words then shift to us.

It's a powerful shift. I can feel his commitment as he looks at us.

"My V Corps teammates," he begins, "we stand here together on the precipice of a great opportunity—a historic opportunity—to make a lasting impact on the lives of the Iraqi people. The road ahead will be bumpy, with unexpected twists and turns, but we will keep our eyes on the destination—a free, democratic, and prosperous Iraq."

As the Corps' lead prosecutor, my criminal law division has a clear mission: to enhance good order and discipline and seek justice within the bounds of the Uniform Code of Military Justice. But in this moment, as Benetti asks us to embrace the chance to create a better life for the people of this war-torn land, I'm inspired to contribute much more.

Benetti continues. "We must extend our efforts beyond the battlefield. The heart of our mission is to provide clean water, reliable electricity, and hope for a brighter future."

I listen intently, hoping for a role in bringing about positive change.

"Since I last departed Iraq two short years ago," Benetti says, "Al Qaeda has grown stronger, and it is more active. But if we continue to play insurgent whack-a-mole, we will never exhaust the endless supply of disenchanted, angry, and unemployed Iraqis. And, worse yet, the continuing violence will turn otherwise friendly Iraqis against us. We must gain the confidence and trust of everyday Iraqis before the situation will stabilize and improve."

Colonel Miller and I nod in silent agreement. When the first clap sounds, we enthusiastically join in the group's applause, filling the atrium with a hopeful, positive energy.

CHAPTER 4

Wolfe
Sunni Triangle, Iraq
21 July 2006

Wolfe flies high over the Euphrates River three weeks after Benetti's command ceremony. The whir of helicopter blades makes communication difficult as Wolfe, Jackson, and Ingram soar over the unforgiving landscape to put eyes on the target. An ancient sheik sits with them, his gaze fixed on the horizon. Normally, Wolfe wouldn't waste his time with a local. However, this guy provides a fragile human link to Major Ingram's intelligence estimates. Wolfe hopes the old guy will confirm everything the Raiders believe about the enemy. Wolfe looks out the window, tracing the riverbank and the ominous outline of the Al Fanni complex with his appraising eyes.

The sheik shifts in his seat and points toward buildings dotting the isolated peninsula. "Those are the ones," he says in heavily accented English, his voice barely audible over the roar of the helicopter's blades. "Al Qaeda."

Wolfe nods, his gaze locked on the buildings.

The old informant continues. "If you strike at the right time, everybody could be there." The sheik's hedging is a reminder that no matter how precise their planning, timing is everything and the outcome will still hinge largely on luck. The helicopter continues its flight and approaches the southern tip of the peninsula. The informant sweeps his hand out in a vague gesture that encompasses the whole expanse. "All Zarqawi," he says.

Mud huts on a canal bank come into view, standing guard like two gritty sentinels. They seem to hold dangerous secrets.

"Men, we have our target," Wolfe says to Jackson and Ingram. Wolfe turns to the informant and looks into his watery eyes. "Thank you, you've given us what we need."

The old man nods and says, "Inshallah."

The helicopter banks and makes its journey back to Tikrit. Wolfe uses the time to work through all the possible contingencies. Now that the sheik has confirmed the brigade's intelligence, Operation Judgment Day is no longer a concept. It's a reality.

Then and there, Wolfe decides that the best course of action will be to bomb the peninsula into the Stone Age. Then his Raiders can sweep across it in waves of controlled violence. They will kill every bomb-builder and sniper they find. And they will finally end Zarqawi's reign of terror over the Sunni Triangle.

Tikrit, Iraq
22 July 2006

The command center's harsh fluorescent lights blind Wolfe momentarily as he enters. One light, in the far corner, blinks annoyingly and refuses to die.

"Goddamn it, Ernie," Wolfe growls, pointing at the offending light.

"Base ops said all work orders must be submitted to local contractors," Jackson explains. "I guess we're trying to grow their economy."

"They can grow my ass," Wolfe barks. "Get someone up there to pull that friggin' bulb!"

Wolfe paces back and forth until the bulb is out. He strides over to the trooper who did the honors, shakes the trooper's hand, and says, "Good work! You don't have to wait around for me, Major Jackson, or some crooked Iraqi contractor to fix stuff. You use your initiative and get things done."

"Thank you, sir!" the young trooper beams, snapping a crisp salute.

Wolfe returns the salute and turns back to Jackson. Both men are restless. The countdown to Operation Judgment Day has been paused. It looms over them like a storm cloud as they wait for a green light from higher headquarters.

Major Ingram enters the ops center. Without a word, he hands Wolfe a folder marked *Secret*. Wolfe opens it, scans the contents, and frowns.

Turning to Jackson, Ingram whispers, "They disapproved our strike package."

"They disapproved both?" Wolfe bellows.

"Yes, sir, both our general request and our more limited strike on Walter," Ingram answers.

Wolfe's grip on the folder tightens. Frustration and disbelief roil within him.

"They want us to go in naked?" Jackson asks Ingram. "This is our one chance to strike a decisive blow, and they want us to go in naked?"

"They're denying us," Wolfe says. "They're sending us into the belly of the beast without any goddamn fire support!"

Ingram nods. "We'll be on our own."

It's a bitter pill to swallow, and Wolfe must now decide whether to send his Raiders into battle against a seasoned enemy without fire support. His mind jumps back to Panama and the horrible day when he lost twelve men. The memory is a painful, stinging reminder of the very high cost of his failure. And goddamn it, it will never happen again.

Wolfe glances at the map, toward the peninsula and its high-priority objectives that Major Ingram had so painstakingly identified. Wolfe hoped that he could largely eliminate the enemy threat before any of his troops set foot on the ground. And now, that course of action has been vetoed by the goddamn armchair quarterbacks sitting in the Al Faw Palace.

Wolfe pounds his fist into an open palm. "Do we go forward as planned, or do we postpone? Both options carry significant risks."

Jackson nods. "If we postpone, we may lose the element of surprise."

"If we go forward," Ingram adds, "we won't be able to properly prep the battlefield."

Wolfe closes his eyes and clears his mind. He considers their options. It's a brutal choice. But leaders must make tough calls, even those forced by chickenshit denials that sting like a dagger in the fucking back. "We move forward," Wolfe growls, his eyes narrowed to murderous slits. "We stick to our plan and take the fight to those ugly fucking bastards."

CHAPTER 5

Jess
Baghdad, Iraq
02 August 2006

The late afternoon sun filters through the windows of Colonel Miller's palace office. I sit, waiting for her to finish a phone call, and admire the family portrait perched on the corner of her desk. I pick it up to take a better look at her husband and son.

She hangs up and I put her family photo back, saying to her, "I'm amazed at how you manage to juggle it all."

She glances at the photo and offers a warm smile. "It hasn't been easy, Jess. I've been fortunate to have a supportive husband and a strong family."

I lean in, eager to hear more. "How did you put it all together?"

Colonel Miller's gaze turns introspective as she reflects. "I grew up on a dairy farm in Minnesota, the youngest of five kids. I attended Catholic school and had a strong sense of duty instilled in me."

"What drew you to military service?"

"Leaving the cows behind," she laughs. "Well, that and I had an ROTC scholarship to attend the University of Minnesota. That's where I met my husband, Mark. He was an EMT, and we quickly fell in love. But soon I had to leave for the Army."

I listen intently as she recounts her early days in the military, her first tour in Korea as a military police platoon leader, and her eventual selection for the Army's funded legal education program, which sent her back to Minnesota for law school. "That's when Mark and I rekindled our relationship," she continues, a fond smile gracing her lips. "We got married shortly after I took the bar exam, and we've been on this journey together ever since."

I can't help but feel a twinge of envy as I listen to her story—the stability of a loving relationship and the support of a partner who is willing to be a stay-at-home dad for their son, Cody, now sixteen.

"I've been blessed," she says, her voice tinged with gratitude. "But it hasn't been without its challenges. There have been deployments, long separations, and moments of doubt. But through it all, Mark has been my rock."

As much as I admire Colonel Miller, when my thoughts drift toward a future beyond Iraq, I imagine living a nonmilitary life.

One option that has always loomed large is to join my father in his comfortable law practice. Now more than ever it's a tempting prospect with stability, financial security, and the opportunity to work alongside my dad. The idea of a more predictable and less demanding life is appealing, especially after the stress of deploying.

There's also the possibility of pursuing a career in prosecution, with an eye toward running for district attorney one day. The opportunity to make a meaningful impact on my community, to fight for justice on a larger scale, and to use my legal skills to advocate for victims of crime excites me. The thought of leading a dedicated team of public servants and implementing policies to promote fairness and accountability is something that exhilarates me.

With both options, there's also the big upside of being able to put down roots and raise a family. It's a dream that I've always held close, the idea of building a life with someone I love and raising children in a nurturing environment. But I've always prioritized my career over my personal life, and the uncertainty of military life makes it difficult for me to imagine how it could ever become a reality while I'm in uniform.

"No matter what the future holds for you," Miller concludes, "at least you'll never be an old woman sitting around waiting for your life to start."

Back in my cubicle, I consider Miller's parting words. Being deployed doesn't seem real yet, but it does make me feel somehow closer to my grandfather. He never spoke about his time in the Army, but my grandmother kept a framed photo of him on her mantel. When I was little, I always asked her to lift me up to get a better look at the photo of my very young grandfather looking so very handsome in his khaki uniform.

When I got older, after my grandfather passed, I'd point to the same dashing photo and ask my grandmother, "What did he do in the Army?"

"I don't know, Jessica. He never talked about it."

"Why not?"

"That was his business. Some men wall off that part of their lives."

Baghdad, Iraq
04 August 2006

I sit in a sweltering up-armored Humvee with my driver, Sergeant Steven Harms. We're stuck in a line, idling at the first of three checkpoints that guard the US Consulate. I try to ignore the overwhelming smell of diesel fumes before it triggers my gag reflex. This is my second trip to the Green Zone to attend mind-numbing rule of law meetings chaired by my State Department counterparts. The first meeting only exposed how frighteningly disconnected the diplomats are from the realities of life outside of their comfortable cocoon. I'm not optimistic that this one will be any better.

I glance over at Harms, his hands steady on the wheel. He is a squat, broad-shouldered New Yorker who exudes cocky confidence. At first glance, he is mean looking, but there's a playfulness in his eyes that takes the edge off his tough exterior. He was born and raised in Brooklyn—a fact he is never shy about sharing—and he speaks in the clipped cadence of the city. An Army court reporter by trade, he possesses a keen attention to detail that serves him well over here. And this isn't his first rodeo; he's on his third tour. He's always on the lookout for trouble, and his reactions to danger are quick, precise, and decisive. I look out the window at the baked streets and buildings, grateful that Harms is at the wheel. In a place where danger lurks, having someone like Harms at your side instills a sense of confidence and reassurance that no amount of money could ever buy.

I gaze at the barren expanse behind us and shift my eyes to the concrete jungle up front. The blazing sun casts dark shadows under the fig trees that line the dusty road. My sweaty fingers slide off the slick plastic stock of my M-16 rifle as my thoughts drift to General Benetti's vision for a better Iraq.

Before he took command, this place had been haunted by a grim statistic—one Iraqi life claimed each day at coalition checkpoints. A chilling tally, and a cruel reminder of the divide that exists between us and them. But Benetti refused to let this situation persist. He challenged us to confront the problem and reason our way to better solutions. My mind retraces his one-line order: investigate each killing. A simple directive, yet it slices through our indifference like a blade. And the results are undeniable, a drop of 85 percent in those deadly check-point killings.

"Capture, don't kill," is another radical shift in Benetti's enlightened approach. No longer do we perceive every shadow as a threat deserving instantaneous death. Now, we aim to subdue rather than obliterate. It is a challenge that tests our mettle, forcing us to see the humanity in those we might otherwise instinctively assume are our enemies.

Radical shift number three, the soft knock, is a law enforcement concept that seems alien to the chaos of war. Yet, Benetti challenges us to adopt this gesture that transcends language to convey the simple idea that Iraqi homes are respected sanctuaries. He believes this modest act will help bridge the chasm between us and them.

Perhaps Benetti's most audacious decree is to compensate surviving family members for innocent lives lost in our wake. The idea clearly springs from Benetti's strong commitment to justice. He wants the Iraqi people to see us as partners, not oppressors. To further this, he wants us to investigate and compensate victims and their families when our bullets go astray.

We inch forward as a gust of wind blows dust across the road. I glance over at Harms. Is there an awareness, a sense of purpose that transcends force protection? General Benetti's manifesto of change has breathed new life into a difficult mission. Through Benetti's progressive efforts, a transformation is taking root. Harms and I are not just a pair of sweaty soldiers sitting out in the oppressive heat. We are emissaries of change. The checkpoint in front of us, once a symbol of fear, has become a testament to our commitment. With each interaction, each knock on a door, each life spared, we inch closer to a better world. Of that, I'm sure.

Baghdad, Iraq
09 August 2006

After wasting all day in the Green Zone, I must spend a late night in the office to catch up on case reviews. Some time after midnight, Colonel Miller comes into the office. She tries to pull me away from my all-night review of criminal charges pending against various soldiers, and I reluctantly follow her down to the windowless, top-secret vault—the SCIF, called "the skiff" for short—to observe real-time reports from a massive air assault operation going down in the Sunni Triangle.

We stand at the edge of a dimly lit, windowless operations center. Miller explains that Operation Judgment Day's mission is to root out insurgents and disrupt their operations. Operational law has never been my thing, but I'm impressed. The room is alive with the low hum of electronics and spot reports barking out of multiple speakers. The sharp radio chatter is acronym-laced and mostly meaningless to me. My eyes are drawn to an array of screens. Ghostly graphics move across them, and I understand they represent flesh-and-blood people moving through the cold, dark desert. The reports coming in provide glimpses of the unfolding events as troops draw closer to what could become a very bloody battlefield. On one screen, the map displays the movement of a ground convoy, the fifteen vehicles snaking their way toward Objective Gaslight. Miller explains to me that it's a crucial part of the operation, sweeping through the area to set up a blocking position to catch any insurgents attempting to flee. The room remains uncomfortably silent as we wait for updates.

Snippets of communication from troops on the ground burst through the steady crackle of radios. The terse exchange of information adds to the tense, uncertain mood in the command center. At around 05:00 everyone's gaze shifts to a large screen, where an aerial view shows an airborne assault force landing on Objective Walter. In a low voice, Miller explains to me that Objective Walter is a suspected Al Qaeda training facility hidden along the Euphrates River. Once a suspected chemical weapons site, it is a high-priority target for our troops. As I watch the images of friendly soldiers moving across the objective on foot, I can't help but hold my breath.

The assault is underway, yet even as the reports pour in detailing the successes of the operation—insurgents neutralized, weapons seized, locals detained—a thread of skepticism runs through me. Despite all of the bravado coming through the radio chatter, it seems we invested a lot of effort to kill and capture a very small group of suspected terrorists and a tiny cache of weapons. The operations guys who seemed so excited a few hours ago, now seem deflated. I'm surprised that General Benetti doesn't express any anger or telegraph any disappointment. I guess Army leaders are expected to keep their game faces firmly in place no matter what they feel on the inside.

My eyes drift to a photo of an Iraqi child on the wall. It's a reminder of our ultimate goal—a stable, peaceful Iraq where the people can thrive. It's a vision that goes beyond the battlefield, a vision that encompasses clean drinking water, reliable electricity, and a sense of security for the people who call this land home. I remind myself that every action, every operation, is a step toward that vision. Operation Judgment Day, for all its violence, complexity, and danger, is part of a larger, multifaceted effort to bring lasting peace and stability to Iraq.

But an undeniable uneasiness lingers. Is the insurgency and counterinsurgency a never-ending cycle of violence begetting violence? Is it an endless struggle that threatens to unravel any progress we make with outreach and reconstruction? While the operation was a bust, maybe that's a better outcome than the seek-and-destroy bloodbath that failed to materialize.

CHAPTER 6

Jess
Baghdad, Iraq
13 August 2006

I step out of my containerized housing unit, or CHU, which is pronounced "chew," and enjoy a deep breath of cool morning air. It is surprising, but even in the blistering summer, the temperature drops significantly at night. While stretching for my run, I ponder the US Army's strange obsession with acronyms. The most famous being POV as a clumsy three letter, three syllable stand-in for "personally owned vehicle," meaning a car. Why would the Army substitute that for a three letter, one syllable word? And downrange, they up the acronym ante by giving the same thing several awkward pseudonyms. For example, my CHU is sometimes called a SEA-Hut or a CONEX, which is short for the "Container Express" shipping boxes. No matter what you call it—CHU, Sea-Hut, or CONEX—it's still my air conditioned happy place.

I start off at an easy jog. In the stillness of the sleeping base, the only sound is the rhythmic beat of my running shoes on the concrete road. A blood-red sun rises slowly over Baghdad, casting a dazzling reflection off the Al Faw palace lake. We seized the palace and made it our Corps headquarters at the end of Donald Rumsfeld's hundred-hour sprint to victory. Pronounced "awful," it isn't actually too bad. Tacky, yes, but tacky comes with running water and air conditioning. In a combat zone, I'll take that every single time.

I pick up my pace and follow a familiar route around the large, man-made lakes that dot our sprawling headquarters. The water sparkles and I admire the tranquility. It stands in stark contrast to the chaos that often defines our daily life here. I run past a smaller lake with twin islands where Saddam Hussein's sons built their palaces. I'm struck by the symbolism. In the desert, water is power. The hierarchical Ba'ath party that once ruled Iraq reflected this in the layout. Saddam's grandiose palace is surrounded by the most water. His sons' smaller palaces, nestled on their twin islands, are surrounded by slightly less life-giving water. The faux-Italian villas that dot the edges of both lakes once housed Saddam's favored Ba'ath party chiefs.

A Muslim call to prayer echoing through the air interrupts my thoughts. It's a hauntingly beautiful sound, a reminder of the cultural tapestry that surrounds us even in the midst of war. I can't help but wonder about the evolving role of Iraqi women. When we invaded, one of the most wanted Ba'ath fugitives was a woman. She was in charge of Saddam's chemical weapons program. Did she have a villa on the water? I wonder.

As I continue to run, I can't shake the thought that there are no longer any high-ranking women in the Iraqi government. The lone woman elected to Iraq's parliament was assassinated shortly after taking office. I shudder at the thought that Iraqi women were better off under Ba'ath party rule. It's a sobering idea, and a reminder of the complex web of power and privilege that Saddam spun as he clung to power for so long.

I finish my run, take a quick shower, swing past the chow hall, and pick up a to-go coffee and a protein bar. By 08:00 I'm at my desk scrolling through the daily MP blotter report.

"Jess, the general wants to see us," Colonel Miller calls, as she heads out on to the third-floor marble balcony that rings the Al Faw's grand atrium.

"Yes, ma'am," I say, grabbing my pen and notebook and following her out at top speed.

I rush to keep up with Miller. Everyone thought she would become the JAG Corps first female general officer. When it didn't happen, she didn't quietly retire. Instead, she extended a year to deploy with Benetti to Iraq. She certainly didn't need to do it to prove anything to anyone, as she'd already deployed to Bosnia and to Kuwait during the first Gulf War. But here she is, back in the sandbox, double-timing down a wide, white marble staircase to see the boss.

I catch up to her in General Benetti's cramped waiting area. She checks in with the commanding general's strapping aide, Major Jimmy Brown. He tells her that the CG is in with CID. Miller and I exchange puzzled looks, wondering what the Criminal Investigation Division is briefing the CG.

Brown says, "I'm sure he'll see you in a minute." He then looks over at me, a fellow Major, and winks. I ignore his playful wink, because it is a universally acknowledged Army truth that a single woman is either a nerd or a whore. I choose the lonelier path of a nerd lacking friends and a social life. Maybe I'm being overly cautious, but I've been twice promoted and have a bright future in the JAG Corps. For now, that's enough.

Brown excuses himself and goes into the CG's office. Miller and I take a seat in the small waiting area, and I lean in to ask, "What's up, ma'am?"

"I don't know. Brown called. He said the general wanted to talk to us right away."

Brown returns and announces, "He's ready."

Miller and I jump up and follow him into Benetti's cavernous office.

"Thanks for coming, Denise," Benetti says. Turning to me, he adds, "You too, Jess." As the general's chief of military justice, I'm his district attorney, but I'm still impressed that the officer in charge of two hundred thousand coalition troops can remember my first name.

Miller and I recognize Colonel Mike Smith and Chief Warrant Officer Four John Valdez standing behind Benetti. Colonel Smith is our provost marshal, or top cop in Iraq, and Mr. Valdez is the special agent in charge of the Baghdad CID office. We all shake hands and then Benetti ushers us over to his oversized mahogany conference table. As is his custom, he avoids sitting at the head of the table and instead sits on the side flanked by Smith and Valdez. Miller and I sit facing them.

Benetti addresses Miller. "Earlier today Mr. Valdez received some disturbing news, and I need your take on it."

Valdez slides a single sheet of paper across the table. "I received an email from Fort Riley's CID. They forwarded a message from a local recruiter who has been corresponding with a medic he enlisted late last year. The medic, Michael Delgado, is currently deployed here, with us."

Miller reads the messages and hands it to me. I scan it quickly, seeing that the original message was sent yesterday, August 12. I read through it a second time because I can't believe what it says. Delgado claims that during Operation Judgment Day his brigade commander, Colonel Michael J. Wolfe, cut the ears off dead Iraqis, presumably to keep them as war trophies.

I feel for General Benetti. The allegation couldn't have come at a worse time. For the past month, he has been dealing with media reports about a massacre in Haditha, a city in western Iraq under our criminal jurisdiction. The reports are months old and implicate a squad of US Marines. As the theater's overall mission commander, the responsibility to figure it out and deal with it rests with Benetti. It has heightened his resolve to act quickly and decisively to any and all battlefield reports of war crimes.

"What do you think, judge?" Benetti asks Miller.

She turns to Valdez. "Who is Private First Class Michael Delgado?"

"He's a medic up in Tikrit. His story seems to check out. During operations junior medics are usually put in charge of the rear-area tactical morgue. In that role, he would help unload bodies from helicopters. He certainly could have seen what he claims to have seen."

"Has he been interviewed?"

"No, ma'am. The CID team at Riley interviewed the recruiter. He swore out a statement that says Delgado is young and eager. The recruiter believes that Delgado is being truthful and must have seen something that deeply disturbed him. He couldn't go farther."

"So, what do we do next?" Benetti asks.

Colonel Miller looks at me to answer. "Sir, you have three options," I say. "You can step back and wait for CID to investigate, step in and personally conduct a commander's inquiry with an eye toward court-martial, or appoint an investigating officer to conduct a fifteen-six investigation for you."

"Good, let's do the fifteen-six. What do we need, Denise?" the CG asks my boss.

"Sir, we'll need you to appoint an investigating officer who is senior to Colonel Wolfe, and I'll provide the IO with a legal adviser. I can have the appointment orders ready within the hour once I have the IO's name."

Benetti confers briefly with Brown, then says, "Brigadier General David T. Lindsay, the deputy commanding general at the 4th Infantry Division, will be the IO. And I want you to assign Major Gilbert to be his legal adviser." He turns to me. "When can you leave, Jess?"

"Sir? Normally the legal adviser briefs the IO, stays on call for guidance, and helps put the findings and recommendations in order." Getting no response, I continue. "The adviser doesn't normally participate in the investigation."

"This time you will," Benetti says and turns to his aide. "Are my helicopters here?"

"Yes, sir. They're here."

"Has Wolfe started R & R?"

"He flies today, sir."

"Okay," Benetti says, turning back to us. "Denise, get me the appointment orders for David Lindsay ASAP. And, Jess, be ready to fly as soon as General Lindsay can go."

"Yes, sir," I answer with a bit of hesitation.

"Do you need anything else?" he asks me.

I huddle with Colonel Miller before responding. "Sir, I'd like to take a court reporter to make verbatim transcripts of the interviews."

"Good, do it," he says. "Anything else?"

Miller and I shake our heads.

The CG stands and we all stand and salute. Once he returns our salutes, we double time out of his office to put it all into motion.

"What's the story on Colonel Wolfe?" I ask with an exaggerated eye roll.

Miller stops on the landing and looks around to be sure we are alone. Leaning in close to me, she says, "Jess, this is serious business. He is a rising star in the infantry, and a bona fide military celebrity."

I give Miller a little shrug to signal that I'm not impressed by Wolfe's celebrity, military or otherwise.

"No, Jess, this is serious. I'll fill you in once we get through the daily huddle."

We go straight to the JAG conference room, where the JAG leadership team is already waiting. Miller meets each morning at 09:00, Sundays included, with us—her deputy, chief legal NCO, legal administrator, and her five division chiefs—to go over our top issues. As the deputy efficiently runs the meeting and goes around the table, each chief briefs the issues that his or her section is currently working on. This takes some time, as Miller gets caught up on what's hot in her administrative law, operational law, fiscal law, military justice, client services, and claims sections.

As the others brief in turn, the memory of a heroic soldier in Panama flickers through my mind like a blurry old-time film. I recall something about a raid on the presidential palace, or was it some other significant location? The details are hazy, blurred by the passage of time. Maybe Hollywood made a movie about it, or was it a book? I furrow my brow, trying to recall. Trying to piece together fragments of a story that feels just out of reach is frustrating. It nags, like a puzzle refusing to be solved. I guess I should look for the film on DVD, or better yet, get the book. I make a mental note to look it up later to quiet the curiosity that keeps tugging at the edges of my consciousness. For now, though, I push aside my fleeting memories and focus on the present. In my brief, I mention that I'll be out advising an IO for the next week and my senior trial counsel, CPT Buchanan, will be the acting chief of justice until the investigation wraps up.

"Thanks, team," Miller says. "Let me know if you need any help. Otherwise, keep up the good work."

We all stand in unison, and Miller invites me back to her office. Once the door is firmly closed behind us, she gives me the lowdown on Colonel Michael Wolfe. He was twice crowned the NCAA's heavyweight wrestling champion. Because he trained relentlessly, and fought ruthlessly, Oklahoma State's student newspaper nicknamed him "the Big Bad." As a young lieutenant, he jumped into Panama with the 1st Ranger Battalion and led his platoon in a daring assault on Manuel Noriega's Comandancia Headquarters. The mission was a huge success and Wolfe was awarded the Silver Star, but twelve of his men were killed. The deadly raid was immortalized in the famous book and Hollywood movie *Killer Elite*. This, of course, cemented the legend of the Big Bad within the tight-knit infantry community. After that, his career went into overdrive. He was a company commander in the 82nd Airborne Division at Fort Bragg and a battalion commander in the 25th Infantry Division in Hawaii. He took brigade command at Fort Campbell just before the Raiders were notified about their upcoming deployment to Iraq. Older and heavier, but still remarkably relentless, tough, and ruthless, he and his Raiders were aggressively hunting for insurgents operating within the Sunni Triangle.

"Is this from the big mission we watched with the operations guys two nights ago?" I ask.

"Yes," Miller says, "and you're going to be in his crosshairs, Jess. So please, watch yourself."

I hold back on giving Miller another eye roll, because watching out for each other is second nature for females serving over here. We are few, and even women empowered with rank and authority but lacking a Y chromosome can feel vulnerable. We remain on guard, even inside the wire, and after dark we instinctively move in pairs, even if it's just to make the hundred-meter midnight trip from our CHU to the latrine.

Back in my cubicle, I log on to my computer and open an appointment memo template, tailoring it for Benetti to appoint Brigadier General David T. Lindsay to investigate the medic's ear-taking allegation. As I type, Miller comes over to check on my progress. "What do I need to know about General Lindsay?" I ask.

"He's the deputy commanding general of the 4th Infantry Division. I've met him a couple of times. He's a bit of a Boy Scout, and I like him."

"What do you mean by that?" I ask.

"Well, he's a straight arrow. A West Point grad who spent most of his career in special ops. He has a well-earned reputation for staying calm under pressure."

"Sounds like a keeper," I say, sending his appointment letter to the printer. While the printer whirs to life, I do a quick Google search for Mike Wolfe.

"That's him," Miller says, looking over my shoulder.

Seeing Wolfe's head-and-shoulder command photo on my screen, I vaguely remember a Panama-era rescue video seen across America on the nightly news. Wolfe has aged and appears to have gained about thirty pounds. He still, however, looks like a man who means business.

With the clock ticking, I jog back to my CHU to pack my rucksack for the possibility of several days away and then double-time back to the palace. At 13:00, General Lindsay unexpectedly shows up for his legal in-brief. Normally, I make office calls to general officers, not the other way around. Lindsay looks younger and leaner than I expected. His wise and lively eyes remind me of a quick-witted college professor, but they are set in the sunburned face of an Old West cowboy. His prominent Roman nose tempers his otherwise boyish good looks. He quickly scans the JAG office with calm awareness. I immediately conclude it would be a grave mistake to underestimate this man.

I quickly brief Lindsay on the allegation and his role as General Benetti's investigating officer.

He nods and asks in a smooth, Midwestern baritone, "Ready to go, judge?"

"Yes, sir," I say, pointing at my rucksack. "Do I need to go and draw a long gun?"

He laughs and shakes his head. "Major Gilbert, we'll be flying with the corps commander's six-man security detail. If both birds go down, and our security detail can't protect us, an extra rifle won't help."

He takes note of the doubt written on my face, glances at his hip and then mine, and says, "Trust me, we'll be just fine with our Berettas."

While he waits, I struggle into my forty-pound flak vest with its ammo pouches and other assorted battle-rattle and ruck up. Downstairs we stride across the palace's airy main hall and exit over the sixty-foot faux drawbridge. Like always, there are soldiers throwing bread to Saddam's "killer" carp.

A short walk away, we arrive at the coalition heliport. Two Blackhawks sit with their rotors spinning. Lindsay's gear is there waiting for him. Baked by the sun and sweating under the oppressive weight of my gear, I wonder why I didn't just join my dad's law firm and settle for the comfort of a country club life. My pity party is interrupted when I spot Sergeant Steve Harms waiting near the lead copter with his court reporter gear. I smile and wave, thankful that Colonel Miller has detailed him to the investigation. The security team is already aboard the trail bird, so we load up, strap in, and are off.

This is my third trip off Victory Base. The other two were

only short ground convoys to attend State Department meetings in the Green Zone. This time won't be as short or comfortable because we're heading north into the Sunni Triangle and Saddam's hometown, Tikrit.

The dusty neighborhoods whiz by under us as our two Blackhawks streak low and fast over suburban Baghdad. It was once a thriving city, but that is now impossible to imagine. Every dusty house looks the same. Their yards are small, square, baked patches of dirt, surrounded by ugly cinder block walls. Every street is filled with trash. The only movement is debris kicked up by our rotor wash. There are no people. I guess they don't have any reason to be outside, because there is no work. No hope. Power lines strung across the dusty walls and houses give it all a tangled, haphazard look. It's hard to tell if the wires still carry electricity. At best, that is a fifty-fifty proposition.

We leave the sprawling city behind, and I look out on the open desert now racing by beneath us. We whiz over a two-lane highway that runs like a faded concrete scar across the desert's chapped, dusty face. We slalom over Iraqi water wells that look like open graves dug into the hard-packed earth.

Directly outside my window, there's a loud whoosh and explosion. A big cloud of sparkling metal shimmers. Before I can process it, we bank away from the cloud. Have we been hit?

We level out, drop altitude to just above the housetops and power lines, and accelerate away from the explosion. There's no smoke, and the hull of the copter seems intact. I close my eyes and pray we'll make it to Tikrit in one piece.

I'm still trying not to shake thirty minutes later when we finally flare and touch down. Harms looks over and gives me a thumbs-up. He is smiling and calm, which I guess should be expected. He was with 3rd Infantry Division during their hundred-hour ground invasion and spent his second deployment convoying through Afghanistan with a rucksack full of cash paying out war damage claims.

CHAPTER 7

Wolfe
Tikrit, Iraq
13 August 2006

Colonel Wolfe takes a short helicopter ride from Tikrit to the sprawling military airfield at Balad. He stands on the tarmac, watching an olive-green C-130 idle under the midday sun. Dust whips around his boots, but he barely notices. He has his rucksack slung over one shoulder. It is heavier with resentment than gear.

Two weeks of mandatory R & R. He didn't ask for it. He didn't want it. And he sure as hell wasn't going to spend it at the beach or on a golf course. He'd spend it at Fort Campbell, shaking hands, doing interviews, and telling the locals how well everything is going in Iraq.

Around him, a few junior soldiers on the same flight nervously clutch their bags or fiddle with their phones. Wolfe ignores them, his jaw tight. He'd rather be back in Tikrit with his Raiders. Judgment Day might not have gone the way he had hoped, but that didn't mean the fight was over. There are still missions, checkpoints, and informants. He could be working towards another Judgment Day where they catch the insurgents off guard. Bottom line, he is needed in Iraq, not back home shaking hands with Kiwanis Club retirees or smiling through puff interviews set up by Fort Campbell's PAO.

He exhales sharply. Operation Judgment Day was supposed to be the hammer stroke. The largest air assault since Iron Triangle.

Textbook shock-and-awe. But the intelligence was thin, and the results were thinner. And while his brigade executed with precision, the outcome didn't justify the hype. Now back home, the Army's propaganda machine is hellbent on spinning it as a great victory. Media interviews. Local TV. A Veterans of Foreign Wars banquet. Even a high school visit. But Wolfe isn't a politician, and this public relations bullshit isn't what he signed up for.

Wolfe clenches his fist. Major Jackson tried to reassure him, told him he would keep things under control while he was gone. But goddamn, command isn't something you take a vacation from. Not in a war zone.

The flight chief gestures for the group to board. Wolfe, normally up front, lags behind. He walks slowly up the C-130's steel ramp, his boots ringing with each step sounding like the toll of a funeral bell. He pauses and takes one last look toward where his men are still operating, patrolling, and hunting for the enemy.

CHAPTER 8

Jess
Tikrit, Iraq
13 August 2006

General Lindsay smoothly rises, steps out of the Blackhawk, and steps off in a practiced crouch. I fumble with my release. Once it pops open, the shoulder straps conspire to grab the gear attached to my Kevlar vest. Harms reaches across and pushes my first aid kit under one strap, I twist, and am free. I stagger under the weight of my gear and underestimate the distance to the ground, almost face-planting. The rotor whirls overhead, creating gale force winds. I'm not ready for the dust, noise, and confusion. Disorientated by it all, I hold my breath and blink away the dust, trying to figure out which way to go. I know walking into the tail rotor is deadly, but I'm not sure which end is forward. Harms moves past me carrying his rifle and two large hard-shell cases that house his recording gear. I follow, sticking close to him until we're out from under the hurricane-force rotor wash. Only then is it possible for me to take a deep breath of the hot, dry desert air.

I catch up to Harms and holler, "What was that?"

He laughs. "First time?"

"What?"

"Don't stress, counselor, it was chaff," he says.

I nod, still feeling awkward and uncomfortable with it all.

"You know . . . chaff?" he says. "The stuff our helicopters throw when radar paints us. You know, to confuse the missiles."

"What? You mean we fired it?" I ask, suspecting that he might be pulling my leg.

"Yeah, it's basically tin foil cut like confetti. Shoulder-fired ground-to-air missiles are the biggest threat to our birds. My first tour we flew high to have more standoff from them but, we learned this only gave the freakin' insurgents more time and space to aim and fire at us. So now, we fly low and fast, especially over towns. And we set our systems to throw chaff at any sign of radar. When it fires, we bank away hoping that the missile locks onto the chaff and not us."

"It didn't seem to bother the general at all," I say.

"You know he was here with SF right after the ground invasion, right?" Harms asks. By SF, he means Special Forces, the Army's soft power on the ground who interface with the local population, train indigenous forces, and navigate the messy and delicate web of tribal loyalties.

"You were here too, right?" I ask. "It must have been an especially challenging time."

"Yeah, the Iraqis welcomed us as their liberators at first. But Rumsfeld's de-Baathification program turned that on its head. An insurgency sprang up over-freaking-night. The newly unemployed cops and soldiers may have been new to guerrilla warfare, but they sure knew how to use AK-47s and rocket-propelled grenades," Harms explains.

A fire-hydrant-shaped officer strides out to greet us out on the expansive airfield. He introduces himself as Major Jackson and explains that the facility was built as a training center for the Iraqi Air Force. Now, one-story concrete blast barriers bisect the runways. Ugly, but a utilitarian way to create a huge parking lot for a brigade's worth of Blackhawk and Apache helicopters.

Jackson escorts us to the DVQ, the distinguished visitor's quarters. "We, ah, we don't get many split-tails this far out," he says to Lindsay, with an apologetic shrug. "So," he says, turning to me, "we don't have any female DVQ latrines or showers."

"We'll be in and out," Lindsay answers. "Sergeant Harms and I can stand watch while Major Gilbert uses the facilities." Lindsay turns to me, "Does that work?"

The split-tail comment catches me off guard and spikes my blood pressure. I'm certain that General Lindsay knows that "split-tail" is vulgar artillery slang for a female. The graphic slur is based upon towed howitzers with extended hitches that open up to become the cannon's rear legs. The crew pries open the legs and then stands between them to ram the round and powder into the breach before firing. Instead of calling Jackson on his choice of words, or Lindsay's silent compliancy, I swallow my pride, nod, and state simply, "That works, sir."

General Lindsay nods and the awkward moment passes without comment.

My DVQ room has the feel of a tired spring break hotel, right down to the sad, stale smells that the overworked air conditioner can't mask. I drop my gear, and we head for the chow hall. Before we can enter the weather-worn former warehouse, we must dry-fire our weapons into clearing barrels. The twin fifty-five-gallon drums are filled with sand and are set into the ground at a forty-five-degree angle.

I unholster my service pistol and notice that I still have a ten-round magazine in it. I should have taken it out when we arrived, so I discreetly drop it into my palm and tuck it into my ammo pouch. I pull back the top slide, look to make sure there is no round in the chamber, let the top snap smoothly forward, click off the safety, point my weapon into the ten-inch hole cut into the top of the barrel, and pull the trigger. The metallic snap confirms to everyone within earshot that my weapon is clear. I click the safety back on and holster my weapon.

Back on Victory base we clear our weapons by rote in two seconds flat, because most of us rarely leave the safe confines of the sprawling base. As a result, we never put a loaded magazine into the wells of our weapons. So, we pull the slide back knowing that the chamber is simply empty, making it merely a ritualistic requirement. Until it's not, because the requirement to lock in a magazine before leaving the base drastically changes the equation.

The danger for the oft-maligned staff "Fobbits" who burrow in like Hobbits, never leaving the safety and comfort of the FOB, is that when they do leave and return to the forward operating base, they forget to take the magazines out of their weapons. When their slides go back, they observe an empty chamber. And when their slide goes forward, it pushes a live round from the magazine into their chamber. Then, when they dry fire—BOOM—a round blasts into the clearing barrel, making lunch a little bit more exciting.

Harms, needing to dry-fire his rifle, nudges me forward. Inside, the Raiders chow hall is only slightly less dilapidated than its dusty exterior. The soldier manning the front desk jumps to his feet and yells out, "Room, attention!" Before Lindsay can respond with "at ease," every soldier in the dining hall jumps to his feet. At Lindsay's command they all sit again, but many eyes linger on me. The cafeteria-style food line features surf and turf, and I happily take a T-bone and a lobster tail for my dinner.

I take a seat with Lindsay and Harms. I'm the only woman in a sea of men, with several openly gawking at me. The way they leer, it seems they haven't seen a flesh-and-blood female in a while.

"It must be hard serving with all the unwanted attention," Lindsay says, looking out across the chow hall. "I sometimes skip chow to avoid all the extra attention I draw as a general officer out in public. And heck, I'm not drawing half of the attention you're getting from these troopers."

"I'm glad that I'm armed," I say, laughing nervously. Trying not to blush, my thoughts turn to Colonel Miller. Even in uniform, she is a head-turning beauty. I can't imagine the savvy it must have taken her to survive the unwanted attention.

"Congress throws piles of money at it, we buy into training developed by academics and self-proclaimed civilian experts, and nothing changes," Lindsay says, pulling my thoughts away from Miller. "What do you think the solution is—more sexual harassment prosecutions?"

"No, sir, my father is an attorney back home and the civilians are much more selective about which cases they take to trial."

"Really? That's hard to believe."

"District attorneys are mostly elected officials. They can't risk trying too many cases that could go either way, and they can't spend lots of taxpayer money trying circumstantial cases they likely won't win."

"So, they don't try the 'he-said, she-said' cases?" Lindsay asks.

"Not unless there is something exceptional about them, and as crazy as it sounds, we do exactly the opposite."

"I don't follow."

"Do you remember last month when General Benetti ordered all females on Victory Base to move in pairs after dark?"

"I do."

"Do you remember why?" I ask.

"Something about a rape behind the female shower trailers?"

"Yes, but the allegation was false."

"What?" Lindsay asks.

"Of course, everyone, including me, took the victim at her word. She swore out a statement saying that a medium-sized, medium-build man of undetermined race grabbed her, pulled her behind the showers, and raped her. She claimed that when she screamed, he ran away. I reviewed her statement with Colonel Miller, and we agreed that the CG should publicize the attack, offer a reward for tips, and order females to use the buddy system after dark."

"That makes sense," Lindsay nods.

"A day or two later, CID asked me to meet them at the shower trailer where the attack allegedly happened. The trailers were snug up against Texas barriers. Not the small Jersey barriers like you see dividing traffic from construction sites, but the ten-feet-tall cement blast barriers. There was absolutely no way anyone could get behind those trailers."

"What happened?"

"The CID agents wanted the green light to title her for swearing out a false official statement," I say. "Instead, I asked them to read her her rights. She waived and during her interview she broke down and admitted to making it up. She couldn't handle serving in Iraq and thought making the allegation was her ticket home."

"Did you prosecute her?"

"Absolutely not," I say, "because if word got out it might chill legitimate reports and trigger a media storm. We didn't want either."

"But we've got to do something, right?"

"She had less than six years of service, so we sent her home and then could administratively chapter her out for the down-range misconduct. But that's not my point. My point is that we initially believed her. We took drastic actions based on our unverified belief that she was, in fact, raped behind the showers. On the civilian side, that isn't as likely to happen. Police, attorneys, and even the general public are more skeptical and need corroboration. We've lost that in the military. Out of our fear of appearing weak, we chase our tails over every allegation."

"So, what's your proposed solution, Jess?"

"Sir, we can only follow procedures and keep an open mind until all of the relevant evidence is in. What more can we do?"

"Okay, that makes sense. So, how do we start our investigation? What are our procedures?" Lindsay asks.

"We normally start with the main witness, get his version down in detail, and talk to others to see if it checks out. Then, we circle back to cover any inconsistencies or omissions with the main witness."

"So, we should talk to Colonel Wolfe first?"

"I think we should interview Delgado first and put Wolfe at the end. Maybe last, before we reinterview Delgado."

Harms raises his hand and tentatively speaks up. "If the alleged ear-taking was part of an operation, couldn't we ask the brigade staff to give us its mission brief and maybe get a copy of their after-action review?"

"We normally don't get access to operational information," I say.

"But this isn't a normal investigation," Lindsay says. "If I request a mission briefing, they will damn sure give it to us."

Lindsay stands, and Harms and I join him, remaining on our feet until the general leaves our table. As Lindsay departs the chow hall, the orderly once again yells, "Room, attention!" bringing several hundred troopers to their feet.

As Harms and I retake our seats, I say to him, "Nice work."

"Really?" he asks with a nervous smile.

"Really," I nod. "I want you to stay engaged and help us get to the truth."

"You got it, ma'am," Harms grins. "My life's mission is not just to survive but to, you know, thrive."

I laugh. "Yes, with passion and compassion."

Harms shakes his head, giving me a tight-lipped grin. "I see what you did there, well played."

In the quiet of my CHU, I reread Delgado's email. For some odd reason my mind drifts to memories of my mother and the struggles she faced as a secretive Latina in suburban Kansas City. Growing up, I witnessed firsthand the subtle yet pervasive prejudices she endured, masked behind polite smiles and casual conversation.

I recall the times at the country club when lily-white women would comment on my mother's beautiful olive complexion, their curiosity piqued by her exotic appearance. "Where are you from?" they would ask, their probing questions fueled by ignorance and entitlement.

"San Diego," my mother would answer, her tone polite but distant. But it was never enough for them. "No, I mean your family," they'd pry. "Italy," she'd finally say, a hint of defensiveness creeping into her voice.

As a child, I never understood why my mother seemed so reluctant to embrace her Latina heritage. Whenever I asked her about it, she'd brush it off with a vague explanation about our extended family in Veracruz, Mexico, insisting that most everyone there had originally come from Italy. Even as a little girl, her explanations sounded evasive, leaving me with a lingering sense of unease.

It wasn't until I was a teenager that I began to piece together my mother's reticence to share her Mexican American background. In my teens, I learned about trailblazing Latina women like Raquel Welch and Linda Ronstadt, whose success and fame belied their Mexican roots. And as I watched Jennifer Lopez rise to prominence as a proud Latina in the mainstream entertainment industry, I realized this was something new.

That's when I began to understand why my mother hid her Mexican heritage. Always surrounded by the country-club types from my father's law firm, my mother chose to navigate the complexities of ethnic identity with discretion. I believe that she did it to shield us from prejudice. I regret that her caution extended to me, because she never spoke Spanish at home and didn't allow me to develop any sense of pride in my heritage. While I'm inspired by my sister Latina soldiers, I feel like an entitled imposter. I guess that's why I'm most comfortable cheering for them from the sidelines.

CHAPTER 9

Jess
Tikrit, Iraq
14 August 2006

To mitigate the impact on the brigade's daily battle rhythm, General Lindsay sets the briefing for 05:00 in the brigade conference room. It's as big and high-tech as any command conference room I've seen at Fort Carson or in Heidelberg.

Jackson is ready at five sharp with his canned PowerPoint slides and well-rehearsed briefing. He starts with the standard introduction. "Sir, as you know, I'm Major Jackson, the brigade S-3 and the acting XO. As requested, I will give you a brief overview of the Seventh Brigade's formations, concerns, and operations, with a deep dive into Operation Judgment Day."

"Please proceed," Lindsay says.

Jackson begins by explaining several complex wire diagrams that show the brigade's subordinate units. "Back at Fort Campbell we expanded from a standard three Air Assault infantry battalion formation to a six-battalion Brigade combat team. Our expanded BCT includes three lift battalions, a reconnaissance squadron, a field artillery battalion, and a special troops battalion. At just over six thousand strong, we deployed topped-off with a one-hundred-percent fill rate."

"Got it," Lindsay says.

"Three months later, in March, we deployed with the 101st

Airborne Division through Kuwait to Tikrit. Our mission is to conduct security operations in the Sunni Triangle. Originally, we fell under the XVIII Airborne Corps, our normal parent unit. Four months in, V Corps deployed from Heidelberg and took the responsibility for theater-wide operations and the XVIII Airborne Corps redeployed to Fort Bragg."

"Got it," Lindsay says, impatiently rotating his hand speed up Jackson.

Jackson clicks through several more wire diagrams without comment and then pauses on a bar chart. "Sir, when we arrived in Salah al Din province, attacks rose slightly, which tracked the general trend across Iraq. The bulk were from roadside bombs, and intelligence indicated the attacks were the work of local insurgents, tribal militias, and Al Qaeda in Iraq."

Jackson advances to a slide with a head-and-shoulder photo shot of an ancient Sheik wearing a white headscarf. "We received information from a local informant that Al Qaeda was using an island, or more accurately a peninsula, along a turn in the Euphrates River as a training base. Our recon indicated the training area consisted of an abandoned school, a petroleum processing plant, and a cluster of houses and small farms near the rural village of Ahradin."

Lindsay nods, signaling Jackson to continue.

"At the brigade's request, special operators conducted raids there and killed sixteen Al Qaeda fighters. They also detained three suspected terrorists. We believed the kills were only the tip of the iceberg, and we immediately started planning a brigade-sized operation. Colonel Wolfe's intent was to begin with a targeted artillery barrage and blocking ground convoy, followed by an overwhelming brigade air assault."

General Lindsay leans forward to take in the spiderweb of colorful graphics. When he leans back in his chair, Jackson quickly cycles through a series of aerial photos with arrows pointing to various dusty structures.

"Our operation grew out of weeks of surveillance. As you can see, the riverbanks and man-made canals are surrounded by tall reeds. This created ideal hiding spots for insurgents to defend the strips of land in between. Our intelligence team worked tirelessly with the Defense Intelligence Agency and Special Forces to understand where and how the insurgents operated there. Our informant claimed the abandoned Al Fanni chemical complex was the main Al Qaeda hideout. He told us that fighters, some of them foreign, trained and built improvised explosive devices on the large peninsula which extended almost two miles along the shallow river. One intelligence report said Al Qaeda's leadership in Iraq had gathered—"

"Got it," General Lindsay interrupts. "Jump to the good stuff."

"Yes, sir," Jackson says, scrolling past a dozen slides. Without missing a beat, he continues. "Operation Judgment Day began on August 9 with a blocking ground convoy, followed by a two-battalion air assault deep into enemy territory. It was the largest and most complex air assault conducted by the US Army since Operation Iron Triangle in Vietnam.

"Iron Triangle?" Lindsay asks. "Isn't it better known today as Hamburger Hill?"

"Yes," Jackson answers, looking flustered for the first time, "that's right."

Lindsay nods, signaling Jackson to continue once more.

"Sir, just after midnight our fifteen-vehicle ground convoy began movement to Objective Gaslight. Their mission was to sweep through the area south and east of the peninsula and set up a blocking position. Objective Gaslight included a gas station, its parking lot, and a small cluster of buildings and metal sheds on the other side of the road. Abu Abdul, who provided military training to local insurgents, was believed to be living at or near Gaslight.

"I'm not interested in the ground convoy," Lindsay says. "Move on to the air assault, please."

Jackson advances his slides and stops on one showing six

Blackhawk helicopters banking in a tight formation. I choke back a chuckle, because the bright blue sky in the canned photo might have been taken in Iraq, but not at oh-dark-thirty when the Raiders had lifted off for battle.

Lindsay lets the obvious error pass, and Jackson starts up again. "At its heart, Operation Judgment Day targeted Objective Walter, an Al Qaeda training facility located on an isolated peninsula along the Euphrates River. Colonel Wolfe and I were together in the command-and-control bird. Once the assault force made contact with the enemy, we landed and coordinated the main assault from Delta Company's command post. By all measures, the seventy-two-hour operation was a resounding success. Eight insurgents, including two foreign fighters, were killed in action. A weapons cache was found and seized, and more than twenty locals were detained and processed."

"Processed?" Lindsay asks.

"Yes, sir. We took their biometrics and checked them against high-value target lists before turning them over to the Iraqi authorities."

"Which Iraqi authorities?"

"Sir, the local police. We had them on standby and allowed them forward once the area was secure. This is always done in strict accordance with unit SOP." Jackson pauses. "Sir, subject to your questions, that concludes my briefing."

"Where's the Old Man?" Lindsay asks.

"Sir?"

"Where's Colonel Wolfe?"

"He departed for R & R yesterday."

This catches me off guard, until I remember General Benetti asking his aide about Wolfe's R & R at the meeting with CID. The Army's rest and recuperation policy allows soldiers to take two weeks leave to break up their one-year deployment. Soldiers eagerly count the days until they can trade their desert fatigues for civilian clothes and escape the scorching heat. Travel is arranged and paid for by the Army, and the travel days don't count against the soldier's time off. Some use their free plane tickets to visit family back home, while others explore distant locales like Australia, maximizing their time away from the front lines.

My own R & R plans are unsettled. Colonel Miller, ever the stickler for regulations, won't let me waive my R & R. She insists that all members of her legal team take mid-tour leave. I'm at a loss for what to do. I don't want to go home until my deployment is complete, and the thought of lounging on a beach somewhere feels like a waste of time. Perhaps I'll go to London? It's a city steeped in history and culture, a place where I could lose myself in museums and galleries, far removed from the daily grind and turmoil in Iraq.

But then again, maybe there's something to be said for going home to the familiar comforts of family and friends, even if only for two weeks. The thought of reconnecting with my mom and dad tugs at my heartstrings, reminding me of the importance of family in a world full of violence and uncertainty.

"Please tell me about the brigade's casualty operations," Lindsay says to Jackson. I push aside my thoughts about R & R and focus on Jackson's answer.

"Yes, sir," Jackson answers. "Per unit SOP all casualties are evacuated by air to the rear area. Of course, mortuary evacs are secondary to medical evacuations, but during this operation we didn't suffer any casualties."

"What about the enemy?"

"Sir, as I said, eight casualties."

"They were evacuated to the brigade's rear?"

"Yes, sir."

"Did you see them?"

"Not right away, sir. Later, I went with the S-2 to photograph them for the intel shop."

"To match them against the high-value target lists?"

"Yes, sir, that's right."

"Did you notice anything weird?"

"No, sir," Jackson answers. "May I ask what this is about, sir?"

"We've had a report that someone took ears as war trophies and the CG has asked me to get to the bottom of it."

"Sir, that didn't happen."

"No missing ears?" Lindsay asks.

"No, sir, absolutely not. I would know about it if it happened."

"Who was in charge of the rear?"

"Sir, it was out on FOB Pitcher. That's our artillery battalion. Lieutenant Colonel Ross is the senior officer there."

"Good, please let him know that I'm coming to see him."

CHAPTER 10

Jess
FOB Pitcher, Iraq
14 August 2006

Heat presses down like a heavy blanket inside the helicopter. Sweat trickles down my back, soaking my uniform. I push my helmet back to wipe my forehead. Looking through a small window, I watch the baked desert whiz by two hundred feet below. The vibration of the rotor blades agitates my jumbled thoughts. I shift in my seat, trying to find a comfortable position. The idea of wearing a moisture wicking sports bra crosses my mind; it would be a great improvement on the sweat soaked bra chafing underneath my body armor.

I glance around. Everyone is enduring the same stifling conditions. I wonder why our gear isn't better suited for this furnace-like heat. I try to focus on the interviews that lie ahead. There's no room for distractions, even if every inch of me feels gross and gritty. As we flare to land, I remind myself to stay resilient. It's all just part of the job, and I need to stay focused on what matters. Still, wearing a sports bra next time isn't a bad idea.

We step off the lead Blackhawk and the rotor wash sends a hot blast of dusty air into my sweaty face. I pull my T-shirt up over my mouth and take shallow gulps of dusty, hot air. Sergeant Harms moves out with his bulky gear. General Lindsay steps out from under the rotor wash and waves the two birds away. I watch the helicopters lift off, thinking, *There goes our ride.* Lindsay sees my forlorn expression and says, "There's no room for aircrews or security details out here."

I look around and see that he's right. Forward Operating Base Molly Pitcher, or FOB Pitcher for short, isn't much more than a few cinder block buildings ringed with a twenty-foot corrugated metal wall to protect the field artillery regiment from snipers. In the distance, there's an aircraft hangar tent that has been converted into a combination gym and chow hall. Extending away from it are rows of shipping containers being used as troop billeting.

A friendly looking, pudgy lieutenant colonel strides out to greet us. He stops short and salutes Lindsay. "Sir, we were expecting you, but I'm a little fuzzy on the purpose of your visit."

"I'll only be here a day or two, Colonel Ross. We need a conference room to conduct a few interviews. Major Gilbert has a list of soldiers I'd like to see."

Ross looks at me with a bit of surprise dancing across his face. He quickly regains his composure, and I hand him a list of names with Delgado and five others on it, including the good Colonel Ross himself.

"Okay . . . I'll get my sergeant major on this right away. I've got a couple of SEA-huts set aside for you. Chow is open if you'd like to eat and get settled, sir."

We stow our gear and head to the chow hall. It is set up to look like a 1950s diner with posters of Elvis, Marilyn Monroe, and the like decorating the partitions between seating areas. They even have white Formica tables and metal chairs with red, padded plastic seats.

While the cheerful intent is clear, the execution falls short because cozy diners aren't normally housed in giant white tents staffed by Indonesian guest workers.

Over some unbelievably juicy cheeseburgers, Lindsay asks, "Where are you from, Harms?"

"I'm from the seven-one-eight, sir," Harms answers with a big smile. "That's the area code for Brooklyn, and I'm not talking about the Burg or down under the Manhattan Bridge overpass. I'm from the real Brooklyn."

"So, Jets or Giants?" Lindsay fires back with a grin.

"Oh, brother," Harms groans. "Let's talk baseball or hockey."

"Mets or Yankees?"

"Pin stripes, please, 'cause the Yankees are the best!"

"The Devils or the Islanders?" Lindsay says, shooting a subtle wink my way.

"Sir?" Harms' face clouds. "Come on, the freakin' Rangers! My boys are gonna hoist the Cup again this season."

"Again?" Lindsay teases. "It's been quite a while since the Blue Shirts had a ticker tape parade down Broadway."

Harms shrugs off the ribbing and excuses himself. Lindsay and I stay put and talk about our interview strategy, and he asks me to describe how these things normally work.

"Well, sir, there really isn't anything normal this time."

"What do you mean?" he asks.

"In a regular fifteen-six investigation, you interview a witness, take notes, and reduce it to writing on a sworn statement form. We can skip all of that because we've got Sergeant Harms. He'll record everything and turn it into a verbatim transcript, just like at a court-martial. If I swear in each witness at the start, we won't need to loop back and have the witnesses read and sign their statements."

"Okay, Judge. You'll handle all the legal stuff, and I'll bat cleanup."

FOB Pitcher, Iraq
14 August 2006

An hour later, Harms tests his courtroom microphones and recording gear in Colonel Ross's command conference room. We arrange the room so that I'm in the middle, General Lindsay sits to my left, and Harms sits to my right. The closed mask microphone over Harms' mouth makes him look like a fighter pilot.

Harms finishes testing his equipment, lowers his mask, and asks me, "Do you know why they're called SEA-huts, ma'am?"

"After the sea-land shipping containers?" I guess. "You know, the ones that load straight off ships onto flat-bed trucks."

"Good guess," Harms grins, "but no cigar."

"Okay, enlighten me."

"It stands for Southeast Asia huts, because they're the same metal containers they used for the troops in Vietnam," he smiles. "I learned that little bit of trivia from the Brown and Root contractor who handed me the keys to my very own SEA-hut on my first tour."

Lindsay enters, ending our banter. Seconds later, Ross knocks and enters. Lindsay directs him to the far side of the table and the single chair facing me.

I look over at Harms to make sure he's recording, then say to Colonel Ross, "Sir, for the record, would you please state your full name, rank, and unit of assignment?"

Surprise again dances across his jolly face. Boy, Ross should stay away from the poker table. But, he quickly regains his composure and says, "Patrick M. Ross, lieutenant colonel. I'm assigned to the 12th Battalion, 3rd Field Artillery Regiment."

"And you are the unit's commander?"

"Yes."

"And the senior officer on Forward Operating Base Pitcher?"

He nods.

"Sir, for Sergeant Harms's benefit would you please answer out loud."

"Yes, I am the senior officer here."

"Do you swear or affirm to tell the truth, the whole truth, and nothing but the truth, so help you God?"

"Yes, ah, am I under investigation or something?" Ross asks, looking back and forth between me and General Lindsay for an answer.

"No," Lindsay says. "If you were suspected of any wrongdoing, Major Gilbert would read you your rights."

I smile and continue. "Colonel Ross, do you recall Operation Judgment Day?"

"Of course."

"Colonel Wolfe held his mission rehearsal briefing here on FOB Pitcher?"

"Yes, that's correct."

"Please tell us about it."

Ross looks up at the ceiling and sighs. He then looks over at Lindsay. Lindsay nods, and Ross reluctantly starts. "Well, on August 8, the ground and air assault forces assembled here at sunset. The operation began at midnight, with the ground convoy leaving for Objective Gaslight to block the insurgents' one overland escape route. One of my Alpha Battery platoon leaders, Lieutenant Sullivan, led the convoy. His mission was to take his convoy of sixteen up-armored Humvees to Gaslight and hold it until released." Ross relaxes a little bit and sits back in his chair.

"Released by whom?" I ask. Ross stiffens in his seat. I sense he has just realized why a general officer has been appointed to lead this investigation. In accordance with Army Regulation 15-6, an investigator must be senior to the subject of an investigation.

"Ah, the mission commander," Ross says.

"And sir, who was the mission commander of Operation Judgment Day."

Ross clears his throat and answers. "Colonel Michael Wolfe."

"Did you have any interaction with Colonel Wolfe during the operation?"

"Of course I did. Many, in fact."

Lindsay leans in and asks Ross, "At any time did you see or hear about anything inappropriate?"

"Inappropriate, sir?" Ross asks.

"Any law of war violations? Any rumors of bodies being desecrated?" Lindsay prompts.

Ross shakes his head. "No, sir, absolutely not. Nothing of the kind."

Lindsay turns to me, "Anything else, Major Gilbert?"

"Yes, sir," I say, turning back to Ross. "Were your men in charge of the rear area during the operation?"

"Yes, my service battery was in charge of the rear."

"Thank you, sir. No further questions."

Lindsay stands, and per military protocol, Ross and I also stand. Harms takes off his mask and turns off his recording equipment. Ross makes his way around the table and approaches Lindsay. "Sir, whatever I can do to help, just let me know."

Lindsay nods. "Please have Lieutenant Sullivan here at zero-eight-hundred, followed by Private First Class Delgado at nine, and the service battery commander and first sergeant at ten and eleven."

Sullivan, of course, is a decoy witness. Lindsay is trying to keep the spotlight off of Delgado for as long as possible. I admire his wily maneuver; he would have made a great attorney. And as a bonus, starting with Sullivan will allow us to warm up and give Harms another opportunity to test his equipment.

As I gather my notes, Harms comes over. "Ma'am, if you like, I can pull the personnel files of each witness so you and General Lindsay can review them before the interviews."

"Great idea."

"Don't worry—I got you." Harms smiles.

"Thanks," I say, secure in the knowledge that Harms has my back. Out here, I'm extremely grateful to have a guy like him watching out for me.

First Lieutenant Sean Sullivan shows up ten minutes early. He's tall, lanky, and confident.

Well scrubbed, he has a fresh haircut and wears a newly pressed uniform. He reports to General Lindsay with a crisp salute and takes his seat across from me. I swear him in, tell him he's being called as a witness, and is not suspected of any wrongdoing.

Thanks to Sergeant Harms' research, we already know that he's twenty-four, single, Catholic, from Cape Cod, and joined the ROTC program at UMass Lowell to pay for college. He's a go-getter, but with only two years on active duty he doesn't have the experience to know how close he is to ground zero of our investigation.

I ask Sullivan a few open-ended questions broken up by a few leading and "what happened next" questions. Sullivan tells us about how his men prepared for the convoy and roared off into the night to seize Objective Gaslight. They had to drive on Route Gold to reach it. It's a two-lane highway running from Fallujah to Samarra nicknamed the "Hajji Highway" due to frequent insurgent attacks along the route. It took Sullivan and his men four hours to get to Objective Gaslight.

"The route was closed by Corps, until my platoon cleared it," Sullivan boasts. "The abandoned buildings on both sides looked like they'd been bombed out during the First Gulf War."

"This is all covered in your after-action report?" Lindsay asks.

"Yes, sir, in detail," Sullivan says.

"You can provide me a copy?"

"Absolutely, sir."

"Did anything significant happen that didn't make it into your AAR, Lieutenant?"

"No, sir," Sullivan says.

"Anything further, Major Gilbert?"

"Yes, sir," I answer and turn to Sullivan. "Did you have any interaction with Colonel Wolfe during Operation Judgment Day?"

"No, ma'am, not directly."

"Anything indirect?"

"Well ma'am, as I said, I heard Colonel Wolfe brief his intent and the rules of engagement at the mission rehearsal."

"At any time during the operation did you see or hear about any law of war violations?"

"No, ma'am."

"Have you heard any rumors about bodies being desecrated?"

Sullivan shakes his head. "No, ma'am. We're aggressive. We're tough. And we're very disciplined. Nothing like that would be tolerated."

Lindsay dismisses Sullivan.

Harms lowers his mask. "He's feigning," Harms says, shaking his head. "You know, puttin' way too much effort into sellin' his bullshit."

I agree but refrain from discussing witness credibility with Harms in front of Lindsay. We have ten minutes before Delgado's interview. I slide a copy of Delgado's ear-cutting email over to Lindsay.

"You know, Jess," he says, "Colonel Wolfe might be innocent."

"I presume it, sir."

"Then please make sure your questions don't plant seeds that erode the Raiders' confidence in their commander."

"Sir?"

"You came pretty close to asking Sullivan if he had heard any rumors that Colonel Wolfe desecrated bodies."

I nod. "I did get close to the line, but I didn't step over it. With Delgado, we don't have a choice and must ask him directly."

A rap on the door interrupts us. General Lindsay opens the door, and First Sergeant Durham escorts Delgado and reports in for both. Lindsay returns Durham's salute. "Thank you, First Sergeant. You can come back in an hour for your interview."

"Sir, Private First Class Delgado has requested that I sit in with him during his interview."

"That's not necessary," Lindsay says, opening the door for Durham to leave.

Javier Delgado sits nervously waiting for our questions. He is very young, very small, and very much out of his element in the presence of officers. I try to be nonthreatening and welcoming as I ask him his name, rank, unit, and duties during Operation Judgment Day.

"Ma'am, I'm a combat medic," he says, fidgeting. "I was assigned to the field morgue during the operation."

Lindsay hands a sheet of paper across the table to Delgado. "Did you send this email to your recruiter?"

Delgado looks like he's about to wet his pants, looking over to me for help.

"Just remember the oath you took," I say, "to tell the truth, the whole truth, and nothing but the truth."

Tearing up, he looks back to General Lindsay. "Sir, do I have to? I mean, if I do, I'm—"

"Listen, son, it's your duty to answer our questions truthfully. Why did you send this message?"

"Because, sir, I saw Colonel Wolfe cut the ears from the dead."

"This is important, Delgado. Tell me exactly what you saw," Lindsay says.

"Sir, the second dust-off landed and I helped the air crew unload four body bags and some weapons. They lifted off, and another medic helped me move the bodies to the shade." A simple soldier wrestling with strong emotions, he speaks in a low, controlled tone. It wasn't rushed. It wasn't rehearsed. And, it had the ring of truth to it.

"What happened next?" Lindsay prompts.

"Another bird landed, sir. It landed close and caused the bags to flap around.

Three officers got out, and one told me to get back."

"Who told you to get back?"

"I don't know, sir."

"Did he have rank like Major Gilbert's?" Lindsay says, pointing at the gold oak leaves centered on my chest.

"Maybe, sir, but I can't say for sure," Delgado says. "But he was Black, that part I'm sure about."

"Who were the others?"

"One was Colonel Wolfe. The other I didn't know."

"Was he also a major?"

"Uh, well . . . he was White. Skinny, tall, and white."

"Do you know the brigade S-2 and S-3?"

"Who, sir?"

"The intelligence and operations officers, Major Ingram and Major Jackson?" Lindsay clarifies.

"No, sir."

"That's okay, Private Delgado," Lindsay says. "What happened next?"

"They went over to the bodies. I moved to get a better look, and the Black officer moved to block my view. The skinny one unzipped a bag and pulled the top back. Colonel Wolfe opened his pocketknife, bent down, and took an ear. The skinny officer closed the bag, and then they did the same to the other two."

"If the Black officer moved over to block your view, how did you see anything?" I ask.

"Ma'am, I couldn't see everything, but I could see around him, and I could see when Colonel Wolfe leaned over to cut off the ears."

"You are one hundred percent sure Colonel Wolfe took the ears, Delgado?" Lindsay asks.

"Yes, sir, hundred percent. I even saw him wipe the bloody knife on his leg down by the top of his boot before he folded it and put it back on his hip."

"What did he do with them?" Lindsay asks.

"Sir?"

"The ears, where did he put them?"

"Ah, I don't know."

"They could still be on the bodies?" Lindsay says.

"No, sir."

"Why not?"

"I know what I saw, sir."

"But not what happened afterward?" Lindsay presses.

"No, sir."

Lindsay dismisses Delgado and we sit in silence. I think about Delgado's initial reluctance to talk. Some soldiers join for the college money, or to learn a trade. Some join to blow stuff up and shoot heavy weapons. But most join looking for a family they don't have anywhere else. For whatever reasons, Delgado signed up. By sending the email, he had forfeited any belonging he had found, because once word leaked that he snitched, he'd be shunned by the Raider pack. His life might even be at risk because he told an outsider a Raider secret.

"What do you think, Judge?" Lindsay asks.

"I think you would have made one heck of a prosecutor, sir," I say with a respectful nod. "I also think Delgado believes he saw Wolfe take the ears, and I think we need to move him back to Victory Base as soon as possible."

Sergeant Harms skips dinner to go over to the Battalion Personnel Action Center and print out personnel files on our FOB Pitcher witnesses. He hurries to my table with a thin file in his hands and the glow of success on his face. He back-briefs me using clipped, efficient military jargon. As expected, both Colonel Ross and Lieutenant Sullivan are squeaky clean.

Then, Harms drops the bomb.

Delgado is pending disciplinary action for a positive urinalysis for marijuana use. The test was administered before the Raiders deployed, but they had an unwritten policy that smoking weed wouldn't get anyone out of their all-expense-paid trip to the desert. In fact, they deferred all discharges for drug and alcohol use until after their return to Fort Campbell.

"Great find, Harms."

"No biggie," he says with a humble shrug.

But it is a big deal. Harms and I both know that this is very big news, because it gives Delgado a motive to fabricate an explosive allegation against the commander who forced him to deploy knowing that he will kick him out of the Army afterward.

General Lindsay radios the flight crew for pickup and notifies Major Jackson that we'll interview him right after lunch. The flight to Tikrit is fast and low. Lindsay, Harms, and I set up in the brigade conference room and then head to lunch. I'm again impressed with the Raiders' menu, which features bacon cheeseburgers and foot-long chili dogs. Well, you know what they say about deployments, "You can go home benching two-fifty or weighing two-fifty—the choice is yours!" And today I decide to throw caution to the wind, and gorge on two foot-longs with lots of onion, chili, and Tabasco.

"Eating like that will shorten your life by ten years," Harms says, grinning.

Lindsay looks up from his baked chicken breast and brown rice. He shakes his head in disbelief like a disappointed father.

"What?" I shrug. "It helps me focus."

"Focus on what?" Harms laughs, "heartburn?"

CHAPTER 11

Jess
Tikrit, Iraq
15 August 2006

Majors Jackson and Ingram are waiting for us when we arrive at their conference room. They pop up and go to the position of attention, until General Lindsay sits and invites them to do the same. Jackson attempts to look relaxed and in control but can't hide that he's wound up tight. His eyes keep darting from Lindsay to Harms and to me. Normally, I'd open an interview with a few easy questions to put the witness at ease. This time, however, I slowly triple check my notes, to give Jackson plenty of time to stew in his own juices.

"Sir, may I ask, why are we here?" Jackson says.

"I've narrowed the focus of my investigation to when Delta Company evacuated dead to the rear," Lindsay answers.

"Shouldn't we wait until Colonel Wolfe returns before investigating his brigade?"

"Colonel Wolfe will have the opportunity to respond once he returns," Lindsay says coolly.

"Sir, that's exactly it," Jackson presses. "It puts Major Ingram and me in a bad spot to answer questions that are better answered by our boss. Would you consider leaving us your questions so we can work up a written response for Colonel Wolfe's review?"

Lindsay pauses and says, "The allegation, which remains unfounded, isn't against the brigade. It's against Colonel Wolfe. We have a report that during Operation Judgment Day he cut the ears from dead Iraqi fighters."

"What?" Jackson starts. "No, absolutely not! That absolutely did not happen!"

Major Ingram clears his throat, and we all wait for him to speak. "Sir," he says, "I have an idea about where this allegation might have started."

"Go on," Lindsay says.

"On the first day of the operation, Major Jackson and I landed with Colonel Wolfe to take photos of the Iraqi fighters."

"The dead ones?"

"Yes, sir, the dead."

"What happened next?" I ask, to keep Major Ingram talking.

"Colonel Wolfe opened the body bags and turned the heads so that I could take front and side shots of each MAM."

"MAM?" I ask.

"Yes, they were just military-aged males at that point, because we hadn't yet positively identified them as high-value targets."

"Did you notice anything unusual?" Lindsay asks.

"No," Major Jackson snaps.

"Major *Ingram*," Lindsay emphasizes, "did you notice anything unusual."

"The men were blindfolded with white engineer tape."

"Blindfolded?"

"Yes, sir, I think that's maybe where the ear misunderstanding started."

"Explain," Lindsays prompts.

"Well, sir, Colonel Wolfe used his pocketknife to move the engineer tape so that I could get full-face photos."

"Why did he do that?" Lindsay asks.

"Sir," Major Jackson interrupts, "Colonel Wolfe should be allowed to answer that question, not us."

Lindsay ignores Jackson, and says "Major Ingram, you're an

educated man. Can you take an educated guess as to why Colonel Wolfe used a knife to remove the blindfolds?"

"The blood, sir."

"Where was the blood?"

"Everywhere. Their hair. Their heads. The engineer tape was soaked in it."

"So, Colonel Wolfe didn't want to get his fingers bloody?"

"Yes, sir. And we needed to PID the detainees."

"PID them?" I ask.

"Positively identify them as high-value targets," Ingram explains.

"Were they?" Lindsay asks.

"No. None were high-value. The first was in our files along with two unidentified boys."

"Boys?" Lindsay asks.

"They appeared to be under sixteen," Ingram says, eyes downcast.

"That was never confirmed," Jackson interjects.

Lindsay holds up his hand to silence Jackson and asks Ingram, "Didn't it seem like something had gone wrong?"

Ingram pauses and then confides, "Yes, sir. I wondered why somebody blindfolded them after they were shot. I thought it was maybe a religious thing?"

"We investigated it," Jackson says.

"Who investigated it?" Lindsay snaps.

"We did, sir," Jackson says. "The brigade."

"I need a copy of it," Lindsay says.

"Sir, we can't release it," Jackson says.

"What? That's unacceptable," I interject. "The corps commander has appointed General Lindsay to investigate the allegation. If you have relevant information, you will release it to him."

Jackson locks eyes with me. "Colonel Wolfe appointed an officer to investigate the deaths and explicitly told us to hold it until he personally reviews the findings and recommendations."

"What was the scope of the investigation?"

"Second Lieutenant Delvecchio was appointed to investigate the combat deaths of the three detainees who were shot trying to escape."

"Second lieutenant?" I ask, not bothering to wait for him to answer. "And you didn't bother to inform your *higher headquarters* about detainee deaths?" I ask.

"The initial report was that they were shot while attempting to escape. So, there wasn't anything significant to report to *higher headquarters*," Jackson says, punctuating it by crossing his arms over his broad chest.

"You will deliver a copy of the complete investigation, including the IO's unapproved findings and recommendations, by seventeen-hundred," Lindsay says.

"Are the PID photos you described included in the report?" I ask Ingram.

"I don't know," he says with a nervous shrug.

"Major Ingram," Lindsay says, "do *you* have the photos?"

"Yes, sir," he says.

"In that case, I direct you to provide copies of all Operation Judgment Day photos possessed by you or your S-2 shop to me by seventeen-hundred today."

CHAPTER 12

Wolfe
Fort Campbell, Kentucky
15 August 2006

Colonel Wolfe hasn't slept more than a few hours since he landed stateside. His BlackBerry shows four missed calls and a message from Ernie Jackson that says, "Call please. V/r, MAJ J." Wolfe isn't surprised by the lack of connectivity in transit, but it really pisses him off. And now, Wolfe's call to Jackson won't go through!

Wolfe's jet lag and worry about the missed calls are a potent combo that prevents him from resting easy during his goddamn mandatory R & R. His dress blues hang in an open closet, standing ready for tomorrow's speech to the local American Legion. A folded note card with talking points from the PAO sits on a small table next to the closet. "Duty, Honor, and American Leadership," are listed as points Wolfe should discuss with the legionnaires.

As Wolfe steps out of the shower, his Blackberry beeps. "Goddamn," he says to himself. Even two thousand miles away he can't make it to breakfast before somebody wants something from him. "Colonel Wolfe," he growls, holding the Blackberry away from his face and trying not to drip on it.

On the other end, Major Jackson clears his throat, wondering if he should make some small talk and ask his boss how it is back in the States. Instinctively, he knows it's the wrong approach and says instead, "Sir, we've got a problem."

Wolfe's mind jumps to the worst things possible: a massive IED attack, fratricide on the battlefield, or a massive outbreak of food poisoning from the chow hall. Realizing that his boss is waiting, Jackson continues. "Corps is up our ass asking questions about whether you cut the ears from the dead during Operation Judgment Day."

"Say that again," Wolfe says slowly.

"They're saying"—Jackson clears his throat again—"that you may have taken body parts, specifically ears, from enemy KIAs during the op. I don't know where it started, but it's out there, sir, and it's being taken seriously."

Wolfe closes his eyes for a second, jaw clenched so tight his molars ache. The room seems to tilt for a moment—not from shock, but from fury. "What!" Wolfe finally barks. "Are you fucking kidding me?"

"Sir, no. I wish I was. I told the general to wait, but he insisted on questioning me and Major Ingram."

"A general? Who?"

"Lindsay."

"One star David Lindsay?"

"Yes, sir, that's the one."

"Fuck me," Wolfe says. "Benetti sent a long-tabbed special forces general to investigate a bullshit allegation that I took ears?"

"Yes, sir, and he's got a JAG major and court reporter swearing people in and taking verbatim transcripts."

Wolfe leaves the steamy bathroom and stands dripping by his bed. His mind races through the absurdity of it. "They're setting me up, Ernie," Wolfe says flatly. "You understand that?"

Jackson doesn't respond right away.

"I want you to get ahead of this," Wolfe continues, voice tight. "Quietly. Find out who said what and who's fanning the flames. Find out and tell me what the hell this is really about."

"Yes, sir," Jackson says. "Understood. General Lindsay ordered

Major Ingram to turn over all Judgment Day photos by seventeen-hundred today. What should we do, sir?"

"Give them to him."

"Roger, sir."

"And Ernie, only give him exactly what he asks for. Nothing more. This guy is not our friend." Wolfe hangs up, tosses his phone onto the bed, and stands there, motionless, the hum of the air conditioner the only sound in the room. He thinks about the ridiculous allegation of taking fucking ears, and about how once an accusation like that is made, the truth doesn't matter nearly as much as the rotten smell it leaves behind.

CHAPTER 13

Jess
Tikrit, Iraq
15 August 2006

Major Ingram knocks on the conference room door at 17:00 sharp. He hands General Lindsey a hard copy of the draft 15-6 report, which the general then hands to me. The report contains the investigating officer's appointment orders, sworn statements signed by Staff Sergeant Fleury and his men, and the photos they took of the detainees and weapons seized on the objective.

The investigating officer's findings stress the squad's strict adherence to unit SOP and highlights their heroics on the objective. He concludes that the detainees were killed while trying to escape and urges Colonel Wolfe to give them Army Commendation Medals with V devices for their uncommon valor.

The statements from Fleury and his men support the findings and recommendation. The statements are all remarkably consistent. They all describe Fleury's amazing shot to take out the first man in the window. They all describe breaching the front door and stress the very humane handling of the male detainees, the women, and their children. They all describe the squad's heroic attempt to save the man who bled out upstairs. They all describe the MAM and their failed attempt to escape. And they all stress that they used the minimum force necessary to stop the escape.

While the report includes before photos of the detainees squatting before the weapons found in the shed, it doesn't include the after photos of the same detainees after they'd been shot. In short, the investigation was a whitewash.

General Lindsay sends Harms to find Major Jackson.

Ten minutes later, Jackson reports, standing stiffly with his right hand touching his temple in customary salute. General Lindsay asks, "Where are the photos Major Ingram took of the dead detainees?" Only then does Lindsay return Jackson's salute.

Jackson drops his salute but remains locked up at the position of attention. "We haven't found them yet, sir," he responds.

"At ease, Major. What do you mean you haven't found them?"

"Sir, there are thousands of Operation Judgment Day photos. Major Ingram is going through them as we speak."

"I instructed him to give all of them to me," Lindsay says.

"Sir?"

"He has them on electrons, right?"

"Yes, sir."

"Then put them on a disc," Lindsay snaps. "In the next hour, I want them all."

Major Jackson returns in twenty minutes and hands a CDROM to Lindsay. The General borrows Harms's computer, and we see Jackson wasn't exaggerating. There are thousands of photos on the disc. Most seem to be public affairs shots taken to emphasize the heroics of Colonel Wolfe and his Raiders.

When General Lindsay stops scrolling and pauses on the first bloody headshot, I gasp. It depicts a thin, bearded man lying in a body bag. The bag is zipped down to his stomach and peeled back to expose his blindfolded head, thin shoulders, and white dishdasha.

Somebody's boot pushes the dead man's grotesquely disfigured head, so his nose points up to the camera. It is hard to tell his age. Maybe twenty-five? Maybe forty-five? Either way, his blood-soaked hair, face, and blindfold leave no doubt as to how he died—a gunshot to the head.

The next photo is even more shocking. It is similar, except the blindfold is being pulled down over the man's face and around his neck by the metal tip of a pocketknife.

"It can't be," I say.

"Wolfe's hand?" Lindsay asks.

"Probably," I say.

Lindsay scrolls back one photo. "It's the same hand unzipping the bag."

I shake my head in disbelief.

"Look closely at the blindfold over the right temple," Lindsay says, pointing at a dark smudge that's only partially soaked in blood.

"What is it?" I ask.

"Powder burn," he says, "from the muzzle blast. He was temple shot from about three inches."

"With his blindfold on," I add.

Silently Lindsay scrolls to the second and third victims, two boys. As Major Ingram had previously noted, both appear to be under sixteen. Both also have the telltale powder burns on their blindfolds, and both feature Colonel Wolfe's hand pulling open the zipper and moving the bloody blindfolds out of the way with the tip of his Raider knife.

"I see how Delgado got the impression that Wolfe took their ears," I say.

"Oh, no," General Lindsay says. He scrolls back and forth between photos. "Look at their hands."

In some photos hands aren't visible, but in several the dead men's hands are zip-tied palm to palm in front of them. "Please tell me this is a Raider SOP for securely transporting bodies in those flimsy plastic body bags," I whisper, unable to process what I'm seeing.

Lindsay scrolls back to the shots of the bound men posing in front of the seized weapons. The three squat together with their hands securely zip-tied palm to palm.

"Sorry, Judge," he says. "They were bound before they were shot. So, what's our next step? Do we report it to CID?"

CHAPTER 14

Jess
Baghdad, Iraq
16 August 2006

I hate to admit it, but I'm happy to be back in the Al Faw palace. Sure, it has all the charm of a rundown boardwalk casino with none of the New Jersey hustle and bustle. And up close, its showy main chandelier is plastic, not crystal. Souvenir-hungry soldiers steal the plastic beads from the matching hallway light fixtures. That battle booty is not exactly high quality, but I guess back home they can tell stories about it.

Another Al Faw oddity is that there's nowhere to sit. The only couch in the whole place is a gaudy, ornamental two-seater that Yasser Arafat allegedly gave to Saddam on some grand occasion. Now soldiers pose on it and sneak a selfie, like goofy teenagers sitting on Santa's gilded throne at the mall. Despite all of it, I'm glad to be back in the air-conditioned safety of our cheesy magic-kingdom headquarters and far away from the Raiders' fanatic loyalty to their vacationing commander.

My first stop is the second-floor lady's room to use a toilet that has running water. As a bonus, the stalls have locks so there's no need to post a guard. The restroom is bus station big. It is really a strange setup for a head of state's palace, but whatever, I'm glad the water runs, and I take my time washing my hands with liquid soap in front of an actual mirror. I take a deep breath and marvel at how the cleaning crew keeps it, and everything else, so well-scrubbed. And best of all, there's no nasty porta-potty chemical smell assaulting my nose.

Up in what was formerly Saddam's domed bedroom, scores of paralegals and attorneys tap on keyboards, taking care of the Corps' legal business. I make my way through a maze of cubicles to Colonel Miller's office. Before I can knock and enter, Master Sergeant Tipton, Miller's senior enlisted paralegal, intercepts me.

"You just back from Tikrit?" he asks.

"Yes, that's right," I answer cautiously, remembering that he wears a Screaming Eagle combat patch. He may have earned it with the Raiders in Afghanistan, who knows? Unit loyalties are often invisible, but they're real and can remain in place for a lifetime. I don't want to share too much information before I know where his loyalties lie.

"It's all over the headquarters about the Big Bad taking ears," he lowers his voice to a conspiratorial whisper. "They say it's true." His face twitches as he licks his lips, waiting for my response.

I don't allow my face to give anything away. "The investigation is ongoing," I answer flatly.

"Yes, of course." He hesitates, licking his lips again, and then continues. "But you must have a preliminary—"

"Jess," Colonel Miller says, coming out of her office to welcome me with a hug. "Are you done?"

"Sort of," I start, and look over at Tipton. "Can we go inside, ma'am?"

"Of course," Miller answers, leading me inside.

Once I close the door, I turn and say, "You won't believe what happened to me up north."

"What?" she says.

"The Raiders told General Lindsay that they didn't have any female latrines or showers for visitors, because they don't get many *split-tails* up there."

"Split-tails?"

"Yes, can you believe it!"

"Was it Wolfe?"

"No, it was his acting XO and operations officer, Major Jackson."

"Let me tell you a quick story," Miller says, motioning me to sit. "When I was interviewing for jobs right after law school, I was in a fancy office with a partner in one of the big law firms. Part way through the interview another partner comes in, interrupts the interview, and starts briefing his buddy on a messy divorce case. He calls the wife 'a real bitch, a slut, and a dyke,' I think were his exact words. Then, he says, 'I need to drain the dragon.' He goes through a door behind the partner's desk and starts to piss. He leaves the door cracked open, and I hear the whole thing. Then, he washes his hands, comes back into the office, smiles at me, and says, 'Hello, little lady.'"

"You're kidding me?"

"No, I kid you not. The interview ended with the first partner explaining that trial attorneys run on brains and testosterone. He asked if I was okay with that kind of environment."

"What did you say?"

"I said yes, but afterward I was certain that it all was a setup. They were testing me to see how much sexual harassment I would put up with, and that's when I decided life in a big law firm was not for me."

"Do you think the Army is any better?"

"Yes. We've got programs and systems for handling exactly those types of situations."

"So, you think I should report it?"

"Heavens no, absolutely not," Miller smiles.

"Then what?"

"The next time you see Jackson, take him aside and tell him that his comment was inappropriate."

"He'll think I'm thin-skinned."

"He'll think you're tough."

"True," I nod.

"Just tell him to knock it off and end it there."

"Colonel Wolfe did not take ears," I say, changing the subject.

"That's good," Miller says, her voice revealing both relief and disappointment.

"But there's more," I add.

"Of course there is," she says, directing me to one of the chairs facing her desk. "Coffee?"

"Yes, ma'am, that'd be great."

She returns with two Styrofoam cups of black coffee. I tell her about the investigation and show her the glossy photo of the bound detainees squatting in front of seized weapons. Then, I show her the three photos of the head-shot, blindfolded men.

"Oh my god! They executed them?"

"The Raiders say no," I answer. "Their draft fifteen-six concludes that the men were shot while trying to escape."

"Shot in the temple?"

"That's their story," I say.

"And they're sticking to it," Miller finishes.

Colonel Miller and I huddle with General Lindsay in the commanding general's waiting room. I pass Lindsay the folder with the 8 x10 glossies.

He flips through them, looks up, and asks Miller, "You've seen them?"

Miller nods.

"And?"

"You don't need a lawyer to tell you what they show."

"True," he agrees, "Where do we go from here?"

"That will be the CG's call," Miller says, as Major Brown calls us into the CG's office.

General Benetti is seated at his conference table. He stands, shakes Lindsay's hand, and pulls out the chair beside him. He then motions Miller and me to sit across from him. "Tell me some good news, David," Benetti says to Lindsay.

"Sir, we've interviewed all the relevant witnesses except Colonel Wolfe. He's on mid-tour leave in the States, and it turns out I don't need to speak with him to make my findings."

"They are?" Benetti asks.

"Wolfe didn't take ears," Lindsay says.

Benetti nods, waiting for the other shoe to drop.

"However, we've stumbled onto something more disturbing," Lindsay says, fanning the photos out in front of Benetti. "Sir, the medic who made the report about the ears actually saw Colonel Wolfe use a pocketknife to slide blindfolds down so that the S-2 could take head and shoulder photos to positively identify the dead detainees."

Benetti picks up a photo and examines it closely. "Headshot at close range?"

"Yes, sir," Lindsay says, handing another photo to Benetti. "And, when evacuated to the rear, their hands were still zip tied."

The man responsible for more than one hundred thousand coalition troops deployed to Iraq, perhaps the most powerful military commander on the planet, is stunned silent. He picks up the last two photos and examines each one. Letting out a long, low sigh, he looks across the table to Miller. "Denise, help me out."

"Sir, we've now got probable cause for murder times three. You could simply send General Lindsay's findings and evidence to CID for criminal investigation."

"Then what?" he asks.

"We wait for the system to work."

"Can I keep the investigation here?" asks Benetti.

"If you mean within command channels, yes, but I recommend against that course of action."

"Why?" Benetti asks.

"Because, sir, it's now a murder investigation and normally that means CID should conduct it."

"That's true, Denise, except CID originally referred the case to us. That, plus I'm not confident the Raiders will cooperate with CID."

Miller nods.

Benetti turns to Lindsay. "What do you think?"

"They'll circle the wagons, sir. Heck, they already have."

"How so?" Benetti asks.

"They did an internal fifteen-six on it, and their second lieutenant IO found that the detainees were shot while attempting to escape."

Benetti spins around and says, "Major Brown, go check if the Raiders sent up a serious incident report on this, or if they reported their fifteen-six through command channels."

"Yes, sir," Brown says, hurrying out.

"Sir," I say, "the Raiders' fifteen-six isn't final yet. Colonel Wolfe told his S-3 to hold it until he returns from leave."

"You've seen it?"

"Yes, sir. The investigating officer is very junior, but on its face his investigation looks solid. Solid, until you see the photos."

"The photos aren't part of his investigation?"

"No, sir," I say, "they aren't."

"Then how did we get them?"

"Sir," Lindsay says, "I ordered the S-3, Major Jackson, to turn them over."

Benetti turns to Lindsay. "You had to order the S-3 to cooperate?"

"The Raiders are very loyal," Lindsay answers.

"To Wolfe?"

"Yes, to Colonel Wolfe."

Brown knocks and enters. "Sir, there's no serious incident report, just an after-action report. The AAR lists eight insurgents, including two foreign fighters, as killed in action and a number of enemy weapons seized. It also mentions twenty locals detained, processed, and released to Iraqi police."

"David, are the three dead included in the Raiders eight KIA?"

"I assume so," Lindsay answers.

"Denise, I want to send David and Jessica back up to Tikrit to finish this."

"Yes, sir, I'll have Jess work up amended appointment orders."

"All right, I want to know if these three were part of the eight reportedly killed in action, why the Raiders didn't report the detainee deaths in a serious incident report, and what is going on with this whitewashed fifteen-six," Benetti says. "Wait, scratch that last part, I don't want to telegraph what I think of their internal investigation. Change it to finding out why they are keeping their findings under wraps."

Miller and I nod, and Benetti stands, signaling that our meeting is over.

As I follow General Lindsay and Colonel Miller out of the CG's office, Major Brown asks me, "Got time for lunch?" Seeing my skeptical look, he quickly adds, "A working lunch."

Brown and I walk over the faux drawbridge and across dusty sidewalks to the huge, air-conditioned tent that serves four meals a day: the standard three, plus a midnight lunch for those on night shift. I fill my tray at the Indian buffet with curries and rice dishes. We find an empty table. Major Brown has loaded up on soul food. By loaded up I mean catfish, ribs, and chicken on one plate, and greens, sweet potatoes, corn bread, and dirty rice on a second plate. Noticing my sideways glance at his tray, he laughs. "My guilty pleasure, and I'm glad they only serve it once a week."

Between bites, I ask him what's up.

"You know the background of this, right?"

I shake my head, waiting for Brown to enlighten me. He tells me that Wolfe had deployed to conduct security operations in the Sunni Triangle six months before Benetti and V Corps arrived to replace the XVIII Airborne Corps.

"Right. You know, I've been here too," I answer, stabbing a large chunk of chicken from my spicy vindaloo. Despite my sarcasm, hearing it from Brown does remind me that Wolfe had a free hand to be as brutal as he felt necessary until Benetti showed up.

"What you might not know, is Wolfe's response," Brown says sharply, not amused by my attitude. "Do you remember when the insurgents blew up the Golden Mosque?"

"Sure, in Samarra. Sectarian violence skyrocketed."

"Right, and the CG flew up to Samarra to calm the local leaders. Wolfe and his staff were also there. Benetti asked Wolfe how much the Raiders were spending on reconstruction and outreach projects. Wolfe said that he refused to risk lives or money on worthless projects."

"Can't the general just order civil affairs to do it?" I ask.

"Wait," Brown says holding up his fork to shush me. "A few weeks later the CG hosted a conference with Iraqi police commanders. Wolfe showed up late, with a brown lunch bag. During the meeting, he held one bacon cheeseburger in each hand, and made a big show of eating them. He even leaned over and offered a half-eaten burger to the Iraqi police chief sitting next to him. The poor guy shook his head and turned a pale shade of green. The CG had me go over and ask Wolfe to leave, and I escorted him out."

"Did you finish his burgers?" I say in perfect deadpan.

"Not the half-eaten one," Brown laughs, but turns serious. "You should have seen the faces of the Iraqi attendees. Wolfe undid everything Benetti has been trying to accomplish."

"They were upset?"

"Yes—and insulted. Benetti was embarrassed and angry. It wasn't good."

"Jeez, you're right. I didn't know."

"Well wait, I've got one more story. In this one, the Raiders saw two insurgents firing mortars and tracked them to a hut. They fired from the air and killed two men and a pregnant woman inside. When we received the spot report, our staff cut an order directing the Raiders to find and compensate the woman's family. Wolfe refused and still refuses to comply, saying the woman and her unborn baby were enemy combatants."

I shake my head in disbelief. It seems that Wolfe's punch-them-in-the-face approach has been on a collision course with Benetti's give-them-a-hand-up approach from the beginning. I wonder why the CG has allowed it to continue? Does Wolfe's fame make him and his insubordination bulletproof? Does the CG hope that General Lindsay's investigation is the golden bullet that finally takes Wolfe out?

CHAPTER 15

Jess
Tikrit, Iraq
16 August 2006

We fly back to Tikrit, and I no longer need to get my bearings. There's no longer an ear-taking red herring to distract me. This time I fly north focused on trapping murderers in their web of lies.

We land, ground our gear, and head to the chow hall for a late dinner. I see Fleury sitting with his men in a far corner. They seem to look to him for comfort. When he spots us, it seems to cut his confidence in half. He's smart and probably realizes that there's nothing he can do. Tomorrow is their day of reckoning, and they will fry.

Over dinner, Lindsay and I talk strategy. It's a rare opportunity, because throughout the investigation, Lindsay has been checking in for reports from his chief of staff. This has given Harms and me the time and freedom to plan witness lists and develop focus areas, but it takes away my chance to mind meld with Lindsay. Sometimes, as I've questioned witnesses, I've been unsure if I've hit all the areas he wanted me to cover. So, when I've asked if he has any follow-up questions, it has been a relief when he says no. Anyway, tomorrow I won't have to guess, because we agree to begin our interviews with the most junior and end with the most senior soldier.

"What about the Iraqi women and children?" Lindsay asks. "Shouldn't we interview them?"

"No, sir, it would just be a waste of our time."

"Why?"

"Iraqi witnesses are difficult to locate, are often reluctant to cooperate, and when they do, are notoriously unreliable."

"Unreliable, how so?"

"To be very kind about it, they exaggerate. For example, when I first arrived, we received an allegation that US troops were stealing watches, money, and cell phones at checkpoints. It was hard to believe, but CID took the case, went to the local unit, and called a phone that had been reported as stolen. Lo and behold, a phone inside a wall locker rang. CID got a search authorization, cut the lock, and recovered half a dozen phones, at least as many watches, money, liquor, and other assorted Iraqi property."

"Case closed?"

"Not really. The soldiers invoked and CID arranged to reinterview the Iraqi victims. To cut to the chase, most didn't cooperate and the few who did had no value as prosecution witnesses."

"Why not?"

"One Iraqi gentleman originally told the Iraqi police that the soldiers took his watch, Samsung cell phone, and five hundred dinars. When CID reinterviewed him, his watch became a Rolex, his Samsung became a Samsung and an iPhone, and his five hundred dinars grew to ten thousand, along with five hundred US dollars. When the file hit my desk, I went to our in-house interpreter to set up an interview to ask the witness about the inconsistencies. The interpreter said it would be a grave error, because asking about it would cause the Iraqi witness to lose face. I explained that if I didn't clear it up before trial, the defense counsel would certainly ask about it at trial and it would be far worse."

"So, what happened?"

"We avoided trial by administratively separating the soldiers with other than honorable discharges. So, no convictions or jail time in a slam-dunk case, but at least we salvaged it a bit by kicking the thieves out."

"And you think that would happen again?"

"Yes, sir. I could give tons of examples, but if we locate them and they are willing to cooperate, I'm certain their testimony would be exaggerated to the point of being unusable."

"Unusable?"

"Maybe unhelpful is the better word," I shrug. "Unreliable and inconsistent testimony creates confusion in the courtroom. That helps the defense, because they'll try to pass it off as proof that the government failed to prove its case beyond a reasonable doubt."

Lindsay nods and sends Harms to set up our interviews. I then brief Lindsay on my plan to catch the shooters in their big lie. He approves, walks me to my SEA-hut, and goes to make a call to his chief of staff.

I turn on my laptop and spend the night reviewing witness statements and transcripts. I sit, surrounded by stacks of documents and reports, in my makeshift office. My mind spins and my body buzzes with anticipation. I pause my preparation to consider a trait that has always defined me—my ability to become completely immersed in whatever task is at hand. It always served me well at law school and in prepping cases as a young prosecutor.

Yes, supreme focus is indeed my superpower. But now, in the middle of this investigation, I wonder if my superpower might also be my Achilles' heel. My ability to focus and sift through mountains of evidence to home in on the important details of the case helps me excel at my job. But in my single-minded pursuit of the truth, I can be oblivious to everything else around me. I know about the dangers that lurk in the shadows and the constant threat of violence. As I pore over the original investigation and review witness statements, I can't help but feel uneasy. I certainly can't afford to let my focus on legal work blind me to the real-world dangers of serving in a combat zone. On the other hand, surrounded by so much macho Raider bullshit, showing fear isn't an option.

I take a deep breath, think of my dashing, young grandfather, and force myself to pause and reflect. Yes, my focus is valuable. It allows me to spot crucial details and assemble them like puzzle pieces into an accurate picture of what really happened. But I must also remain vigilant, aware of my surroundings, and cognizant of the fact that the Raiders view me as a threat.

Tikrit, Iraq
17 August 2006

I rise early, eat breakfast, and go to the brigade conference room to help Harms set up. About half a dozen Raiders are already waiting in the narrow hallway.

Lindsay enters behind me. "First Sergeant," he calls out.

"Here, sir!" Durham barks.

"We don't need everyone here. We'll start with Willowby now and Gruber at oh-nine-hundred." Lindsay hands Durham a copy of the list Harms delivered, saying. "Send them on the hour, in this order."

"Yes, sir," Durham answers and turns to his men. "You heard the general. Go to chow, go to the gym, whatever. Fleury, here's the list. Have your guys report back here, ready to go fifteen minutes before their show time. Got it?"

"Yes, First Sergeant," Fleury answers.

As Lindsay and I step inside the conference room, a nervous energy bounces around in my stomach. In some units, there is an unspoken bond that is so tight and intense that it eludes description. Warriors don't often discuss it outside the brotherhood of arms. Even among themselves, they don't talk about it much. Will I be able to get Fleury and his men to spill the beans? Hopefully General Lindsay's presence will help break through their stony wall of silence. Sergeant Harms is already setting up and testing his equipment. He finishes and gives me a thumbs-up. I ask him to invite Private First

Class Charles A. Willowby to join us.

Willowby enters, his boyish face flushed. He shuffles indecisively, then realizes that the general is waiting for him to report. He finally snaps to attention and throws a nervous salute. Lindsay returns it. I know from reading the IO's draft findings that Willowby is one of the trigger men, but with his chubby face and panicky eyes, I can't shake the idea that it all must have been Fleury's idea. Sure, Fleury didn't pull the trigger, but—

"Take a seat, son," Lindsay says, bringing me back to the task at hand.

Willowby takes his seat directly across from me, his gaze deliberately avoiding mine.

It's like I'm invisible to him. Hmm, I guess he doesn't like women in uniform. I can't wait to begin, because it's likely that he'll underestimate me. That will blind him to the fact that a woman is boxing him in. At least, I hope it will—until it's too late for him to distance himself from his crime.

I read him his rights and inform him that he is suspected of killing a detainee. I expect the allegation to shock him, but he isn't fazed. He verbally waives his rights and signs a Department of the Army Form 3881 to memorialize his waiver of his right to talk to an attorney or remain silent.

"Please stand and raise your right hand," I instruct. "Do you swear to tell the truth, the whole truth, and nothing but the truth, so help you God?"

He nods.

"Please answer out loud for the benefit of our court reporter," I say, looking over at Sergeant Harms.

"Yes, ma'am," he answers, looking away like a child corrected for picking his nose.

I ease into my questioning by asking him about his role in Operation Judgment Day. He starts in about Al Qaeda terrorist training facilities, Special Forces shootouts, and all the military-aged males having been positively identified as enemy.

"Please stick to only what you saw, heard, and did," I instruct. "Do you understand?"

"Yes, ma'am," he answers. "But I did hear 'em say that all them ragheads was terrorists."

"Let's just stick with what you personally saw and did, clear?"

"Yes, ma'am."

"What happened when you landed on Objective Walter?" I ask, and he describes maneuvering with Staff Sergeant Fleury to assault the first house.

"And you met no resistance?"

"Yes, ma'am."

When I prompt him with the tried-and-true "What happened next?" he tells me about flying to the second house, and Sergeant Fleury shooting the man in the window. He tells me about the men in the living room, the ones who hid behind women and children. "He ain't even close to active surrender," he complains. "We shoulda just plugged 'em right there."

Lindsay asks, "What does 'actively surrender' mean to you Willowby?"

"Well, sir, they gotta git their hands up over their heads."

"What if I only get my hands up to my ears, like this?" Lindsay asks, raising his hands to demonstrate.

"Then, you ain't actively surrendered."

"And you can shoot me?"

"Yes, sir—gotta. Got to shoot. Shoot to kill."

Lindsay frowns and lowers his hands. His face darkens and the mood in the room changes. The only one who doesn't seem to notice the change is Willowby. So, I seize the moment and ask him, "Later you did plug them, right?"

"Yes, ma'am," he says, smiling proudly.

"Tell me about it. Every detail you can recall, please." I break eye contact with him and pretend to read something on my legal pad.

Nice and casual, Jess, I coach myself.

Don't spook him. He's almost there.

"Well, they are dangerous fellas, ma'am. Very dangerous," he starts, and then spins a story about how his heroics prevented the escape of the "ragheads" and saved his squad from certain death.

"So, it's your testimony that you chased and butt-stroked the first runner to the ground?" I ask, feigning wide-eyed admiration.

"Yes, ma'am, that's right."

"And it's your sworn testimony that this runner reached up and grabbed the barrel of your rifle?"

"Yes, ma'am, he did."

"And you shot him as he tried to wrestle your weapon away from you?"

"Had to—it was him or me."

"And where did you shoot him?"

"On the ground, ma'am."

"No, where on his body? His face? His leg?"

"Center mass, ma'am."

"Dead center?"

"Yes, ma'am, right through the heart."

"Okay, now please explain to me exactly how all of the bodies fell."

He nods, and like a proud tabby cat presenting a dead mouse to its owner, he offers me one gruesome morsel after another about how each detainee fell dead.

"Would you please draw a sketch showing me where each fell in relation to the house?" While Willowby sketches his death map, I turn to Sergeant Harms and say, "Please let the record reflect that the witness is drawing a diagram, as requested." When he finishes, I inspect the diagram and slide it over to General Lindsay. He nods and slides it back.

I hand it back to Willowby, saying, "Please draw an X to show where each detainee started and an arrow to show which way he ran." Once again, I make a verbal record of the witness's compliance, inspect his artwork, share it with Lindsay, and hand it back to Willowby.

"Now, please mark the one you killed as X-1, the one Specialist Gruber killed as X-2, and the one Specialist Taylor killed as X-3. Can you do that for me?"

"Yes, ma'am. I ain't never gonna forget it."

Once he finishes, I take the diagram, show it to General Lindsay, and hand it to Harms, saying, "Please mark the witness's diagram as Exhibit Seven for identification."

I turn back to Willowby and say, "I'm now handing the witness three photos previously marked as Exhibits One, Two, and Three."

Willowby doesn't know exactly what is going on, but he realizes that I'm a threat to him and his made-up story.

"Go ahead, Private Willowby," I say, "please take a close look at them." I turn toward Harms and continue. "For the record, they are head and torso photos of the three detainees killed by you, Gruber, and Taylor on Objective Walter."

"So what?" Willowby shrugs.

"No, please, pick them up and take a closer look," I instruct and pause for a long ten count. Only when the silence becomes unbearable do I ask, "How do you explain the detainees' zip-tied wrists?"

"You can run and skedaddle zipped," he says, pushing the photos away.

"No, please keep them in front of you," I say. "I've got a few more questions about them."

Willowby blushes and then looks over to General Lindsay for help.

Lindsay sits stone-faced, offering no quarter.

"Please look again at Exhibits One, Two, and Three," I say, slapping them down in front of him like a blackjack dealer. "We'll call them the after-photos, okay?"

Willowby nods reluctantly.

"Let the record reflect that the witness has nodded in the affirmative," I say. "Now, Private Willowby, please explain the bloody blindfolds wrapped around each man's head."

"Ah—they musta done it after. Like some raghead thing about covering the eyes or something."

"Really, that's your story?" I ask, again pausing to let it all sink in. "Please explain the powder burns for me."

"The what burns, ma'am?"

"The *powder* burns," I say, pointing to the scorched temple area on the bloody headband in the photo closest to me. "See the dark, circular burn pattern at the temple here, and in the same spot on the other victims?"

"I don't see anything, ma'am," he says, defensively crossing his arms over his chest.

"Look closer," General Lindsay says, "because they are there, Private Willowby."

Willowby squints, making a good show of following the general's order.

"Do you know what they mean?" I ask.

"Jack shit, ma'am," he blurts, projecting paper-thin false bravado.

"No. Temple shots," I state flatly. "From a handgun about three inches away. How do you account for that?"

"I already been cleared, ma'am," he says. "Been investigated and cleared, so accordin' to first sergeant, this ain't nothin' but double-damn jeopardy. Sides, everybody knows the colonel wanted them dead."

"At ease, Private," Lindsay snaps.

Willowby jumps to his feet, braces at the position of parade rest, and flushes bright red. He apparently knows that even when provoked by a mouthy female officer like me, soldiers should never lose their shit in front of a general.

"Be seated and take a breath," Lindsay says, and gives Willowby a moment. Once Willowby seems to regain some of his shattered composure, Lindsay then asks, "Why do you believe Colonel Wolfe wanted them dead?"

"He told us to kill 'em all," Willowby says. "It's how you get in the club."

"The club?" Lindsay asks.

"Yes, sir, when you get a knife from the colonel."

"For what?"

"For killin' 'em."

"Killing who?"

"The MAM. All them there military-aged males."

"And you've been initiated into the club?"

"No, sir, gotta get a Raider knife from the colonel."

"And, you don't have one?"

"No, sir, not yet, but when the colonel gets back, I'll get mine. First Sergeant will make sure. You get a kill, you get a knife. That's the deal."

Lindsay turns to me. "Anything else, Major Gilbert?"

"Yes, sir," I manage, flipping through the bloody photos. When I find one with a clear shot of Colonel Wolfe's hand moving the blindfold with his knife, I hand it to Willowby and ask, "Is that the knife you're talking about?"

He looks, smiles, and says, "It is, ma'am, and I'm gonna get me mine lickety-split."

I turn to Harms. "Please note the witness has positively identified the knife held by Colonel Wolfe in a photo to be marked as Exhibit Eight."

Behind his mask, Harms nods.

Lindsay turns back to Willowby. "Listen to me very carefully, because I am about to issue you an order. Do not discuss your testimony with anyone. Do you understand?"

"Yes, sir."

"You will go back to your quarters and will not discuss your testimony or this investigation with anyone except me or Major Gilbert. Understood?"

"Yes, sir."

"If anyone tries to talk to you about it, you will report the contact to me. Is that clear?"

"Yes, sir."

"You are dismissed."

Willowby stands, salutes, and waits for the general to return his salute. Then, he departs.

The thought of Wolfe egging on young soldiers to kill with the promise of a cheap pocketknife, is ugly and tragic. Here I was, the big bad prosecutor looking to box in and take down this ignorant knucklehead, and all he was doing was trying to fit in. He was just mirroring what he saw around him and trying to live up to what his leaders expected.

I try to breathe evenly, not get upset, and keep my gaze steady. My heart is breaking, but I have a job to do. I will deal with the morality of it later, because if I dwell on it now, it will leak out through my eyes. And that would be unacceptable, wholly and completely unacceptable in this environment. Now, I need to push it aside and resolve to deal with it later.

CHAPTER 16

Jess
Tikrit, Iraq
17 August 2006

Specialist Jackson J. Gruber is next. Sergeant Harms' research tells us that Gruber is from Texas. His grandfather fought in Vietnam, and his father served in Berlin as the wall fell. As soon as Gruber turned eighteen, he went to a recruiter and signed up for the family business.

As I read him his rights, Gruber does his best to project confidence. Like Willowby, he elects to waive, and I use the same tactics to expose his equally obvious lies. This time, however, when I show the grisly head-shot photos, Gruber's face twists into a mask of grief, and tears flow before he can get his hands up to hide them. He takes a couple of seconds, lowers his hands, and confesses that Taylor passed him Fleury's pistol after shooting the first prisoner. Trembling, Gruber admits that he shot the second prisoner in the head.

"Why?" I ask.

"I don't know, ma'am," he says, choking back snot and sighing. "Maybe because Sergeant Fleury asked for volunteers?"

"He did what?" I ask.

"He asked us who wanted to be in the club, um, right after Top asked him why we had live detainees."

"First Sergeant Durham was there?"

"No, over the radio."

"Got it." I nod. "What happened next?"

Gruber starts talking in a soft monotone, as if on autopilot. He describes how the dead, stacked side by side in bloody robes, looked like Hollywood mummies. He finishes by describing how difficult it was to shove them into the flimsy body bags.

"Is there anything else you want to add?" I ask.

"We all just wanted to do what infantrymen are supposed to do—fight. But instead of facing us like men, they hid behind their women and children," he says, choking up again. "It was all cleared by higher. We followed orders," he says, sniffing loudly and wiping the back of his hand across his nose. "We'll be okay on this, right?"

"That's not something we can decide today," Lindsay answers in a near whisper. He then gives Gruber the same warnings and orders not to talk to anybody about the investigation. Gruber acknowledges the order, stands shakily, salutes, and leaves.

We sit silently for a few minutes. When he thinks, Lindsay doesn't need to fill silence with idle conversation. That's ideal, because I need every second of down time to process, plan, and stay one step ahead of the Raiders and their various versions of the truth. Lindsay finishes thinking and looks over at me. "Who's next?"

"Taylor, sir."

"Good, let's start."

I nod to Harms, who goes out to call Specialist William B. Taylor. He's a wiry, brainy-looking kid, and based on Harms' research, we know he is from Cleveland, married, and recently became a father. Early in the deployment, Taylor impressed First Sergeant Durham by volunteering to clean Iraqi remains out of a truck. And right after Operation Judgment Day, First Sergeant Durham recommended Taylor for promotion to Sergeant. That promotion, of course, is on hold.

I read Taylor his rights, tell him that he's suspected of murdering detainees, and ask him if he wants to waive.

Taylor sits, silent.

I ask him again if he wishes to waive and speak with us and watch his face for a glimmer of realization. There is something there. Maybe guilt, shame, fear, or remorse, but I can't quite read it. Maybe he's just struggling to absorb an allegation that doesn't quite compute. Maybe, like a badly transplanted organ, his sense of honor is rejecting it.

"Murder?" he answers and turns to Lindsay. "Sir, how can anyone here be accused of murdering terrorists? That's what we were sent here to do."

"Are you waiving your rights?" Lindsay asks. "That has to happen before we can discuss what is or isn't murder."

"Sir, you and I both know that they would have done far worse to us if they'd had even half a chance."

"Are you waiving?" I ask Taylor.

"No, ma'am. I've already said all that matters."

"Then, thank you for your time," Lindsay says and stands.

We all stand and Taylor salutes Lindsay. When Taylor departs, I let out a silently held breath.

"He has a point," Lindsay says.

"Against lawful combatants," I agree, "but not prisoners."

We have twenty minutes before our next interview. Harms uses the time to get me up to speed on Raymond L. Fleury. He is a twenty-three-year-old staff sergeant from Eastern Kentucky. His father drifted away when he was young, and his mother died from cancer. Raised by an aunt, he dropped out of high school. He enlisted in August 2000, completed his GED in the Army, and was rapidly promoted. He graduated from Airborne, Air Assault, and Ranger schools, and was chosen to be a drill instructor. Predeployment, he taught himself basic Arabic. He seemed on his way to more fast-track promotions.

That is, he was until he met First Sergeant Durham.

First Sergeant Durham noted in one of Fleury's monthly counseling statements, "You are a strong mentor to your soldiers.

Well-liked, but you trade discipline for affection. For example, you swam in an irrigation ditch with your men. This must stop. Joe doesn't need a buddy with stripes, he needs a leader who enforces standards." Ouch, I bet high-achieving Fleury didn't like being called out for being "a buddy with stripes" who failed to enforce standards.

Lindsay returns at 10:59. Exactly one minute later, Staff Sergeant Fleury knocks, enters, and reports. Fleury's demeanor is technically correct, but it's somehow slightly off. His pride seems AWOL, and in its stead is a facsimile of a soldier trying to cover for its absence.

I ask Fleury to take a seat and read him his rights. He signs the waiver form, and I start to set him up for the questions that will come right after I confront him with the grisly head-shot photos. But it isn't necessary. I can already see defeat in his eyes. Maybe somewhere deep down, he knows what he and his men did was wrong. Or more likely, Willowby or Gruber have talked, and Fleury is already aware that we know what really happened. Fleury is certainly savvy enough to realize that the military justice system will spring into action to hold him and his men accountable for the battlefield executions.

So, I just let Fleury talk. He describes shooting the man in the window. How his men stacked and breached the front door. How the Iraqi men hid behind the women and children. Unprompted by me, he describes how his men took the three men outside, zip-tied and blindfolded them, and sat them cross-legged in the dirt. He claims that when he radioed in a request for a dust-off, First Sergeant Durham responded, "Why in the fuck do you have detainees?"

Fleury takes a deep breath, shakes his head in a silent expression of regret, and describes how the blindfolded men fidgeted. He says they turned their heads, seeming to try to catch the meaning of his words. He pauses, looks down at the floor and says, "Then, I asked, 'Who wants to be in the club?'"

"Asked who?"

"My men," he sighs, looking up. "My guys."

"Why?"

He smiles and shakes his head.

"Why did you ask for volunteers?" I press.

"To kill the military-aged males . . . as ordered," he adds, trying to inject some confidence into his wavering voice.

"Ordered?" General Lindsay interrupts. "By whom?"

"By Colonel Wolfe, Captain Foote, First Sergeant Durham, hell, everybody, sir."

I press my luck and ask, "Did you know it was wrong?"

"Wrong?" Fleury shakes his head and laughs. "Sure, whatever you say, ma'am. But orders are orders."

"Do you think this is funny, Sergeant Fleury?" Lindsay snaps.

"No, sir," Fleury says, straightening in his seat. "But how am I supposed to answer the major's question? I called for a dust-off and was second-guessed. My guys for sure heard the radio call." An uncomfortable silence settles as two men size each other up. Fleury finally asks, "What other option did I have, sir?"

It's hard for me to read Lindsay's expression. Anger? Empathy? Breaking the silence, he answers, "That's why we're here, son. To figure it out."

To keep things moving, I quickly follow up. "What happened next?"

Fleury retreats to a sanitized version of events. He mechanically tells us that before he or his guys could do anything, the Iraqis started to squirm. He claims that he and his men were forced to kill the Iraqis to prevent their escape.

Anger wells up inside me. I slap a gruesome head-shot photo down in front of Fleury like a Blackjack dealer slamming down bust cards. "Forced to kill this blindfolded man?"

Slap! "And this one?"

Slap! "And this one, too!"

"Yes, ma'am," Fleury says, looking away from the photos, "that's my story."

I stare at him in disbelief.

He keeps his eyes averted, unable to make eye contact with me.

"Look at the zip ties on their hands," I say.

Fleury doesn't respond.

"Look at the bloody blindfolds on their heads."

Fleury remains silent.

"Look at the powder burns on their temples."

Fleury glances at the photos. He seems to recognize the significance of the powder burns, and quickly looks away, remaining silent.

"You executed them," I state flatly.

A tear slides down Fleury's sunburnt face. "No," he whispers more to himself than to me, "we didn't have any other option."

I wait a beat. Deciding to come at things from a completely different angle, I inject all the compassion I can muster into my voice. "Sergeant Fleury, please explain to me why you and your men didn't have any other options." Fleury wipes his face with the back of his hand. He looks over at Lindsay, as if to get permission.

Lindsay nods.

"The last full moon," Fleury says, choking up, "I saw a bloated, shattered head. It stared down at me and asked *why*?"

Lindsay and I wait for Fleury to continue.

He shrugs and looks down at the floor. "I mean, I don't know. You know?" He rubs the back of his hand up his tear stained cheek. "I just don't fucking know."

"Staff Sergeant Fleury," I say, leaning in and trying to pull him back. "I've dealt with the aftermath of many terrible things. Talking about it will help. Please, keep going. Tell us what happened."

In a detached, far-away voice he says, "It started with the mission rehearsal out on FOB Pitcher. We got there in the late afternoon. It went from daylight to dark in a quick minute, and we huddled behind a rusted-out shed to stay warm."

As he continues, Fleury's voice gets stronger. Everything falls away and it's like we are there with him. He describes diesel engines whining in the distance, rotors beating from above, helicopters landing and their blades whirling to a stop. Fleury and his men shift back and forth in the darkness trying to warm themselves. They all need sleep, but they won't get any until after the Big Bad gives his rah-rah speech.

"Think we gonna git some action, Sarge?" Willowby asks. "I gotta kill me a doggone raghead. I'm a-gonna git in the club this time," Willowby boasts, bouncing back and forth on the balls of his feet.

Fleury explains that this wasn't anything new. "What he lacked in discipline, Willowby always made up with enthusiasm. But everybody saw his paper-thin bravado for what it was," Fleury smiles, "everybody, except poor old Willowby."

Fleury switches back to FOB Pitcher. Just before midnight, the Raiders form up. Floodlights kick on, illuminating Colonel Mike Wolfe. He stands, superhero style with hands on hips, ready to brief his beloved Raiders.

"This ain't no drill, boys," Wolfe bellows. "Last month the insurgents there chased out a special forces team. Every military-aged male on that island is already positively identified as an enemy. Don't sit back and react to hostile acts, lean forward and take the first goddamn shot. Kill those ugly motherfuckers on sight. Is that clear?"

"Yes, sir!" the Raiders answer in an animal roar.

"We are the alpha mother-fucking predators. No warning shots," Wolfe shouts. "We own the sky! We own the night!"

"Hoo-ah," six hundred men primed to face death shout back at him.

"Did you buy it?" I ask Fleury.

"Buy what, ma'am?"

"Wolfe's 'rah-rah' speech?"

"Yes, ma'am," Fleury answers. "He left no doubt about what we were facing and what he wanted us to do."

"So, what happened next?"

"Major Jackson briefed. He told us that a ground element would roll out and cut off the only land-based escape route. We would then attack three separate objectives from the air. Delta drew Objective Walter, the most built-up site. It has a two-story house, some old bunkers that were blown back in the first Gulf War, and some outbuildings. We expected the biggest fight right there."

"And then?" I ask.

"Colonel Wolfe spoke again. He said that he would dismount with the Death Dealers on Objective Walter."

"Death Dealers?"

"Yes, ma'am, that's what he calls Delta Company—his Death Dealers."

"What happened next?" I ask.

"Colonel Wolfe released everyone, and I took my squad back behind the shed. I grounded my gear and told my guys to do the same and get some shut-eye. Willowby was still worked up. He shook his head like a nervous hen, saying, 'Too jacked to sleep, Sarge.' Specialist Taylor cracked, 'Lighten up, Francis,' and we all laughed, because Francis is his nickname for Willowby."

"Tell me about Taylor," I prompt.

"He's a good soldier and I recommended him for promotion just last month. He has discipline and a killer work ethic. Right after we deployed, his wife had a kid. He didn't complain about it, not once. It is a little weird when he quotes Nietzsche about not becoming monsters and such, but I trust him."

"Got it, he's a good one." I nod. "So, what happened next?"

"Well, everyone laughed at Taylor's dig, except Willowby. But Taylor's put-down did shut Willowby up, and we all needed sleep."

"And then?"

"We did the rucksack flop and caught some shut-eye. I was out cold until First Sergeant Durham kicked the sole of my boot. 'Fleury, get your ass up. The Big Bad wants a word,' he said. So, I got everyone up and joined Delta around Colonel Wolfe. He said that our company led the brigade in confirmed kills and told us what a bunch of bad asses we were. He reminded us that the green berets just got their butts kicked on Objective Walter and that it's still crawling with Al Qaeda. 'We're going to finish the fucking job this time,' he said. 'Come off the aircraft hot and do the same when you kick in the doors. Don't pause to clear rooms, just toss in a grenade and clear rooms by fire!'"

"What happened next?"

"First Sergeant called Martinek and Gomez forward. During a cordon-and-search mission a while back, they had greased a couple of MAMs. That put Delta's body count into triple digits." Fleury pauses, as if to carefully choose his next words. He shrugs and then says, "At least this time we killed MAMs. It makes me sick when we add women, children, and dogs to our kill board."

"Children and dogs?" Lindsay says. "Please explain."

Like a kid asked to rat on his older brother, Fleury looks back at Lindsay with wide eyes. He pauses, clears his throat, and then answers, "Sir, Captain Foote and First Sergeant Durham wanted us to have the highest kill count in the brigade. Sometimes to support their intent, we'd get creative in adding kills to the board."

"Who's the 'we' getting creative, Sergeant Fleury?" Lindsay asks.

"Ah, sir, ah . . . I guess all of us," Fleury stutters, looking away to a far corner of the room to avoid seeing the disappointment in Lindsay's eyes.

After an uncomfortable silence, I jump back in. "What happened after the first sergeant called the two soldiers forward?"

"Excuse me, ma'am?" Fleury asks.

"After the first sergeant called the two soldiers forward, what happened?"

Fleury nods and answers, "Colonel Wolfe praised Martinek and Gomez for their bravery and passed each one a Raider knife when he shook their hands."

"What is a Raider knife?" I ask.

"A pocketknife that has the Raider logo. Here, I've got mine," Fleury says, taking the knife out of a pouch clipped to his belt. He hands it across to me. It's just a simple pocketknife with an olive-green plastic handle emblazoned with the brigade crest. *I could get one like it at Walmart for about five dollars*, I think, as I pass it to General Lindsay.

"How did you get it?" Lindsay asks.

"From the colonel, sir," Fleury answers. "I had a kill early on."

Lindsay nods and hands the knife back to Fleury.

"What happened next?" I ask.

"Willowby said he was going to get one, and I told him that he could have mine. 'Don't count,' he said, shuffling from side to side, ''cause you gotta git it from the Big Bad.' Just about then, the ground force roared off into the desert. I hoped we'd be able to get a little more shut-eye before we mounted the Blackhawks."

"Did you?"

"No, ma'am. I sent my guys back to the shed and went over to see Captain Foote and First Sergeant Durham."

"Why?"

"To tell them that I didn't have such a great feeling about going in so hot."

"What did they say?"

"First Sergeant Durham said that the houses on Walter were enemy targets. He added, 'Are you going soft on me, Ranger-boy?'"

"Why did he add that?" I ask.

"To piss me off, I think," Fleury says.

"So, what did you do?"

"I didn't appreciate being called soft. So, I ignored him and turned to Captain Foote. I told him that nobody else goes in that way, and we'd risk killing innocent civilians. 'Nobody is innocent over here,' he said, ending our conversation."

"What happened next?" I ask.

"I dropped it and went back to my guys. I mean, if they want us to go in so damn hot, I'll go in hot. What's the point in pushing back?" Fleury says shrugging. "About an hour later we boarded the helicopters. Almost everyone was asleep by the time we level off. With six months in country, we could get shut-eye just about anywhere."

"Then what?" I ask.

"Our bird banked, and I saw tracer rounds arcing up. 'Huh,' I thought, 'maybe for once our intel isn't total bullshit.' The six copters carrying my platoon peeled off, taking us to the mud-brick buildings on Objective Walter. We flared and touched down. Inside the helicopter, I couldn't see much, but when we hit the ground, I saw everything just fine. Anyway, we exited, and I led my guys toward the largest mud-brick building. We formed a skirmish line and moved forward, firing. It took a minute for me to realize that nobody was shooting back."

"What did you do?"

"I yelled, 'Hold fire!' We crept forward and stacked at the front door. On my signal we burst through and cleared the building room by room, but it was empty. I called it in. Captain Foote acknowledged and ordered me to relocate to a cluster of houses a mile to the north. So, we went back, loaded up, and took off. The sun was coming up, and the sky was getting lighter. We landed a hundred yards in front of a two-story house with a corrugated metal roof. This time we didn't fire. That is, until I saw movement in a second story window. I couldn't tell if it was a curtain fluttering or a man. Time slowed. I dropped to a knee, took aim, and fired two quick shots. And the shadowy figure dropped."

"Then what?"

"The double-crack of my shots somehow sped everything up. I felt the sun on my back, and felt like I was standing naked, exposed in the open. I rush forward with my squad. We made it to the house, stacked and breached the front door. Inside, three military-aged men were hiding behind four women and two children."

"What happened?"

"I sent Alpha team to clear the upstairs and kept Bravo downstairs to guard the people. We zip-tied everyone, including the women and kids. I told Smith and Jackson to take the men outside."

"And then?"

"Private Taylor yelled from upstairs, 'One down!' I double-timed to him and saw Taylor crouching beside an old man lying on the cracked tile floor. I pushed Taylor away to get a better look. The old guy was about a million years old. He was bleeding out and gummed the air like a dying fish."

"What next?" I ask.

"Taylor and Gruber carried him outside for MEDEVAC. I knew he was dead and said, 'Hold up, guys. He's done.' They stopped and put him down right where we had just lined up to breach the front door. For some reason, Bravo followed us outside and brought the women and children. The women saw the old guy and started to cry. 'Hey, take them inside,' I yelled. I mean, the dead guy might have been their father. Right? So, I went back inside to calm them down. I said in Arabic, "If you've done nothing wrong, everything will be all right." But it didn't work, and they kept wailing."

"What did you do next?"

"We searched the rest of the house and its outbuildings. In a falling-down shed we found a weapons cache. We stacked three AK-47 assault rifles, two ammo cans, and two bayonets in front of the three military aged males and took photos. Then we used white engineer tape to blindfold the men. I told Taylor and Gruber to bag the dead guy and put him out beside the landing zone with the weapons. Then I radioed in our status and requested a pick-up—one casualty, three MAM detainees, and the weapons."

"And what happened?" I ask, holding my breath.

"First Sergeant Durham says, 'Why in the fuck do you have three MAMs who should be dead? Over.'"

"And?"

"I answer, 'Roger. Over,' and Durham says, 'Out,' and clicks off. Even through the static, I could hear the anger in his voice. So, I reconsidered my options," Fleury says. Choking up, he reaches for his water bottle and takes a sip.

I sense that he wants to keep talking, so I give him a few extra seconds to regain his composure and then I go to the heart of the matter. "Will you please tell me about the killings?"

"Yes, ma'am," he answers. In a detached monotone, like a Catholic confessing his sins, he describes it all. He switches back to the present tense, as if he's back on the objective. He asks his men for volunteers to join the Big Bad's club. Willowby double-times over. Then, Taylor and Gruber come over. Fleury unholsters his pistol and hands it to Taylor. Fleury grabs the first MAM by his bony shoulder and pulls him to his feet. Taylor raises the pistol and shoots the man, point blank, in the head. The guy jerks, goes slack, and falls to the ground.

"Why did you hand your weapon to Taylor first?" I ask.

"He's a rock and I knew he wouldn't flinch."

"What happened next?"

Fleury tells us that he pulled the second guy to his feet. Gruber shot him cleanly through the temple, dropping him instantly.

Then, the third guy started to squirm. "He was the smallest, a kid really," Fleury says.

"And?"

"And he tried to wriggle away. So, I pushed him to the ground. He wailed, just like the women. So, I got mad and jerked him to his feet."

I sit patiently waiting for Fleury to continue.

He stares into space, as if reliving it and describes Willowby shakily raising the pistol, jerking the trigger, and firing a grazing shot across the kid's skull, snapping his head to the right. His body spins with it, and he lands on his side, bleeding and zipped. The kid tries to crawl away but can't. 'For fuck's sake, finish him!' I yell."

"Then?" I ask.

"Willowby loses it, ma'am. His bawling matches the kid's wailing sob for ugly sob. I can't take it, so I grab the pistol from Willowby, put my boot on the kid's back to pin him down, and blow the top of his head off." Fleury looks down at his lap and stops talking.

Afraid that he's about to start crying himself, I ask him, "What happened next?"

"I stepped over his body, removed my helmet, and sat in the doorway of the house. I buried my face in my hands. I mean, God damn, if you're going to do something, do it right! Don't make them suffer." Fleury sighs and looks out across the table for some sort of affirmation from Lindsay. Getting none, he turns back to me and continues. "I ordered Willowby to bag the bodies. Taylor and Gruber went over to help, and I yelled, 'No, just Willowby!' But they stayed and unrolled the body bags." Fleury pauses and again looks down at his hands. They are clasped so tightly that white knuckles bulge against his chapped skin.

"Then what?"

Fleury unclasps his hands and wipes them on his pants. He looks up and says, "I watch it all like we are underwater. You know, muffled and in slow motion? They stuffed the dead guys into the black bags. Their heads wobbled. They wobbled like buckets of pudding when my guys pulled the zippers shut."

"What happened next?"

"I told my guys to stack the bodies over with the old man. Then, I keyed my radio and called in a dust off for the four casualties. I stood in the shade, over by the house, watching choppers come and go. I don't remember anything else, until the Iraqi cops arrive."

"Why were police there?" I ask.

"To collect the women and children," he says. "The police cut the zip ties off them and put them in a van. The women started wailing again. They pointed at me and my guys. An Iraqi cop came over, got in my face. 'This is why the Iraqi people hate you!' he yelled." Fleury looks around the conference room with vacant eyes. I slide him a bottle of water. He opens it and takes a drink. "The Iraqi police left," he says. "We were alone. Nobody talked. Nobody looked at each other. We were feeling it."

"Feeling what?" I ask.

"I don't know—shame?" Fleury answers with a defeated shrug. He then tells us that at about noon Colonel Wolfe declared the objective secure. Captain Foote then ordered Fleury to extend his hunt for insurgents to the mouth of the peninsula. "I keyed my radio, 'Same rules of engagement, over?' and Foote responded, 'Affirmative, same. Nothing's changed. Out.'"

"Then what?"

"We left the shade of the house, climbed over a dirt berm, and found a low-slung house circled by a rusty chicken-wire fence. A goat grazed underneath laundry drying on a line. I ordered Alpha to flank the house, while Bravo laid down suppressive fire."

"Then what happened?"

"I told Bravo to shoot high, to avoid killing any noncombatants," Fleury says. "A fat military-aged male with a bushy black mustache ran out of the house. He was wearing a white man-dress and held a baby in front of him!" Fleury pauses, takes a swig of his water and continues. "I mean, who in the fuck uses a baby as a shield? What kind of trash does that?" His question is clearly rhetorical, and I wait silently for him to pick up where he left off.

Fleury looks over to Lindsay and Lindsay says, "So, what happened to the fat man?"

"I yelled at him, sir. I yelled, 'Yalla! Yalla!' But the guy, he doesn't hurry." Fleury pauses, struggling to maintain his composure. "Gruber grabbed the baby. Taylor grabbed the man and dragged him back into the hut. I followed and heard Taylor beating the man."

"Did you move in to stop him?" I ask.

"Taylor's wife had just had the baby," Fleury says. "That's got to matter, right? I don't have any kids and I'm still disgusted by it."

"Okay, so what happened next?"

"Some of my guys pushed past me and pulled Taylor off the MAM. I posted a guard on the guy and sent Taylor and the others to search the farmyard. They didn't find anything, so I'm wondering why in the hell did the fat guy use the baby as a shield."

"Then what?"

"We zipped and blindfolded the MAM and I led him back over the berm. I called it in, and a chopper landed. We handed him and the baby over for transport to the rear.

I turn to General Lindsay, "Any questions, sir?"

"Why didn't you shoot the fat man?"

"He had the baby, sir."

Lindsay nods and issues Fleury an order to refrain from talking about the investigation. Fleury stands, salutes, and walks out of the office with his head hung low. I start to speak, and Lindsay raises his hand stopping me. "Not now, I need a minute."

We sit in silence. Lindsay closes his eyes and sits perfectly still. Harms takes off his mask, gives me a thumbs-up, and flashes me his pearly whites. Lindsay sighs and opens his eyes. "Okay, Jess, we can talk now. There are a few inconsistencies, but what Sergeant Fleury said seems plausible."

Plausible? He gave us everything! I think. Instead, I ask, "What inconsistencies, sir?"

"First Sergeant Durham questioned Fleury about evacuating the first set of military aged males as detainees, and no questions were raised later when the same men were dusted off as KIA. Then, Fleury dusts off the fat man and baby and there is no push back."

"Why does that jump out as inconsistent, sir?"

"The initial rebuff and the later failure to ask questions happened at two different locations and at two different levels of command," Lindsay explains. "Durham is operating down at the Company level and the dust-off landed in the brigade's rear."

"We'll have to ask First Sergeant Durham and Colonel Ross about it," I say.

"Yes," Lindsay says, standing. "We most certainly will."

Lindsay leaves and I watch Harms pack up his court reporter gear.

"Damn, he took the loss," Harms says. "That was some real talk."

"He sure did," I agree, still shocked by Fleury's decision to admit how the killings really happened.

CHAPTER 17

Jess
FOB Pitcher, Iraq
18 August 2006

Investigations can take on lives of their own. Yesterday, during Fleury's interview, new facts crashed in like stampeding buffalo. Touching down in the dusty heat of FOB Pitcher, I expect the pace to accelerate. Sure, we will have the speed bump of getting Delgado to acknowledge that the photos show Wolfe lowering bloody blindfolds, rather than taking ears, but it will largely be housekeeping. The bigger task will be to corroborate Fleury's testimony about the Big Bad's kill-them-all order. Will Lieutenant Colonel Ross come through? That's the question, for now.

Ross must recognize that Wolfe's brash cult of personality is dangerous. Like a short fuse connected to an overfilled powder keg, one spark could set it off to kill blindly. But will Ross stand up and acknowledge it? Maybe. Maybe not. But I'm confident that he'll truthfully answer my direct questions about what he saw and heard at the mission rehearsal. Sharing his opinions could go either way, because Raiders don't seem to know who they are without the Big Bad, and most certainly wouldn't dare to be disloyal. But who knows, maybe with Colonel Wolfe away on leave, Ross will have the backbone to tell us what he really thinks.

Hustling off the birds with our heads bowed under the swirling blades, we head straight to battalion headquarters. General Lindsay checks in with Ross while Harms and I set up in the conference room. Twenty minutes later, Lindsay joins us, and Delgado reports. I swear Delgado in, go through the legal formalities, and turn to the heart of the matter. "I'm handing you photos marked as Exhibits One through Eight. Do you recognize them?"

"Uh, yes ma'am," Delgado says, looking at them. "I think so—"

"Do they accurately depict the bodies you saw on the first day of Operation Judgment Day?"

"Yes, ma'am, they do."

"How many people were present at the scene with the bodies?"

"After I helped the helicopter guys unload them, it was just me."

"Until Colonel Wolfe and the others arrived?"

"Yes, ma'am."

"I'm showing you Exhibit Five, do you recognize the person's hand in the photo?"

"No, ma'am."

"Is it possible this is Colonel Wolfe's hand?"

"Um, I guess so," he stutters.

"Do you recognize the knife?"

"I don't, ah, I'm not—"

"Does it look something like the knife you thought Colonel Wolfe used to cut the ears off of the dead?"

"Yes, ma'am."

Lindsay holds up a hand, interrupting me, and asks Delgado, "In the photos, do you see how Colonel Wolfe is using his knife to pull down the blindfolds? From such a distance, could you have maybe mistaken that motion for cutting off ears?"

Delgado sits bolt upright, takes a gulp of air, and looks up at the ceiling. He seems to be holding his breath and I'm afraid he's going to pass out. He finally shifts in his seat and starts breathing again. Flushed and sweating, he looks at the photo and stutters, "Yes, sir."

"Relax, son. Nobody's trying to put words in your mouth. We just need to make sure these photos cover what you saw and not something else. Do you think you might have mistaken what they show for somebody taking ears?"

Delgado blushes and follows Lindsay's eyes back to the slim stack of photos. He shuffles through the first few, nods his head. "Yes, sir, it's possible."

"It's okay," I interject. "We only want the truth. After seeing the photos, do you still stand by what you reported to your recruiter?" I pause, hoping he'll willingly recant, otherwise I'll be forced to switch to plan B, a brutal cross-examination about his drug-bust-fueled bias against the Big Bad, his lack of ability to see the reported ear taking from where he stood, and his dereliction in failing to verify that the ears were in fact missing from the bodies before emailing his erroneous account to his recruiter. It would be the opposite of the old saying 'this is going to hurt me more than it's going to hurt you' because my plan B cross is designed to destroy the poor kid's credibility. I don't want to do it, because I respect Delgado's courage and don't relish the idea of tearing into a young Latino.

"No, ma'am. I mean, I thought—" Delgado answers, allowing me to push my cross-examination notes to the side.

"Don't worry," Lindsay says. "You did the right thing. We looked into it and found these photos. It's okay to now realize you didn't have quite as clear a view as you thought. The important thing is that you knew something was wrong and reported it."

Delgado nods, stands unsteadily, and makes a defeated, half-hearted gesture that almost resembles a salute. General Lindsay skips his normal warnings. Private Delgado, eyes downcast, silently exits. I feel bad for Delgado, but I'm glad that we've cleanly closed out that part of the investigation.

I look forward to our next interview with Lieutenant Colonel Pat Ross. Harm's research shows exactly what I expected: a devout family man with a sterling military career. Once he's seated and sworn in, I jump right in. "Sir, a few preliminary questions. Your Battalion hosted the mission rehearsal on the eve of Operation Judgment Day?

"Yes."

"Would you please tell us about it?"

"Well, it was pretty standard."

"Please take us through it."

"It hit the high points of the operation and tracked the operation order. Major Jackson should be able to provide you with a copy."

"Sir, we need to know what you saw and heard that night. When Colonel Wolfe briefed the brigade combat team, what did he say?"

"He covered the high points of the operation. It tracked the published operation order."

"What specifics do you recall?"

"Our mission was to neutralize Al Qaeda," he says. "The objective was flanked on three sides by the Euphrates, and it would trap the terrorists."

"Did he tell everyone to expect to be shot at coming off the helicopters?"

"I'm not sure about the exact words he used."

"But he used words to that effect?"

"Yes, to that effect."

"Did he say only military-aged males would be on the objective?"

"Yes, words to that effect."

"Did he say shoot first and kill them all?"

"I don't recall."

"You don't recall the mission's rules of engagement?"

Ross shifts in his chair, then goes back to ramrod straight. "It's all in the operation order. If you want the exact verbiage of the ROE, you'll find it there."

"Sir, soldiers at the briefing have been consistent in reporting that Colonel Wolfe said that the whole area was a suspected Al Qaeda training facility and that all military-aged males had been positively identified as enemy. Is that what you recall? Did he tell the troops to take the first shot and kill everyone on sight?"

Ross takes a deep breath. His easy demeanor changes. He licks his dry lips but can't hide the nervous tic under his left eye. He looks over at General Lindsay. His breath comes out as a sigh and his shoulders deflate. He turns back to me, and says that as darkness fell, Wolfe addressed his Raiders. He told them that they would soon be face-to-face with the strongest enemy they'd ever meet.

"Did Colonel Wolfe give the order to shoot all of the military-aged males on the objective?" I ask.

"Yes," Ross answers.

"Jim," Lindsay interjects, "what were his exact words?"

"He said, 'Come off the birds hot. Don't wait, take the first shot.'"

"Who can corroborate it?" Lindsay asks.

"What?" Ross asks, taken aback. "Everyone, sir. Colonel Wolfe put it out to the whole formation."

"Who will give it to us straight?" Lindsay presses.

Ross relaxes a bit, maybe realizing that Lindsay is trying to protect him. "Maybe the snipers? Jeffries and Krupa, I think. They were attached to my ground force and were surprised by Wolfe's shoot-first ethos."

Tikrit, Iraq
18 August 2006

It's a short hop from FOB Pitcher back to Tikrit to interview Delta Company. We land, ground our gear, and go to the conference room to set up. The air conditioning inside is an absolute godsend. Sergeant Harms and I shed our heavy battle-rattle. We ground our long sleeve camo tops and enjoy the feeling of the cool air drying our damp moisture wicking T-shirts.

General Lindsay steps into the room just as we finish arranging the chairs. He glances from me to Harms and back to me. "Please get back into your proper uniform," he says, his tone firm, "and stay that way."

I look down and see that my T-shirt is clinging in all the wrong ways. Embarrassment floods through me and my cheeks heat up. Did the general notice? I wonder. Probably, and the thought makes my stomach twist. I nod, mumble an apology, grab my ACU top, and slip it back on. Harms follows suit, both of us moving with haste. The awkward moment feels much longer than it is, and I remind myself that it's a lesson learned. I must be vigilant and aware of my surroundings, especially out here. Harms and I silently settle back into our tasks. Harms sets up and tests his equipment and then leaves to gather intel on Captain Foote and First Sergeant Durham. I push my embarrassment aside by concentrating on my interview notes.

"Help me out, Jess," Lindsay says. "What do we know, and what do we still need to find out?"

"Well, sir, we've got probable cause for murder times three against Fleury and two of his men. The photos corroborate their inculpatory statements. So, we're solid there."

"It doesn't sit right, does it?"

"You mean the shoot-them-all order, sir?"

"That and the radio call."

"Technically, Wolfe and Durham could be charged with conspiracy to commit murder, which carries the same penalty as murder—"

"For giving orders?"

"Yes, sir."

"And that would do what, exactly, for Fleury and his men?"

"Nothing, sir, because obedience to orders is never a defense."

"Ah, the legacy of the Nazi war crimes trials at Nuremberg."

"And the mobsters in New York and Chicago."

"Excuse me?"

"When a mob boss orders a hit, he's just as liable for it as the guy who pulls the trigger. The order giver and the shooter are equally liable for the crime, and the shooter can't use his obedience to the order to escape liability. Legally, it's the same here."

"Isn't that for a military jury to decide—"

A sharp rapping on the door ends our discussion. Harms enters, looking like he just won the lottery.

"All right, Harms, spill it. You've clearly got something good," Lindsay says.

Harms sits across from us in the witness chair. He puts a folder down and begins telling us about Captain Geoffrey Foote's background. Foote grew up in Connecticut, attended a Catholic high school, and was senior class president. He was a soft-spoken, bookish cadet at West Point and shocked his classmates by choosing to go into the knuckle-dragging infantry rather than a more technically demanding branch. In the infantry, he religiously embraced the warrior ethos of closing with and destroying the enemy.

Harms then turns to the second file belonging to Foote's first sergeant, Eric Durham. "Durham. He grew up in Missouri and had been in the Army for eighteen years. He's your typical tough first sergeant who uses rough humor and sarcasm to lead his troops," Harms says. He pauses and then continues. "Some of Durham's men think he intentionally oversimplifies things to up the company's body count."

"How?" Lindsay asks.

"Foote and Durham have pushed their guys to be the most lethal Raiders. They stressed it throughout the train-up. Due to their over-the-top emphasis on killing, they are known throughout the brigade as Wolfe's 'death dealers.'"

"And?" Lindsay says, allowing a little impatience to creep into his voice.

"And the men sometimes include noncombatant casualties in their body counts. That, and they sometimes carry their aggressiveness to the extreme. Early in the deployment, Durham led a convoy that came under attack. They returned fire, killed one enemy sniper, and detained the other. Durham had the dead sniper stripped and tied to the hood of a Humvee. Durham then led the convoy through the nearest village to show everyone what happens if you mess with the Raiders. An embedded reporter was there. Here's the story he published about it," Harms says, handing us photocopies of the magazine article.

I glance down at the date of publication and say, "This was long before V Corps got here, months before General Benetti took command."

Lindsay finishes the article, shakes his head, and pushes it back across the table to Harms. "Anything else?"

"Sir, the Raiders use kill boards to track how many MAM each company kills. Foote and Durham liked the distinction of being in first place and didn't want anyone to surpass them."

"Let's talk with Foote and Durham first thing tomorrow morning," Lindsay says, excusing himself.

Captain Foote enters, formally reports to General Lindsay, and looks over at me. Surprise flashes across his face. He's apparently surprised to see a female officer at the table. He is smaller and more corporate than I expected. Most of the Raiders have their hair cut very short in either a high-and-tight, a Mohawk-like cut favored by paratroopers, or simply shaved down to the skull. Foote, by contrast, has his jet-black hair grown out and parted on the side like an evangelist. As he sits, his eyes rove over my chest and then glide to my nametape. I silently curse whoever moved rank insignia from the collar to centered on the chest. Whoever it was clearly didn't have breasts.

"Hello, Major Gilbert," Foote says, taking his seat.

This is Wolfe's death dealer? It's not too hard for me to imagine this guy as the squeaky-clean, Jesus-freak who brown-nosed his way to being first captain at West Point, but it is very hard for me to imagine him as Wolfe's Death Dealer. And creepy Geoff surely didn't need a full three count staring at my chest to figure out my rank. I guess what my granddad said is true: "Sitting in church to be a better Christian is a lot like hanging out in a garage to be a better mechanic—just being there isn't enough." I wonder how long it will take for Geoff to figure out that it's my job to expose him and make him pay for his sins? My battle plan is simple. I will ask him open-ended questions and let him talk through his deployment chronologically. Then, I'll circle back to ask him pointed questions about specific events and finish with a cross-examination about any inconsistencies or omissions.

My open-ended questioning strategy costs us an hour while Foote regales us with his heroic version of events. He tells us about the midnight mission rehearsal and his belief that terrorists were hiding on the peninsula. "Based on the brigade's intelligence, all the buildings on the peninsula belonged to Al Qaeda," he emphasizes. "Delta was at the tip of the spear, and when we landed, we were ready to kill on sight."

"Is that what happened?" I ask.

He shakes his head. "Not right away."

"What happened right away?"

He tells us how the operation unfolded. His story tracks with Major Jackson's slick presentation, minus the fancy PowerPoint slides. Foote tells us about how his company led the brigade in confirmed kills and finally ends his story with he and Durham arriving back in Tikrit with all of their men safe and sound.

Now, I finally get to go to work and surgically poke holes in Foote's self-aggrandizing tale. I start by asking him if he recalls Wolfe presenting knives to two troopers shortly before liftoff.

"Yes," he answers.

"Did Colonel Wolfe tell you and your Raiders to be the dominant predators? To be alpha killers?"

"I don't recall," he snaps. "You should ask Colonel Wolfe about it. He'll be back soon."

"But you do remember Colonel Wolfe giving two of your soldiers Raider knives?"

"Yes, ma'am."

"Do you remember why?"

"Yes, ma'am."

"Was it because they'd recently killed military-aged males?"

"It's because they did their job."

Sometimes my temper causes me to take a risk, and Foote's evasiveness is starting to bother me. So, I ask him, "Do you have a Raider knife?" Holding my breath, I wait for his answer.

"No, ma'am."

"Why, don't you do your job?"

He smiles. He looks over at General Lindsay and then looks back over at me and shrugs. "Of course I do my job."

"But you haven't killed a MAM?"

"No."

"Do you know Staff Sergeant Fleury?"

"Of course I do."

"Do you recall talking with him about his reluctance to go in hot, with guns blazing?"

"No, ma'am."

I pretend to review my notes to buy myself some time. Fleury had convinced me that he didn't buy into the Raiders shoot-first mentality, and I believe he went to Foote and said that he wasn't comfortable with going in hot. I decide to go with a frontal assault and ask, "You didn't talk with him about the mission's rules of engagement?"

"I briefed everyone on the rules of engagement."

"And they were?"

Foote lets out a sigh. "That is in the operations order."

"Indulge me, please."

"Take the first shot, and if necessary, call in the heavy artillery." Foote smiles.

"Is that what you did?" I ask.

"Excuse me?"

"Shoot first?"

"It was status-based targeting. We didn't need to wait for a hostile act or hostile intent, because the objective had been pre-PID for us by higher."

"Did you call in the heavy artillery?"

"No." Foote scowls. "We wanted to, but higher disapproved our requests for artillery."

"Why?"

"I don't know." Foote shrugs. "Maybe because they sit in an air-conditioned palace hundreds of kilometers from the fight."

"So, you don't know."

"No, ma'am, but I do know that Colonel Wolfe doesn't hide out in some far-off palace like General Benetti."

Lindsay raps the table sharply with his class ring, the same ring on Foote's hand. "Captain Foote, you know better." The general stares at Foote for a few seconds. "Do you believe that General Benetti was born a general? Do you honestly think he's never been in harm's way?"

Foote turns bright red and apparently thinks the question is rhetorical, because he doesn't answer.

Lindsay waits.

"No, sir, I don't," Foote finally says.

"I didn't think so," Lindsay says and continues. "This denial of air support is covered in Major Jackson's operation order and after-action report?"

"Yes, sir, it should be," Foote answers.

I wait a five count and then ask General Lindsay, "Sir, do you have any follow-up questions?"

"No," he says, and then gives Foote the standard "don't talk about the investigation or your testimony" warnings. Once Foote leaves, Lindsay turns to me and says, "Let's talk to the first sergeant after lunch. I'm going to get a copy of the operations order."

As soon as the door closes behind Lindsay, Harms shakes his head. "Jeez, you woulda thought."

I shake my head, too, knowing exactly what he means.

"You know, light does travel faster than sound, so some peeps can seem pretty damn bright until they open their traps. But hey, you really shut down that thirst bucket," Harms grins.

"Thanks, but help me out Harms. What is a thirst bucket?"

"A creep," Harms laughs. "You know, some horndog who's trying way too hard."

General Lindsay returns and hands me the operations order. I must read it twice to believe my eyes. It says:

> *Identification of Enemy Forces: Enemy forces will consist of Al Qaeda in Iraq. They will be dressed in traditional LN garb and attempt to blend in with the surrounding population. Intelligence reports that Objective Walter is abandoned and unoccupied by civilians. Therefore, all military-aged males on Objective Walter are to be assumed to be enemy forces unless there are clear signs to indicate otherwise. We will aggressively seize Objective Walter and kill all Al Qaeda. On-scene commanders will make maximum use of on-call rotary wing aircraft and indirect fire to minimize US casualties and destroy retreating enemy forces. On-scene commanders will accept risk to inflict maximum casualties on the enemy.*

I hand it back to Lindsay, with a simple, "Wow. Kill them all."

Before we can discuss it further, First Sergeant Durham knocks, enters, pops a crisp salute, and takes his seat. He is a lean, sharp-eyed, and weathered warrior. He would clearly be more at home leading Pickett's charge at Gettysburg than seated across the table from me. I decide that rehashing Foote's overview of their deployment would be a waste of time and jump straight into the critical areas.

"First Sergeant, do you recall the firefight that was later reported in the popular press?"

"I'll never forget it, ma'am."

I hand him a copy of the article, and ask, "Have you read it?"

"Yes, ma'am."

"Does it accurately cover what happened?"

"Pretty much," he says, crossing his arms.

"Did you or anyone else receive a Raider knife for taking out the sniper?"

"Yes, ma'am," Durham answers. "I put the KIA up on the company's kill board and reported it to the brigade headquarters. When I know who scores the kill, I pass it along."

"Why?" I ask.

"It's SOP."

"And is it also a standard operating procedure that the trooper then gets a Raider knife?"

"Well, I don't think it's written down," he says, scratching his chin in thought. "That's just how it works."

"Do you recall what Colonel Wolfe said about the ROE for Operation Judgment Day?"

"Yes, ma'am, I do."

"What did he say?"

"Objective Walter was preidentified as an enemy target used by the Al Qaeda."

"Colonel Wolfe said to kill all MAMs?" I ask.

"Yes."

"And you expected everyone on the objective to be a military-aged male?"

"That's right. We had solid intelligence."

"So, the order was to kill everyone?"

"That's right, ma'am. It was status-based, pure and simple."

"When you arrived, were there any women?"

"Yes, ma'am, there were some."

"And children?"

"Yes, but no women or children were hurt."

"Any men too old to be considered military-aged?"

"That's hard to say," Durham hedges.

"Afterward you learned that the man in the second-floor window, the one that Sergeant Fleury shot, was approximately seventy years old?"

"Yes, ma'am, but who's to say he wouldn't shoot at us if he had the chance?"

"At the mission rehearsal, do you recall Colonel Wolfe presenting Raider knives to two of your soldiers?"

"Yes, I do."

"Please tell us about it," I say.

Durham walks us through asking Colonel Wolfe to present the trophy knives to the two troopers who had recently killed MAMs. Once Wolfe agreed, Durham gathered about a hundred Delta troopers into a loose circle to watch Colonel Wolfe praise the men for their bravery, welcome them to the elite who had answered the call, and present them with their knives.

"Did Staff Sergeant Fleury come talk to you and Captain Foote after the ceremony?"

Durham's eyebrows spring upwards in surprise. "Yes, I believe he did."

"What did he want?"

"He was worried about going in so hot." Durham shrugs.

"Please explain," I say.

"In a normal mission, like a cordon-and-search mission, soldiers breach an entryway with weapons ready, but they hold their fire unless there's a hostile act or hostile intent. A hostile act is being shot at or attacked. A hostile intent is when somebody aims their weapon at you."

"So, normally they don't fire unless fired upon or if somebody is about to fire on them?"

"That's right."

"And that's what Fleury wanted?"

"Something like that, I guess."

"Do you remember Fleury requesting air transport for three detainees?"

"Not specifically, no."

"Would it surprise you to learn that half a dozen soldiers heard Fleury call to request transport of three detainees, one casualty, and a small weapons cache?"

"No, it wouldn't surprise me."

"Would it surprise you if the same soldiers said your response was, 'Why do you have detainees who should be dead?' or words to that effect?"

"No, I guess not."

"What did you mean by 'detainees who should be dead?' Were you implying that Staff Sergeant Fleury should kill them?"

"Ma'am, I can't answer that question because I don't remember the radio call. If people say I said it, I won't dispute it. Things were moving fast, and I was in contact with soldiers on multiple objectives."

"Is it possible that Fleury took the question as you second-guessing his decision to take prisoners?"

"I don't know, ma'am. The ROE was very clear, but I'm not a mind reader. You'll have to ask Fleury about what he thought."

"Did it surprise you when Fleury later called in a request for transport of four casualties?"

"They died while trying to escape."

"So, the four KIA didn't surprise you?"

"No, ma'am—in combat nothing surprises me."

CHAPTER 18

Wolfe
Fort Campbell, Kentucky
18 August 2006

Colonel Wolfe answers his BlackBerry before it can ring a second time. He's been waiting for this call. The clock on his nightstand reads 2345. His dress uniform hangs limply on the closet door, the ribbons and badges catching slivers of light from the lone desk lamp. He doesn't even bother sitting up and just presses the phone to his ear, jaw clenched. "Jackson," he says.

"Yes, sir. It's me." Major Jackson's voice is quieter than usual, as if the walls in his operation center in Tikrit have started listening. "The investigation has shifted."

Wolfe stays silent.

Jackson exhales before continuing. "Lindsay and his legal team are not focused on ears anymore. It's fallen off their radar."

"Good," Wolfe says, but the tension in his jaw doesn't ease.

"No, sir, not good." Jackson pauses. "Worse, they're now asking about what happened to the Judgment Day detainees on target. The rumor mill's on fire, and Lindsay's staff is asking pointed questions."

Wolfe sits up in bed. "What questions?"

"Whether the detainees were executed after we had them in custody."

The silence on Wolfe's end is long and cold.

Jackson presses on. "They're re-plowing the same ground as our

15-6. They've asked for SITREPs and internal comms logs. They've interviewed Captain Foote, First Sergeant Durham, Staff Sergeant Fleury, and other soldiers on Objective Walter."

"Remind me, have I signed off on the 15-6 officer's findings and recommendations?"

"No, sir, but it was clear that Fleury and his men shot the insurgents as they tried to escape, and that's how the investigating officer wrote it up. Do you want me to scan and send his draft report to you?"

Wolfe exhales slowly through his nose, jaw clenched so tight his temples pulse. "No, keep it close hold for now," he says, voice low and deliberate. "This isn't about the truth, Ernie. It's about theater optics. Benetti doesn't like the way we do business and he wants to make me pay for it."

Jackson says nothing.

Wolfe stands, running a hand down his face. It's not fear that tightens in his chest—it's anger. He's seen this before. The quiet start of a campaign, not against the enemy, but against our own.

"Let me be very clear, Jackson," Wolfe says. "No one was executed. Not by me. Not by my orders. Anyone saying otherwise is lying."

"Yes, sir."

"And you?" Wolfe asks. "You keeping your head?"

"I am, sir."

"Good. Track who Lindsay talks to and find out what they tell him. Start with Foote and Durham."

"Yes, sir," Jackson says.

"And remember, only give Lindsay what he asks for. Nothing more," Wolfe says and hangs up. He then stands in the silence. Another sleepless night. Another wasted day away from his Raiders. As soon as the base personnel and travel offices open, Wolfe is going to end this bullshit and get on the first flight back to his guys.

CHAPTER 19

Jess
Baghdad, Iraq
19 August 2006

First Sergeant Durham gave it to us game, set, and match. He corroborated Wolfe's kill-them-all order. He verified Fleury's reluctance to go in with guns blazing, and even admitted he wouldn't be surprised if soldiers heard him challenge Fleury's request for the transport of detainees. That's why it surprises me when General Lindsay insists that we fly back to Baghdad to interview the snipers, Clayton Jeffries and Zach Krupa, about the Raiders' aggressive rules of engagement and deadly targeting of all military-aged males.

Harms comes up with nothing on Jeffries or Krupa, and it's Lindsay who fills us in on their backgrounds. It turns out they are much more than a two-person sniper team. They are assigned to a special ops unit based out of Fort Bragg. Lindsay divulges that he has "some experience" with the unit. While he doesn't know either soldier, he knows they are thoroughly vetted, highly trained, and extremely experienced. They also fall outside of Colonel Wolfe's chain of command and cult of personality.

As advertised, Jeffries is an impressive soldier. He listens intently to my questions, answers succinctly, and doesn't hide the ball. He confirms Wolfe's order to kill all MAMs and adds that sometimes Special Forces has extremely permissive ROE, but he had never seen such broad discretion given to a regular Army unit.

"What about in conventional force-on-force warfare?" Lindsay asks.

"Status-based targeting is standard in conventional war, but I haven't had the pleasure yet. As far as fighting in an insurgency, I'll stand pat with my first answer. I have not seen another regular unit switched to status-based targeting over here."

Lindsay nods, and I continue. "Did anything of note occur during the convoy?"

"We reached Objective Gaslight after five hours on the road. Gaslight was a rundown gas station surrounded by a concrete parking lot, with a cluster of bombed-out buildings across the street. Lieutenant Sullivan, the Delta Company platoon leader in charge of the convoy, noticed handprints painted on the buildings. Since handprints are used as covert symbols of the insurgency, Sullivan had his men dismount and search the area. Off in the distance, they spotted two men digging in a field. Sullivan ordered his men to shoot them, but the men were out of range."

"What happened next?" I ask.

"Sullivan wanted Krupa and me to try. So, we climbed onto the roof of a building and used a scope to take a better look. The men were just farming, and Krupa told Sullivan that the men were not a threat. Sullivan disagreed and ordered us to kill them."

"Did you believe that the mission ROE allowed you to kill them?"

"I didn't see any reason to do it."

"But," Lindsay interrupts, "did you think that the ROE permitted Sullivan to give you that order?"

"Sir, I honestly don't know. I just knew it was fucked up."

After waiting a three count, I ask, "What happened next?"

"Krupa told me to shoot and miss. So, I fired three short rounds. The men dropped their tools and ran. Sullivan and his men drove out into the field and detained them."

"And?" I prompt.

"They were just farmers."

"Did anything else happen that morning?"

"Lots, ma'am, Sullivan was really on a roll."

"Then please, take us through it."

"The Raiders found a family—a man, his wife, and their three children—in a house just south of the gas station. The man claimed he was the local sheikh and told us that Al Qaeda fighters came every few weeks, forcing him to feed and house them. He claimed they were currently training at a farm several miles away. Sullivan radioed Captain Foote and said he had an informant who could identify insurgents and asked permission to raid the farm. Foote said yes and gave Sullivan two Apache helicopters in support. Sullivan gathered everyone together for a mission briefing and reminded us to go in hot and kill everyone."

"What did you think of it?" Lindsay asks.

"I thought it was reckless—reckless as hell."

"Which part?"

"All of it, sir," Jeffries says. "We didn't know the sheikh and had no idea about his motives or reliability. We didn't know where he was taking us. And, we had no idea who we would find."

"Go on," Lindsay says, "tell us what happened."

"The sun was up, and people were out. They stared at us as we rolled by, and they didn't seem happy to see us. The Humvees cordoned off the building, and half a dozen of Sullivan's soldiers dismounted. They approached an unarmed Iraqi man sitting on a wooden block. He was dressed in a white dishdasha, and he was reading a newspaper. The sheikh told Sullivan the man was an insurgent leader."

"And?"

"Sullivan yelled, 'Kill him!'"

I take a deep breath and ask, "Did they?"

"No, ma'am. They looked to their team leaders for the green light. They held their fire and detained the man."

"Anything else?" I ask.

"Oh, yes," Jefferies smiles, "the sheikh told Sullivan there were more insurgents in a house down the way. Sullivan radioed in a request for Apaches to fire Hellfire missiles at the building, but the pilots were busy elsewhere. So instead, Sullivan ordered one of his MK-19 gunners, who manned a grenade launcher mounted on the top of a Humvee, to fire on the house. As soon as the grenades hit, Iraqis bugged out in vehicles and on foot."

"Then what?" I ask.

"Sullivan and his men started shooting. Dust and smoke were so thick that it was hard to see what was going on. The young soldiers seemed to think we were under attack and were firing wildly. Krupa and I were shouting, 'Cease fire!' But it didn't make a damn bit of difference. Then, two Black Hawk helicopters landed. First Sergeant Durham and two squads were there to reinforce us. Durham found Sullivan and asked, 'What the fuck is going on?'"

"First Sergeant Durham was there?"

"Yes, ma'am."

"Are you sure?"

"One hundred percent," Jefferies answers. "He took charge, got everyone to stop shooting, and organized tending to the wounded."

"He did what?"

"He took charge. He sent soldiers to search the apartment building across the street, saying, 'See those water tanks on the roof, studs? That means that there are people, probably families, living in there. Unless you're fired upon, no more shooting. Just take it slow and easy, and we'll be okay.'"

"Was it okay?" I prompt.

"As good as it could be, ma'am."

"Please elaborate."

"They did find families inside. One guy attempted to escape cradling a baby. In total they detained twenty-one men, six with known ties to Al Qaeda."

"I didn't see Sergeant Krupa. Is he available for an interview?" Lindsay asks.

"No, sir," Jefferies says.

"Why not?"

"He's at Landstuhl," Jefferies says, his voice trailing off. "Evacuated, sir."

"What happened?" Lindsay asks.

Jefferies shrugs, "Roadside bomb."

Lindsay nods and dismisses Jefferies. He then turns to Harms and me. "Meet back here at seventeen-hundred sharp, packed for another quick trip up north."

Lindsay leaves and Harms hooks his thumb toward the empty witness chair. "He's a hunnit,"

"He's what?"

"A hundred percent solid," he says. "You know, the whole truth and nothin' but."

I sit and contemplate how Sullivan and Durham's actions on Objective Gaslight fit into the larger issue of command climate and leader culpability.

"We out?" Harms asks, snapping me out of my thoughts.

I nod and add, "I'm going to swing by my CHU, get some fresh clothes, take a quick shower, and go brief Colonel Miller. I'll meet you at the helipad."

Freshly scrubbed and refreshed, I climb the wide marble steps flanking the airy atrium. I recall the class Sergeant First Class Viñas gave to deploying JAG females. Her gruff advice seemed silly at the time and out of place for soldiers like me who serve in a safe space like the Al Faw palace. But now, after coming back from Tikrit, I appreciate her blunt words. I knock on Miller's door and wait for her to answer.

"Come in," Colonel Miller calls.

I step into her office. She's seated at her desk, reviewing a stack of documents. She looks up and offers me a small, welcoming smile. "Jess, what can I do for you?"

"I wanted to update you on the investigation and on a separate note also thank you for setting up the females' predeployment meeting with Sergeant First Class Viñas," I begin, taking a seat across from Miller. "Sergeant Viñas's advice was . . . well, it was very direct."

Miller raises an eyebrow. "Okay, shoot."

"Well, the investigation seems to be wrapping up."

"Good."

"Everyone we've interviewed confirms that Wolfe issued a kill-them-all order during the mission rehearsal."

"What?"

"Yes, ma'am, and I believe his order was the proximate cause of the killings."

"Of detainees?" Miller asks. "Did he order the killing of detainees?"

"Not specifically, but he did tell his men that there would be no noncombatants on the objective and to come off the birds hot. He specifically did give an order to kill everyone, which certainly implies that no prisoners should be taken."

"Okay, but tread carefully with your proximate cause theory, because General Lindsay might see things differently," Miller says. "So, what about Sergeant Viñas' briefing?"

"Well, when she gave it, I wasn't a fan. Even after working here at the palace, I thought she went too far. I mean, she didn't hold back. She told us to get rid of the makeup and cut our hair short, get on the pill, and avoid falling into the trap of being a "Queen for a Year" while downrange. At the time I felt it was too blunt."

"And now?"

"After spending time with the Raiders, I see her point. First, there's very few women, in fact none at the battalion level and below. Second, the men are more likely to stare and make comments.

During his interview, Captain Foote flat out undressed me with his eyes. What if I was an enlisted female under his command? The idea makes my skin crawl."

Miller nods. "Viñas has lots of deployment experience. She wanted to prepare her sisters-in-arms for the challenges specific to female soldiers."

"True," I agree, "but there is a line between coddling and holding someone down."

"Do you really want to stand by that analogy?" Miller laughs.

"No, ma'am, I guess not," I answer, pausing to choose my words more carefully. "But her 'get on the pill' advice threw me, and I felt her overall approach seemed too rough. I knew her intent was good. However, her scared-straight act was too much."

"Did you talk to her about it?"

"I stayed behind and asked her about her recommendation to get on the pill."

"And?"

"She claimed it makes periods less painful and messy, and that a down-range pregnancy could be career ending."

"She's not wrong," Miller says. "Every time we MEDIVAC a woman on no notice, everyone assumes it's because she's pregnant. Our new scarlet letter is a P, I guess."

I nod. "I've heard stories about deployment policies where all women testing positive for pregnancy receive an Article 15 for either adultery or fornication, depending on their marital status."

Miller leans back in her chair. "That's true, Jess, and it's exactly why I asked Viñas to give the talk. She is direct, but she can communicate in a no-bullshit way that wouldn't sound authentic coming from me."

"Maybe hold some follow-up sessions for women serving in remote locations? We could address their concerns and questions more gently. You know, let them know there is a support system running all the way back to you."

A look of concern clouds Miller's face. "Did anything happen to you up there?"

"To me? No, nothing criminal. Up in Tikrit, things are different. Guys openly leer. Here there's a robust female presence. Up there, there's almost none."

"You're right—I should circle back and check on our women, especially the ones in remote areas. I'll have Viñas make calls and follow-up with our paralegals."

"Thank you, ma'am," I say. It's moments like these that remind me why I chose this path—to make a positive difference and help ensure that every soldier feels supported.

CHAPTER 20

Wolfe
Fort Campbell, Kentucky
18 August 2006

Colonel Wolfe enters the base personnel office with his fists clenched and boots hammering the tile with controlled fury. Every junior officer and soldier in his path steps aside instinctively. No one wants to be in his way. No one asks questions. They know better.

He shoves open the door to the travel section without knocking. "Where's Lieutenant Fraser?" he snaps.

A specialist behind the front desk blinks, startled, and points without speaking.

Wolfe's already moving, turning the corner and slamming open the inner office door.

Fraser, a pale adjutant general officer with glasses too big for his face, jumps to his feet. "Sir—"

"I've been here for eight goddamn days, and my leave form still hasn't been processed. My travel is hung up, and now I'm being told I'm not authorized to schedule my return flights until you amend my goddamn paperwork!"

Fraser opens his mouth and closes it again.

"I'm a brigade commander," Wolfe growls. "I should not be waiting for you to complete my goddamn paperwork to get flights back to my unit in Tikrit."

"Sir, I understand, but your leave and R & R travel was approved in theater. We have to coordinate with them before amending anything. You're also considered high-profile and public affairs must approve changes to your schedule—"

"Stop talking," Wolfe snaps. "I will not be boxed in by travel clerks and public affairs handlers who think they can hold a battlefield commander hostage."

The desk phone on Fraser's table buzzes quietly and Fraser knows better than to answer it.

Wolfe ignores it and continues, "Let me make one goddamn thing clear, *Lieutenant*. My men are in Iraq. They're out there getting mortared while I sit here being told it's hard to amend my travel orders. That is one hundred percent unacceptable!"

"I'll try to escalate, sir," Fraser stammers.

"No," Wolfe snaps. "You will not try. You will do. Call whoever you need to. Cut through whatever red tape is choking this post, and get me on a flight today!"

Fraser nods furiously, reaching for his phone.

Wolfe takes one last, hard look at him before turning on his heel and storming out, his rage echoing behind him in the stunned silence of the travel section.

Balad, Iraq
19 August 2006

The desert heat hits Colonel Wolfe like a slap the moment he steps off the C-130 onto the sun-blasted tarmac at Balad Air Base. He squints into the light, adjusting the strap on his rucksack, boots grinding against the grit on the runway as he moves toward his waiting Blackhawk helicopter. His face is drawn, shadowed with fatigue. Out of frustration he went out of pocket to buy commercial tickets to Kuwait City, and then he bullied his way onto military flights to Baghdad and on to Balad. It was twenty hours of transport hell with three layovers and one missed connection in Paris. All that ass pain and he only managed to shave two days off his planned return from R & R. But at least now, he's back where he's supposed to be.

"Sir," the door gunner standing at the skid of the Blackhawk says as he comes to the position of attention and salutes his commander.

Wolfe returns the salute, hands his rucksack to the trooper, and climbs aboard. He's happy to hear the big turbine engine whine and feel the rotor blades spin as he buckles in and puts on a headset. He toggles his microphone and says one word to the pilot, "Headquarters."

"Yes, sir," the pilot answers. The Blackhawk rises, tips forward, and races above the desert floor at breathtaking speed. Wolfe leans his head back against the seat and shuts his eyes. His mouth tastes like stale coffee, he hasn't showered in two days, and he has hardly slept in almost three. But there's no time for that now.

When they flare and land, Wolfe makes a beeline to his brigade headquarters building. Soldiers inside snap to attention as he walks in. He gives a curt nod, not slowing his pace. "Where's Major Jackson?" he asks a duty NCO.

"In the operations center, sir."

Wolfe pushes through the door. The hum of monitors and the low murmur of staff chatter dies. Major Jackson stands at the central table, looking over a stack of printed reports. He straightens as Wolfe approaches. "Sir, it's good to have you back."

"Thanks," Wolfe replies. He plants his hands on the edge of the map, and fixes his eyes on Jackson. "Let's go to my office so you can update me on the investigation."

Jackson nods, and follows Wolfe up the hallway. Once behind the closed door, Jackson begins. "Lindsay has interviewed about a dozen personnel. Most are from Delta Company. His focus is squarely on whether detainees were executed postcapture on Objective Walter."

Wolfe's jaw tightens.

"Are they focusing on anyone in particular?" he asks.

"Fleury. Gruber. Willowby. And Taylor."

Wolfe grunts. "What about me?"

"Not directly, but they are looking into command climate, ROE interpretation, and whether your commander's intent left room for ambiguity. Lindsay is coordinating with JAG. There's chatter at Corps that they're trying to make the case that this was systemic."

"Systemic?" Wolfe mutters, almost to himself.

Jackson lowers his voice. "They are asking about the briefings we gave at the mission rehearsal. They're asking everyone, from colonel to privates, about whether you told them to kill every military-aged male on the objective."

Wolfe leans back slightly. For a moment, the room is silent except for the quiet hum of a generator.

"Benetti wants me out," he says. "I didn't play Benetti's bullshit 'hearts and minds' game. Instead, I took the fight to the enemy. That doesn't play so well on CNN."

Jackson nods, but says nothing.

"Fine," Wolfe says, straightening in his chair. "Let Lindsay dig. Meanwhile, I've got a war to run. We've got guys out in sector tonight?"

"Yes, sir. I've got a briefing ready for you."

"Good," Wolfe says, glad to be back at it again.

CHAPTER 21

Jess
Tikrit, Iraq
20 August 2006

Our flight is pushed back because General Lindsay must deal with an emergency over at the Fourth Infantry Division. As we lift off, the sun sets. We cut through the desert darkness and two hours later flare and land on a remote pinpoint of light near Tikrit. General Lindsay leads the way off the bird.

"Come on, Jess, let's check in with the commander," he yells once we're out from under the roaring rotor wash.

As we enter the low-slung brigade headquarters, an enlisted orderly sees the star on Lindsay's combat vest and jumps to his feet, calling the building to attention.

"At ease," Lindsay says. "We're here to see the colonel. He's expecting us."

"Yes, sir!" the young soldier barks, and escorts us to Colonel Wolfe's office. The walls, hanging blinds, and ceiling fan are all flat white. The flooring is a light gray, soundless laminate. There are two black leather office chairs facing Wolfe's expansive granite-topped desk. The Big Bad is seated in a black leather executive's swivel chair, which is carefully centered behind the desktop. Apart from the laptop computer, a small black coffee maker, and a plain white coffee mug that looks as if Wolfe walks it over from the chow hall each morning, the room is empty. For some reason, this surprises me.

Wolfe rolls his chair back, rises silently, and steps forward to shake Lindsay's hand. His massive, meaty paw is attached to a massive, meaty man. He looks over at me and nods, acknowledging my presence. He then motions us to sit before returning to his swivel seat behind his oversized, empty desk.

I feel uncomfortable and out of place seated across from Wolfe. The room itself is as spartan and colorless as Wolfe's desk, and the space feels impersonal, but with Wolfe's dominating presence it feels way too close and intimate. I'm glad he didn't offer to shake my hand.

Wolfe takes the initiative and says, "Sir, I imagine our meeting is purely a formality?"

Lindsay says, "No, it's not."

Wolfe's eyes grow dark, and his mouth tightens. The man has charisma, no doubt, but his pungent, alpha-male arrogance repulses me. Suddenly, the full force of his nickname hits me. It doesn't just spring from childish wordplay; it oozes from him. He is big. He is bad. And he is clearly a very dangerous man.

"Okay, let's knock this out and get it over with," Wolfe says to Lindsay. "Ask me whatever you need to close this thing out, sir."

Lindsay looks over at me and I shake my head, because we can't let Wolfe hijack the interview. It has to be done correctly and on our terms.

"If it helps end this nonsense, I didn't take any goddamn ears," Wolfe booms a little too loudly. I understand his anger. By all accounts he loves his men, thrives on high-pressure situations, and lives for the Army. After twenty years of leading soldiers, it is still his passion. And now, because of some little shit who claims he saw Wolfe take ears, it's suddenly all in jeopardy. For an officer as dedicated and driven as Wolfe, that's unacceptable. But so is battlefield murder.

"Sir," I say to Lindsay, "we need to follow the standard of taking sworn, verbatim statements for this investigation."

"Who asked you, *Major*?" Wolfe spits at me, his eyes narrowed to angry slits.

"We'll interview you in your conference room tomorrow at oh-eight-hundred sharp," says Lindsay, standing to leave. "Does that work for you, *Colonel*?"

Wolfe stands, nods, and fumes. As we leave, his eyes are easy to read. His entire military career he has excelled at identifying and eliminating threats. He now views us as a threat.

Tikrit, Iraq
21 August 2006

Harms and I rise early to set up the conference room. General Lindsay has given me the green light to question Colonel Wolfe, with Lindsay batting clean-up. I stayed up drafting lines of inquiry and cross-referencing my questions with known facts and transcribed testimony.

"How are you doin', ma'am? Holdin' up?"

I force a smile. "Yes, of course. And you?"

"Gucci," he grins, giving me a thumbs-up.

"Harms, you got me again," I shrug. "What's Gucci?"

"You know," he laughs. "No problem 'cause everything is just so damn fine."

Lindsay enters and we discuss whether I should read Wolfe his rights. Lindsay doesn't want me to read him his rights while he and his Raiders are conducting combat operations. I hold my ground because that's what the law requires. We finally agree that I don't have to inform Wolfe that he is suspected of committing war crimes, specifically being an accessory before the fact to the premeditated murder. Instead, I'll generally inform him that he is suspected of dereliction of duty for failing to adequately supervise his troops during Operation Judgment Day. This should be sufficient to put him on notice about the nature of our investigation without inflaming him to invoke his Constitutional rights.

Helping Harms run cords and test microphones eases my nerves, but adrenaline still courses through my veins, readying my body to fight or flee. It's no wonder, because the Big Bad rattles me. Everything about him is intimidating. That, and throw in the fact that Colonel Miller and Lieutenant General Benetti will review my questions and Wolfe's answers. All of it pushes my nerves to the breaking point. My stomach clenches. My bottom-line fear is not so much of Wolfe jumping across the table and attacking me, but of falling short in bringing him to justice. That poor little hick Willowby is without a doubt an idiot. I'm convinced that his bloodlust was not fueled so much by a bigoted hatred of Muslims, but in his desire to conform. He simply wanted to be a member of the club. Wolfe's club, to be precise. And that's just it. I know I can convict Willowby in my sleep. What kept me up last night, however, is the fear that a lack of intuition or skill on my part might allow Wolfe to escape his criminal culpability.

Lindsay enters the conference room at 08:00 sharp. "Ready to go, Jess?"

"Yes, sir," I answer.

"Harms?" Lindsay asks.

Harms nods and gives a thumbs-up. We all sit silently waiting for Wolfe to arrive. I review my notes and my stomach lurches again. I'm beyond thankful that I chose to skip breakfast.

A few minutes after eight o'clock, we hear Wolfe's voice echoing in the hallway. It is not so much loud as assertive. It cuts through the background noise.

My stomach clenches again, bringing a sour taste to my mouth. Instinctive fight-or-flight responses, I guess, but flight is not an option. I'm here to read the Big Bad his rights, to ask him hard questions, and to create an airtight record. I sit up straight, prepared to face the man behind the booming voice. I breathe deeply and picture myself asking well-composed questions and having the confidence to give him the space to answer and trap himself with his own arrogant words.

Wolfe strides in without knocking or reporting. Before he can take charge of the situation, Lindsay says, "Good morning, Colonel. Please take the seat across from Major Gilbert."

"Is this necessary?" Wolfe says, pointing with his chin toward Harms and me.

"It is. Once you take your seat, Major Gilbert will read you your rights."

"For taking ears? You know damn well that's a load of crap."

Lindsay looks over at me, giving me the green light to answer Wolfe's question. "Sir, for suspected dereliction of duty during Operation Judgment Day."

Wolfe's jaw drops and confusion flashes across his broad face. He turns back to Lindsay. "Because some punk says I cut off some goddamn ears?"

"Please let Major Gilbert finish," Lindsay says. "She'll get the formalities out of the way, and then we'll talk on the record."

"Sir," I start, "you have the right to remain silent, you have the right to consult with an attorney. As I said, you are suspected of dereliction of duty for failing to properly supervise your subordinates during Operation Judgment Day. Do you understand?" With smoldering hostility, he nods.

"Sir, for the record you must answer out loud. Do you understand the allegation?"

"Yes," he says, looking like he wants to vault across the table and rip my throat out.

"And you understand your rights?"

"I said yes, *Major*."

"Thank you, sir," I say, sliding a Department of the Army Form 3881, Rights Waiver Statement, across the table to him. "Would you please memorialize your waiver by signing block 3, in Section B?"

"What?" he growls, squinting at the form.

"Here, sir," I say, pointing, "right below section A."

Wolfe shakes his head and looks up at Lindsay, silently asking him to stop this madness. Lindsay, stone-faced, turns and looks at me.

"The print is very small," I say. "Would you like me to read it to you?"

"No," he snarls with animal ferocity. "I can read the damn thing myself."

He leans back and takes his time. When he looks away from the page, I follow his eyes. They bore into the general's star centered on Lindsay's chest. Then, Wolfe looks back at the form. I can see wheels turning. Will he waive? Of course he will. It's hardwired into his DNA. But he sure isn't enjoying it. Rights waivers are for common criminals, but he must sign it before he can defend himself. He signs with a violent scribble and shoves the paper back to me.

I pick it up, saying, "I have retrieved a DA 3881 from Colonel Michael Wolfe. His election to waive his rights will be marked as Exhibit 59." I rise and walk the document over to Sergeant Harms, who finishes mouthing my words into his face mask. He takes Wolfe's waiver, stamps it with practiced efficiency, and places it in a fat binder.

An atavistic, animal emotion pitched somewhere between fear and rage flashes across Wolfe's face as he considers the irony of a one hundred-thirty-pound female questioning his battlefield leadership. Wolfe may have been born to be a general and is undeniably adept at leading the Army's toughest men, but I am also very good at what I do. Nervous energy buzzes through my body, prepping me for battle. I am ready. The Big Bad is on my turf. I start my questions the same way I have a hundred times. "For the record, you are Colonel Michael H. Wolfe?"

"Yes."

"You are the commander of the Seventh Brigade Combat Team?"

"I am."

"Please tell us about the Operation Judgment Day mission planning."

"Insurgent attacks in Ramadi, Karbala, and An Najaf rose slightly when we arrived. Most were IED and our intelligence indicated it was the work of local insurgents, tribal militias, and Al Qaeda in Iraq. They were using an area along the Euphrates River as a training base. It consisted of a cluster of farmhouses, an abandoned baby food processing plant, and a few bombed-out bunkers. Special Forces raids in the area killed thirteen Al Qaeda, but the attacks continued."

"So, what did you do?"

"I had my staff begin initial planning for an operation designed to disrupt Al Qaeda operations and to kill or capture members of Al Qaeda in Iraq."

"Sir," I interject, "would you please tell us about the mission rehearsal you held at Forward Operating Base Pitcher?"

Wolfe turns to Lindsay. "Is this necessary, sir? I've got a war to fight."

"Answer her questions, Colonel, and you'll get back to your brigade."

"What was your question?" Wolfe says in a low rumble. There is something savage in his thinly concealed rage and it is more intimidating than if his voice had been at a full roar.

"The mission rehearsal at FOB Pitcher, what happened there?" I repeat.

"Nothing happened."

I reach for my water to give myself a second to regroup. I take a sip. I must shorten my questions and put Wolfe on a leash or else I'm going to lose control of the interview. I set my water bottle down and say, "Sir, as darkness fell on August 8, you addressed your ground and air assault forces. What did you tell them to expect on the objective?"

"I told them it belonged to Al Qaeda, that they should go in expecting hostile fire, and to be ready to kill them before they have the chance to kill you."

"So, nothing about disrupting or capturing?"

"Excuse me, do you think this is funny?" Wolfe snaps.

"Nobody's laughing, sir. I'm simply trying to make an accurate record of what happened."

"What happened is that we kicked ass, and everyone came back in one piece."

"Sir, we'll get to that in a minute—"

"No lawyer tricks. Let's get to it now."

I pause and fight an internal battle about when exactly I should set aside my prepared questions and let Colonel Wolfe sow the seeds of his own destruction. "Yes, sir. Please continue."

"After I lost my first man, in Panama, I resolved to never let it happen again."

I wait, silently hoping that he'll continue.

Filling the silence, Wolfe continues. "I lost Staff Sergeant Jack Carter." The way he lingers on Carter's name is an act of penance. Clearly, the loss still stings. "From that day forward, I resolved to never lose a man due to lack of preparation. To never underestimate the enemy."

"And how did that play out at the mission rehearsal?" I ask.

"I was painfully aware of the danger my men would be facing. I told them that they were going to be shot at coming off the helicopters."

"Did you tell them to shoot first?"

"Of course," he growls.

I decide now is the right time to ask the big question, "Sir, did you tell them to kill all military-aged males on the objective?"

Wolfe leans forward and begins to answer but suddenly stops and leans back in his chair. He blows a frustrated sigh out through his nose. "Really? That's it?" he asks me. He turns to Lindsay. "You want to know about the friggin' rules of engagement?"

Lindsay nods.

"Sir, did you tell your men to kill all military-aged males on the objective?" I ask again.

"I designated the target area hostile in advance and authorized my Raiders to engage targets first instead of waiting for a hostile act or hostile intent. Given our intel, it was crazy to wait and take fire before engaging the enemy."

"So, did you tell your men to kill all military-aged males?"

"When you fight a brutal, unconventional enemy, Major, you don't do it with one hand tied behind your back," Wolfe snaps. "If the intel was good enough for the artillery guys, it was sure as hell good enough for my infantry guys."

"So, you did order your men to kill all military-aged males on the objective?"

"No, I never specifically stated that *every* military-age male should be killed, just that my guys didn't have to wait and could take the first shot."

"That seems to be the same thing, sir. Can you please explain the difference?"

"The difference is that I didn't authorize my men to wantonly kill every man on the goddamn objective, as you cleverly imply. I only made it clear to my men—men going into harm's way—that the individuals on the objective were preidentified as combatants and could be targeted unless they made a clear and unequivocal action to become a noncombatant by standing still with their hands raised above their heads."

"What if they didn't get their hands up in time?" I ask.

"Listen, little lady," Wolfe growls, stabbing his finger at me, "this isn't a video game. It's life and death, and I refuse to put my men in any unnecessary danger. The wild card in every movement to contact is always how the men will react when shots are fired. Will they fight or wuss out? That's the vulnerability of every foolproof plan—the goddamn fools who carry their rifles into battle. Will they fight? Well, I decided to make it easy for them. None of this 'let's wait for hostile acts or intent' bullshit. My Raiders flew into battle knowing that they were authorized by me, the on-scene commander, to take the first shot." Wolfe shifts his gaze to Lindsay. "Shoot first, right? That's how the West was won."

There it is again. He keeps returning to it, like the tongue returning to a chipped tooth. He's deathly afraid of losing a man. He's also deeply disturbed by having me openly question his combat leadership. Tough; life is hard. "Sir, would it surprise you to learn that no less than fourteen soldiers of varying rank recall you ordering them to kill all military-aged males on the objective?"

"It was approved by higher."

"Excuse me?" I say. "Please explain . . ."

"Based on our intel, I sent up a fires request through Division to Corps. I wanted air strikes and an artillery barrage to prep the battlefield before we went in. Everyone supported it, but because I wanted to use bunker busters, it had to go up to SECDEF for approval. Some old Pentagon maps from the First Gulf War listed the food processing plant and the bunkers there as suspected WMD sites."

"And?" I ask, trying to hide my unease.

Wolfe, his confidence restored, rumbles on. "I was worried about going in without air and artillery support. Then, when we were rereading the ROE, we saw that it said, 'Members of designated groups can be declared lawful armed combatants by the on-scene commander.' Well, I'm the on-scene commander, I thought. Why don't we just go in hot and shoot these guys on sight? Bottom line— it was my call," he says, shutting down my line of questions.

Rattled by his answer, I loop back to a safe question. "So, if I understand correctly, it does not surprise you that your soldiers recall you ordering them to kill all military-aged males on the objective?"

"Move on, please," General Lindsay says to me.

"Yes, sir," I say. I scan my notes to buy a little more time to collect my thoughts and then remember that the Raiders don't adhere to General Benetti's warning shot policy. I take a calculated risk and ask Colonel Wolfe, "Sir, does your unit have a standing order against firing warning shots?"

"Yes."

"Under whose authority?"

"As the on-scene commander, I always have the inherent authority to make higher headquarters' policies more restrictive."

"How exactly is skipping straight to shoot to kill more restrictive than following the Corps' published escalation of force rules?" Lindsay asks Wolfe.

"Sir, I have access to information about the local conditions and may restrict my troops as conditions dictate. Here, conditions don't allow the luxury of firing warning shots. We don't shoot to scare, only to kill. That is the very definition of more restrictive, sir."

Lindsay takes a deep breath, shakes his head, and turns to me, "Any follow-up questions, counselor?"

Before I can get a word out Wolfe says to me, "We requested a legal review from our division headquarters before I issued my more restrictive escalation of force orders. If it helps, counselor, I can provide a copy to you."

"Yes, that would be helpful," I say, wondering what kind of legal gymnastics could possibly lead to the conclusion that a "shoot to kill" order is somehow more restrictive than the requirement to fire warning shots before shooting to kill. Like a mistuned guitar plugged into a thousand-watt amp, Wolfe's explanation is loud, fuzzy, and wrong. General Benetti's intent was clearly to stop the unnecessarily killing of Iraqis at checkpoints, and Wolfe's semantic games simply can't navigate around the fact that "shoot to kill" flies in the face of his corps commander's clear intent to de-escalate the violence.

I take a sip of water and review my notes, before switching to a new line of questioning. "Sir, do you recall presenting Raiders knives to two of Captain Foote's men right after the mission rehearsal?"

"I do."

"What was that about?"

"I give them out the same way other commanders give out challenge coins."

"Sir, why knives?"

"Most soldiers like knives better than coins."

"What did those two soldiers do to earn their knives?"

"They did their job to the best of their abilities."

"By killing Iraqis?"

"That's what combat soldiers must be ready to do."

"And that's how your Raiders get a knife? How do they get in the club?"

"There's no club, Major, and I give knives for lots of reasons."

"But, if a kill goes up on the board, you give the shooter a knife?"

"Listen, most soldiers don't want to shoot. When they do, they sometimes feel guilty. I don't want them to hesitate. I don't want them to feel guilty. The kill boards and knives help to socialize them so that they do their job and get home in one piece. Do you understand?"

Before I realize it, I'm nodding in agreement. I take a sip of water to break his momentum, check my notes, and ask, "Sir, during Operation Judgment Day, did you help your S-2 photograph dead Iraqis?"

"Yes," he answers and keeps right on talking. "We are required to take head and shoulder shots to compare against known high-value targets."

I show Wolfe the photos and ask him if that's his hand in the photos.

"Yes," he says.

"Sir, did you notice that the men were bound and blindfolded?"

"Of course; I'm not blind."

"And you didn't report it to higher?"

"I made a preliminary inquiry and was told that the military-aged males were killed while trying to escape."

"While bound and blindfolded?"

"JAG advised that I should appoint a fifteen-six officer to investigate, and that's exactly what happened."

"Who at JAG?"

"I don't know, some staff officer at Division."

"And the results of the investigation?"

"I don't know," he scowls. "Instead of reviewing the findings and recommendations, I'm here with you."

"Sir, I have a copy here. Would you like to review it now?"

"You have a draft copy, counselor. It won't be final until I approve the findings and recommendations."

"Sir, would it surprise you to learn that the draft report does not include any mention of your rules of engagement?"

"Why should it?" Wolfe asks. "Even with status-based targeting, the ROE has nothing to do with it. Everyone knows that prisoners are not lawful combatants."

I turn away from Wolfe to Lindsay, a look of fierce satisfaction on my face. Wolfe's words are damning, and he doesn't seem to know it. "Sir, I have no further questions. Do you have any?"

"No," he says. "Colonel Wolfe, may I see you outside?"

"Yes, sir," Wolfe says, rising and following the general out.

Harms lowers his mask and makes eye contact, the two of us aware that Lindsay's presence is the only thing keeping Wolfe and his Raiders in line. I shiver at the realization that he and his men view us as the enemy from within. And way out here in the Sunni Triangle, we have no backup, except each other.

CHAPTER 22

Jess
Tikrit, Iraq
21 August 2006

General Lindsay returns to the conference room with a casual, "At ease." Harms and I continue gathering up the assorted microphones, cords, and recording equipment. Once packed, Harms asks if there is anything else he can do for us. "No, go grab some chow and be ready to fly this afternoon," Lindsay says.

Harms leaves, and Lindsay and I are alone. "Sir, may I ask what you said to Colonel Wolfe?"

"Sure," Lindsay says, leaning back in his chair. "I told him not to worry about the investigation. I told him to concentrate on safely redeploying his Brigade back to the United States. I also asked him for the legal annex his team worked up to support status-based targeting." Lindsay slides a thin file across to me. "Review it and tell me what you think." I read through it twice. The dots all seem to connect, but the final answer—a free-fire zone on the objective—doesn't compute.

"Well, counselor, what do you think?"

"I'm not sure," I admit. "On the surface, it does seem to add up. Al Qaeda is a terrorist organization. The available intelligence did indicate that the area was used by Al Qaeda. Based on that assessment, the prior corps commander did approve the Raiders' request for artillery and aerial bombardment to prep the battlefield.

Only the old suspicions of weapons of mass destruction derailed it at the Pentagon."

"The ROE did not differentiate between direct and indirect fire," Lindsay adds, "but it did say that with positive identification terrorists could be engaged and destroyed. The Raiders reasoned that because their troops would be limited to using small arms on the objective, there would be less collateral damage as compared to artillery strikes or aerial bombardment."

I catch myself nodding in agreement and then shake my head. "Still, I can't wrap my mind around the lawfulness of an order to land and kill everyone."

"Kill all *military-aged males* on the objective," Lindsay says.

"Yes, but Colonel Wolfe told his men that the area had been pre-PID, and only military age members of Al Qaeda would be on the objective."

"And, he was wrong," Lindsay says.

"Sir, you are an infantryman and spent a lot of time in Special Forces. In your experience, how should it work?"

"In a status-based operation, before soldiers can lawfully kill, they must first identify combatants by name and prove, with reasonable certainty, that they are members of a terrorist organization. Wolfe's argument is that the intelligence his unit gathered made it reasonably certain that anyone there would be a member of Al Qaeda. Neither Corps nor SECDEF second-guessed his conclusion that only combatants would be present. So, to Wolfe, giving his guys the green light to go in shooting was the same as the SECDEF giving the Air Force the green light to fly over dropping bombs."

"So, he used the denial to justify the order he gave to shoot everyone his men encountered?" I ask. "Does it sit right with you?"

"No, it doesn't," Lindsay says, his face grave. "Go pack and I'll meet you for lunch. We'll have to sort this out back in Baghdad."

Baghdad, Iraq
22 August 2006

During our flight back to Victory Base, I ponder the rules of engagement. The ROE, as supported by Wolfe's bombardment theory, was to shoot all military aged males on Objective Walter. That's where Al Qaeda was supposedly training, and it matches the area Wolfe wanted to bomb. But the soldiers at the mission rehearsal understood Wolfe's kill-them-all order to encompass the whole peninsula. The ground force leader, Lieutenant Sullivan even understood it to apply to his blocking position at Objective Gaslight. Still, even limited geographically to Objective Walter, the order to kill all MAMs doesn't seem lawful.

I get some odd looks wearing my battle-rattle in the palace, but I want to talk to Colonel Miller about the ROE right away. I stop at my cubical to check email and when I look up from my screen, I see Colonel Miller. She invites me back to her office, pours two cups of coffee and says, "Well, what was it like up there?"

I pause to think. "Cultish."

"Most commanders are charismatic and cultivate loyalty within the ranks—"

"No," I interrupt. "It's more than unit pride. It's a wall of silence and without General Lindsay—"

"Okay, I get it," Miller leans in, "the Raiders serve in a man's Army."

"No, they serve in *Wolfe's* Army. He's the alpha and the omega. They'll kill for him. They'll die for him. And they'll for darn sure lie for him. I didn't believe that the first casualty of war is the truth, until I went to Tikrit."

Miller nods, "And when truth dies, justice is also a casualty."

"The shooters really didn't have a choice," I shrug.

"They made a choice," Miller stated flatly. "They pulled the triggers."

Miller and I discuss Wolfe's theory on the ROE and I'm still struggling to deconstruct it. The law of war is just that—law. The

Geneva Convention, The Hague Convention, and scores of other treaty-based rules that the United States signed and agreed to follow are commonly called LOW and must be followed by our troops. ROE, on the other hand, is battlefield guidance tailored to a specific mission or situation and given to the troops by their commander. The most famous ROE was issued to the troops by one of the commanders at Bunker Hill: "Don't fire until you see the whites of their eyes."

I make no progress with the murky LOW and ROE mess bobbing in my mind. Tired and frustrated, I head back to my SEA-hut for some shut-eye. As I cross the palace moat, one of Saddam's killer carp breaks the surface. The scare interrupts my muddled, circular thoughts that are still swimming in circles like the stupid fish.

Okay, ROE can't ignore LOW because LOW is law and must be followed. Rockets and bombs can't distinguish between combatants and noncombatants, so they may rely on vetted intelligence to comply with LOW. But soldiers on the ground can see the difference between a combatant pointing a rifle and a noncombatant cradling a baby. And that's the difference! Wolfe can't rely on intelligence to give a kill-them-all order, because the LOW requires his soldiers to distinguish between combatants and noncombatants before shooting. The law of war doesn't allow it, and no mental gymnastics with the ROE can make Wolfe's kill order legal. I turn around and double-time back to my cubicle, call Lindsay, and tell him about my epiphany.

"Okay, Jess, write it up," he says. I hear a flicker of uncertainty in his voice. Is he skeptical? Does he feel a pull of loyalty to justify the actions of his fellow infantrymen? Is he looking for a way to justify Wolfe's crazy order?

CHAPTER 23

Jess
Baghdad, Iraq
23 August 2006

General Lindsay set a two day suspense for me to draft his findings and recommendations. The ear-taking allegation is easy to address. The criminal culpability of Fleury and his men is also straightforward. Wolfe's command climate and the Raiders' misapplication of the ROE are much harder to pin down. I want to fix the blame on Wolfe, but Lindsay isn't so sure about it.

I close my eyes, sit back, and think about the holy trinity of law enforcement—means, motive, and opportunity—but what about obedience? What if Fleury's sole motive was to follow Wolfe's ROE and Durham's implied order? The Big Bad openly declared a free-fire zone on the objective. He effectively gave his men the green light to kill them all and let God sort them out. Come to think of it, I'd like to do something like that to Wolfe, Jackson, Foote, and Durham. That is, court-martial them all and let God sort them out.

A chirp from my computer interrupts my thoughts. The chirp is my mom calling for our Sunday video chat. I take a deep breath, realizing that I missed our call last week because I was flying north with Lindsay and Harms. I steel myself for the conversation ahead. It's been a grim week, and I can't talk about any of it, because the last thing I want is to worry her. My computer chirps again and I answer. My mom's broad smile fills the screen.

"Hi, Mom," I greet her, mustering my own smile.

"Jessica, how are you?"

I know she really wants to ask about the dangers I face over here, but she won't. She's too polite, too afraid of burdening me with her worries. So instead, she asks the same question she always does. "What's it like over there?"

I can't paint an accurate picture of the harsh realities over here. The flat, dusty landscape, the relentless heat, the constant threat of snipers and mortars. Instead, I give her my standard vague response. "It's challenging, Mom, but we're making progress."

"Everyone here is so proud of you for serving your country," she says, wiping her eyes and blowing her nose with a tissue.

Her words tug at my heartstrings, a bittersweet reminder of the sacrifices families make for their soldiers and the nation. Like many first-generation Americans, my mother's patriotism is turbocharged. I want to tell her that patriotism alone won't bring an end to the suffering and violence over here, that we need more than just words to make a difference. But I bite my tongue, knowing that it's not what she wants to hear.

"Thanks, Mom," I reply. "I appreciate your support more than you know."

After the drama passes, we fall into an easier rhythm of conversation. My mom tells me about the latest happenings back home. As our conversation continues, I can't help but feel a pang of guilt. I wish I could be more honest with her, to share the full extent of my fears and frustrations. But I know that she worries enough, and the last thing I want to do is add to it. So, I plaster on a smile, masking the turmoil brewing beneath the surface, and carry on with our conversation, grateful for the brief respite from the harsh realities over here.

I catch up on emails and case updates, and eat dinner alone. Back in my CHU, I'm restless and can't sleep. My thoughts drift to my grandfather. I know from his photo that he was enlisted and my grandmother said that he served in Korea. I wonder why he never talked about the war. Did he receive an order to kill noncombatants over there? If the dashing young soldier I saw in Grandma's photo would have received a kill order from a gruff commander like Wolfe, would he have been able to push back? Or would he have been too young and eager to question Wolfe's authority? I hope he served at the headquarters, like me, and never had to make a tough call in the heat of battle. How could he—or anyone—live with it?

I sleep restlessly until a vivid dream jars me awake. A weird mashup of Korea and Iraq lingers in my foggy brain. My grandfather and Fleury stand together in a barren desert firing killing shots into kneeling prisoners to win cheap plastic knives. Damn Colonel Wolfe! Damn him to hell for turning brave men into killing machines. It's no wonder some men choose to wall it all off. Who on earth could live with the guilt of killing to win the approval of a commander who keeps score on dry erase kill boards?

Baghdad, Iraq
22 August 2006

The next morning, I enjoy a twenty-minute early morning walk from the Al Faw Palace over to the division headquarters on Zee Lake. In Iraq, water represents prestige, wealth, and power. To reward the party faithful, Saddam built waterfront properties near his splashy island palace. Zee Lake was built in the shape of the letter Z to maximize the number of faux Italian villas that could be put along the water's edge. Saddam's boys, Uday and Qusay, had a double-island lake, also ringed with villas, a mile or so down the road. I sigh and admire the expensive properties, sparkling water, and ornamental gardens, before heading into the division headquarters for my meeting with General Lindsay.

The deputy commanding general's spotless office is nestled in the windowless interior. The clean, antiseptic space stands in sharp contrast to the dust and grime outside. It's a quiet, almost tranquil venue for us to discuss the evolution of the rules of engagement, the situation-driven rules that govern our actions in this ever-shifting theater of war.

"Back when the Third Infantry Division rolled into Iraq as the breaching force, it was a different world," Lindsay begins. "The battle lines were much clearer. Combatants wore uniforms and carried arms openly. It was possible to visually distinguish them from noncombatants."

I nod, memories of the chaos and uncertainty surrounding what became our astonishingly successful hundred-hour dash to Baghdad and unconditional victory.

"Yes, sir, but as the mission and conditions changed, we had to adapt the ROE over and over. It grew to be indecipherable, with its dozens of pages and then edits, changes, and a cluster of classified directives. Now, only a few legal advisers who specialize in operational law can navigate through the maze."

"Job security for JAG attorneys," he laughs. "The core, though, remained constant."

I lean forward. "But when Colonel Wolfe and his men arrived in 2006, the ROE had been updated to guide an occupation force, not a breaching force. It was no longer about shooting on sight, but about reacting to hostile acts and intent force protection."

"Exactly," he replies, his fingers tapping on his desk. "And it's all distilled in the wallet-sized card each of us carry. We're trained to respond with force only when faced with hostile acts or intent. Hostile actions, they're clear-cut. A civilian firing a rifle at a soldier crosses the line, instantly making him a lawful target."

I nod. "But establishing hostile intent, that's where it often gets murky. Like when a civilian drives his car toward our forces. Is it an act of hostility, or just driving?"

General Lindsay's sigh is heavy, a reflection of the moral

dilemma that haunts every decision made over here. "That's the crux of it, and when force is used, it must remain proportional to the threat. In that car scenario, there's a spectrum. It goes from firing warning shots to shots to disable the vehicle before resorting to shooting the driver."

His words remind me of the weight of responsibility that comes with every decision made by our troops operating outside the wire. The ROE attempts to mitigate uncertainty with a simple moral compass. In the midst of it all, the ROE grounds us and allows us to make reasonable split-second decisions about who lives and who dies. As we continue our conversation, I realize how the rules must balance restraint versus the use of deadly force while remaining simple enough for our troops to follow when lives depend on their split-second decisions.

Lindsay checks his watch and stands. "Sorry, Jess, I've got to get to my sync meeting."

"Sir, you've given me plenty to think about. I'll work on your findings and recommendations tonight."

"Thanks. Send them and I'll review them tomorrow morning," he says, stepping out to take on another of his never-ending tasks.

It's late, and when I return to the ornate room that was once Saddam Hussein's bedroom, there is only one light on. I drop my stack of papers at my cubicle and make my way back to Colonel Miller's corner office. Technically, her office is also a cubicle, because there is no practical way to extend her walls to the domed ceiling, but she has a door.

"Jess," Miller says, looking up from her computer screen. "How are you doing?"

"Lots to do," I answer. "I need to draft Lindsay's findings and recommendations tonight."

Miller nods. "The investigation brought in some big surprises. The unlawfully killed detainees, the miscommunications, the blurred lines of command, maybe even Colonel Wolfe's outright insubordination." Miller leans against her desk, her gaze steady. "Stick with the basics. Combatant immunity protects lawful combatants from criminal liability for killing other combatants. The rule seems clear, but events on the ground can quickly muddy the waters. Keep it simple. Were the Iraqis combatants when Fleury and his men killed them?"

"No, but what about their rules of engagement? I know that obedience to orders is never a defense, but it doesn't change the fact that an order to kill every military aged male was in place."

"Jess, you must acknowledge the chaotic nature of warfare as we do our best to uphold the principles we hold dear. Wolfe and Fleury will both say that they were only following orders, but neither may use combatant immunity as a shield for their unlawful actions," Miller says, her tone firm.

"How do we balance accountability with the realities of the battlefield?"

Miller offers a knowing smile. "We advise. Commanders decide. It's a mantra you will carry throughout your career. Our role is to provide counsel, to ensure legality, but the final decisions always rest with the commanders we advise."

I go back to my cubicle. The weight of it settles over me. The words I choose will play a pivotal role in Lindsay's recommendations and Benetti's decisions. I glance at the stack of papers on my desk: interview transcripts, gruesome photos, notes, regulations, and legal citations. As I work, I remind myself that the path to justice can be complex, and my duty is to navigate it with precision tempered by common sense. I work all night and at daybreak, I'm finally satisfied with my thirty-page memo that lays out what happened during Operation Judgment Day and who should be held accountable for the killings. I'm particularly proud of one passage: "But we must also acknowledge that in the fog of war, confusion can cloud judgment." It's the language I used to mitigate the harsh sting of criminal liability I assigned to Private Willowby, Specialist Gruber, Specialist Taylor,

Staff Sergeant Fleury, First Sergeant Durham, and Colonel Wolfe.

My eyes burn with weariness. I email my drafts to Lindsay, swing by the chow hall for an egg white omelet, and head to my hootch for a power nap.

CHAPTER 24

Jess
Baghdad, Iraq
25 August 2006

I sleep late and make it to the office just before lunch. My first stop is to check in with Colonel Miller. I take a deep breath as I enter her office.

Colonel Miller looks up. "Major Gilbert, come in," she says, motioning to the chair across from her. "I bet you're here to talk about the criminal liability of First Sergeant Durham, Captain Foote, Major Jackson, and Colonel Wolfe."

I nod, taking my seat. "Yes, ma'am. I've been thinking a lot about it. Fleury and his men are clearly liable for the premeditated murder of the detainees. The circumstances, including Wolfe's order may serve as extenuating and mitigating factors but absolutely may not serve as a defense."

Colonel Miller leans forward, her eyes sharp. "And Foote? And Durham? They shot down Fleury's concerns at the mission brief. And what about Durham's radio call: 'Why do you have detainees?'"

"I've also given that a lot of thought." I pause, gathering my thoughts. "I think that it's much like the first Iraqi man Fleury shot through the window."

"How so?" Miller prompts.

"Foote and Durham were at the mission rehearsal and heard Wolfe's order to kill everyone on the objective," I explain. "When

Fleury second-guessed Wolfe's order at the mission brief, the sharp response from Durham and Foote made sense. Later, when Fleury made the first call to request a dust-off, Durham's question still made sense."

Miller's eyes narrow slightly. "But it could have been a veiled threat or a blunt reminder about Wolfe's order. Doesn't that fit the legal definition of accessory before the fact?"

"Yes," I agree. "And that's why I've given it so much thought. It's like Fleury's first kill that morning. While I don't like that he killed the old man in the window, I can't in good faith charge him with murder because he reasonably thought, based on all the facts and circumstances, that the old man was a combatant. He was wrong, but when he shot, he didn't possess the mens rea to support a murder charge."

Miller nods slowly. "And you believe it's the same for Durham?"

"Not exactly the same," I clarify. "Similar, though, because at the time Durham was probably confused about what was going on and might have legitimately wondered why Fleury and his men had taken prisoners. Later, Durham knew the intel was wrong, and he prevented the Raiders on Objective Gaslight from indiscriminately shooting noncombatants."

"And Foote?" Miller asks.

"He's a selfish, self-promoting officer," I say, allowing some frustration to creep into my voice. "But if I give Durham a pass, I can't turn around and charge Foote with a crime."

"The cover-up, maybe?" Miller suggests.

"No," I respond, shaking my head. "The investigating officer was a lieutenant appointed by Wolfe, and the IO's findings and recommendations were still in draft form when Major Jackson turned the report over to us."

Miller sighs, rubbing her temples. "Well, what about Wolfe?"

I pause, choosing my words carefully. "I am morally convinced that Wolfe's order to kill everyone on the objective set the conditions for the murders. He incited his men and empowered them to cross the line from lawful combat to premeditated murder."

"So, you think Wolfe is criminally responsible for the three detainee deaths?" Miller asks.

"Yes, ma'am," I say firmly. "Wolfe's actions and orders directly influenced the behavior of his men. He set the conditions that caused them to believe what they did was lawful. While they can't use his order as a defense to their crimes, his culpability is clear because he was reckless. He abused his authority to stretch the ROE to justify his kill order, and he failed to uphold the standards expected of a seasoned brigade commander."

Miller's eyes narrow slightly. "Go ahead, Jessica. Walk me through your prosecution theory on Wolfe."

"I can prove he intentionally set the conditions for the murders," I say. "His order to kill everyone on the objective, coupled with his fiery rhetoric, created an atmosphere where his men felt compelled to do just that."

Miller leans back in her chair, crossing her arms. "And you think it's wise for the Army to roll the dice and prosecute him for it."

"Yes, ma'am," I respond. "I think we have a strong case. Durham would not have questioned Fleury and Fleury would not have killed the detainees in the absence of Wolfe's illegal order. They believed what they were doing was not only acceptable but expected."

Miller's expression is guarded. "You realize the risk involved, right? Wolfe is a high-ranking officer with a lot of connections. He's Hollywood famous for his heroics in Panama. In his defense, he might put the Army and its ROE on trial. A trial could turn into a media circus and badly backfire."

"I understand the risk," I say, leaning forward. "But we shouldn't ignore the plain truth. Wolfe's leadership played a significant role in the deaths. He knew or should have known better, and he should be held accountable."

Miller sighs, her eyes searching mine. "Jess, I've been doing this a long time. Sometimes, going after senior officers isn't as straightforward as it seems. Higher-ups might not support this. They might view it as undermining the chain of command and discrediting the US Army."

"I get that," I reply, my tone passionate but respectful. "But if we don't prosecute commanders like Wolfe, what message does it send? That senior officers are above the law? That they won't face consequences for their reckless actions? Accountability should apply to everyone, regardless of rank."

Miller rubs her temples, clearly torn. "But there's also the pesky matter of proving Wolfe's intent. We need to prove that Wolfe intended for his men to interpret his orders as a green light for murdering detainees. His kill-them-all order doesn't quite get us there, because he thought everyone on the objective would be combatants."

"We have sworn testimony from multiple soldiers of all ranks about Wolfe's rhetoric and the environment he created," I argue. "And we can prove Wolfe's intent by showing the cause-and-effect relationship between his orders and the actions of his men. A reasonable commander knew, or should have known, that the kill order would expose any noncombatants to lethal fire. Fleury made that very point to Foote and Durham, about going in so hot, before the Raiders even lifted off."

Miller remains silent for a moment. Finally, she looks up, her expression resolute. "No, Jess. I can't back you on this. Fleury and his men will face trial, and we'll find another way to deal with Wolfe and the Raiders' chain of command." Miller offers a small, encouraging smile. "Trust me, Jess. They will pay. You ensure that the trigger-pullers face the music, and I'll work on the rest."

I leave wanting to trust Miller, but the whole thing just doesn't sit well with me. I grew up believing in truth and justice. I believe in the rule of law, and the idea that no person should be above the law. But isn't that exactly what Miller is proposing? Fleury and his men will face consequences publicly, in accordance with the

Uniform Code of Military Justice, while Wolfe and his staff will be dealt with quietly outside of the public eye. That insults the bedrock legal standard of equal justice under law, and I'm puzzled at Miller's insistence that I focus only on the culpability of the trigger pullers.

Back in my cubicle my computer pings and I open a "SEE ME" reply from Lindsay. I see an opportunity, because while Miller and I advise, it will be Benetti and Lindsay who decide. I grab my case file and enjoy a brisk walk over to the general's headquarters. Iraqi sunsets don't linger, and the cool air on my face is a welcome relief from the baking sun. I make my way through the busy headquarters, knock, and enter General Lindsay's spotless, quiet refuge.

"Major Gilbert, please have a seat. I've read your drafts. We need to talk about General Benetti's directive regarding use of deadly force investigations."

I'm caught a little off guard by the topic. General Benetti requires a full investigation each time deadly force is used in theater. It was an epic shift in perspective, an acknowledgment that Iraq was no longer a battlefield. Benetti's intent was to shift our thinking away from combat toward the measured use of power. "Yes, sir," I start, "he's adamant about ensuring accountability for every trigger pull. He believes that the unique circumstances of each situation demand a closer look to assess whether we employed the minimum force necessary."

General Lindsay nods, his fingers drumming on the table. "The evolution of our focus, from offensive combat power to defensive force protection, has certainly brought with it new challenges. My issue is that the classified ROE lists two dozen designated terror groups, including Al Qaeda, as enemy forces. And because Al Qaeda conceals itself among noncombatants, it makes switching to status-based targeting nearly impossible for our troops on the ground."

"That's the crux of it, sir. The absence of uniforms, the blurred lines between friend and foe, it's a complex situation that escapes an easy solution."

Lindsay's eyes narrow. "I guess that's why on-the-ground

judgment calls can't be standardized. What might be clear-cut in one scenario could be unclear in the next."

"It's also about establishing a climate of accountability," I add. "To ensure that we're reacting with appropriate and measured force. Each bullet fired has consequences, and we need to be reasonably certain that firing was the only option."

Lindsay nods. "Sure, he wants all of us to walk the fine line between assertiveness and restraint. We, of course, must also strive to minimize collateral damage, bearing in mind that these are split-second decisions."

"The only way to know if deadly force was the right call is to examine each incident individually," I add.

"That's true, but to the trigger-puller an investigation can seem like a veiled threat." He pauses, looking into the middle distance. "Have you ever heard the saying 'It's better to be judged by twelve than carried by six'?"

"No, sir."

"Twelve are the jury and six are the pallbearers. Grim, I know, but you should think about it before you pass judgment on the soldiers who must decide, in a fraction of a second, whether to shoot or hold fire. It's easy to Monday-morning quarterback use of force from the safety of a division headquarters."

Lindsay stands to go. I take the cue and gather my things. As I walk back to the Al Faw palace, the weight of his last comment lingers. In this ever-shifting landscape, where allegiances blur and danger lurks, Benetti's requirement to investigate each use of deadly force serves as a powerful reminder to be careful. While my role is to ensure accountability, I can surely sympathize with soldiers who would rather shoot and be judged in court, than hold fire and pay for it with their lives. How should that color the tone of Lindsay's findings and recommendations? Fleury and his men didn't decide whether to shoot or hold fire in a split second. To the contrary, they deliberately chose to shoot blindfolded and zip-tied detainees.

Baghdad, Iraq
26 August 2006

After a broken night's sleep and a quick breakfast, I head back to Lindsay's office. He has set this time aside to discuss a particularly delicate matter—the legal framework for targeting positively identified members of listed terror groups. I have to admit, trying criminal cases is much easier than trying to untangle the ROE. Maybe I should just ask him for a workspace in his office. Compared to my workspace, Lindsay's office is an oasis that allows for quiet deliberation. As I wait for him to look up from his screen, the intricate web of legal authority defined in the ROE swirls in my mind.

"Let's dig into the targeting of positively identified members of terror groups," General Lindsay begins.

I nod, bracing for a trip into the twisting labyrinth with a true Jedi master. "Yes, sir. The concept of positive identification is central. The standard set within the ROE hinges on a reasonable certainty grounded either in current intelligence or direct observation."

General Lindsay's brow furrows, his eyes reflecting deep, firsthand experience with the concept. "And to establish PID, commanders need a specific form of intelligence, correct?"

"Yes, sir," I confirm. "Tips from at least two credible informants must corroborate the target's affiliation with a listed terrorist organization. Commanders must meet this threshold before any kinetic action can be taken."

A thoughtful silence settles between us. Lindsay waits a beat and then continues. "Okay, once PID is established, it must again be confirmed immediately before the strike. This ensures that the intelligence is not stale, no variables have shifted, and the target's status hasn't changed."

I nod. "Exactly, and the concept of proportionality extends in regard to the means of engagement. Whether we employ precision munitions, snipers, or a Special Forces raid, the emphasis is on minimizing collateral damage."

"But our current ROE doesn't differentiate between direct and indirect fire," Lindsay says, his expression solemn.

"True," I say, recalling the specific language of the ROE. "But for aerial-delivered munitions, in areas where collateral damage risk is zero, an on-scene commander can call in air strikes on PID targets. When collateral damage risk is low—defined as one-to-five noncombatants at risk—a two-star division commander can approve the strike, and in high-collateral damage areas—where six or more noncombatants are at risk—the decision escalates to the three-star corps commander," I finish, completing the decision-making hierarchy.

General Lindsay leans back, his gaze distant. "These estimates, they're generated through a formal targeting process."

"Yes, sir. Colonel Wolfe and his staff started down that path—"

"Until the Pentagon disapproved their strike package," Lindsay says, completing my thought.

Walking back to the palace, the conversation with General Lindsay turns circles in my mind. The flawed command decisions that led to killings attempted to factor in the relative value of human life. Even after-the-fact, Lindsay and I struggle to weigh the value of lives. I can't escape the idea that every command decision can carry profound implications, and there are no easy answers when things go completely wrong.

CHAPTER 25

Wolfe
Tikrit, Iraq
26 August 2006

The sun is low, casting long shadows across the cement as Colonel Wolfe walks alone toward the chow hall. Dust clings to his boots, and the ever-present hum of generators buzzes in his ears. It's the one lull in his schedule—twenty minutes for dinner and a reset before evening handover and his next round of updates.

Halfway down the row of concrete barriers, something catches his eye. A young trooper with a rifle slung loose over his back squats near the edge of a Jersey barrier. He's crouched low, hand extended, fingers gently offering scraps of something greasy to a trembling, skeletal dog. The mutt's ribs show through dust-caked fur. Its ears twitch nervously, but it inches forward, tail low, hunger overriding its fear.

Wolfe makes a sudden, purposeful turn and strides straight toward them. The trooper looks up, confused at first, then alarmed. Wolfe's boot swings hard. It slams into the mutt's ribs with a hollow thump. The dog yelps and crashes sideways, legs scrambling and pawing the air. Before it can right itself, Wolfe lifts his foot high and stomps on the struggling animal's head. The dog wriggles under his boot and somehow breaks free. It yelps and disappears between two barriers before Wolfe can deliver a killing blow.

Wolfe turns on the trooper. "Do you want to explain to me what the hell that was?" he snaps, voice sharp enough to slice steel.

"Sir, it looked hungry," the soldier stammers, eyes wide.

"You think we're here to open a goddamn petting zoo?" Wolfe thunders, stepping in close. "You think this is fucking summer camp? That furry goddamn friend of yours is a threat. That mutt could be carrying fleas, rabies, you name it. And the next time you're out on patrol, you might be too busy tossing Milk-Bones to notice a kid with a grenade under his shirt!"

The soldier swallows hard.

"We are not here to give handouts and make friends. We are here to stabilize our AO and get our asses back home in one piece. Distractions like that goddamn dog can get you killed." Wolfe stares the young trooper down another beat before turning away, his jaw clenched tight.

By the time Wolfe finishes chow and reaches the operations center, the irritation hasn't faded. He finds Jackson reviewing SIGACTs and tosses the incident at him like a grenade. "Publish an order," Wolfe says. "Effective immediately—all strays on base are to be shot on sight. Dogs, cats, goats, I don't care. I don't want another goddamn bleeding heart trooper kneeling in the dirt feeding a stray when he should be on guard."

Jackson hesitates just a second too long.

"Problem?" Wolfe asks, gaze hard.

"No, sir," Jackson says. "I'll write it up."

Wolfe nods once and turns away. There is simply no goddamn room for sentiment in war.

Major Jackson makes his way from the operations center to Wolfe's office. He knocks and meekly asks, "Sir, I'm going to grab a midnight cheeseburger. Do you want anything?"

"Hey, Ernie, come in. Grab a seat."

Jackson takes a seat, and Wolfe leans back in his swivel chair, putting his boots up on the corner of his granite desk. "You think we've got time to plan and execute one more mission?"

Jackson offers a noncommittal shrug.

"Come on, Ernie," Wolfe says, sitting up. "Don't you love it when the choppers knife through the darkness, humming with energy?"

Jackson nods.

"One thought runs through my mind—close with and destroy the enemy! Guys like us, we were put on earth to close with and destroy the enemy."

Jackson smiles and waits for Wolfe to continue.

"And it's a beautiful goddamn feeling when the helicopters swoop down. There's something cold and powerful in the descent," Wolfe says, leaning back. "It's like eagles diving to attack their prey. It's beautiful in its purity—death from above moving in for the kill with such single-minded focus."

"Don't let Benetti's investigators hear you talk like that, sir," Jackson laughs. "They'll send you to Leavenworth for it."

"One thing you gotta learn, Ernie, the Army is a mean old cunt. If you don't learn to love her, if you don't mount up and fuck her, she'll fuck you and throw your broken body to the side. Ain't nobody gonna throw me to the side. Nobody."

CHAPTER 26

Jess
Baghdad, Iraq
27 August 2006

I rise early, looking forward to a solitary run around Victory Base. Sometimes when I'm struggling to understand the twisted facts of a case or the application of various legal rules and their exceptions, I untangle everything during a run. I start out slowly and pick up my pace. My mind wanders to a discussion about negligent discharge cases that Miller and I had with Benetti early in the deployment. Most of the offenders were senior NCOs and officers, and the more senior the offender the more likely it was that the unit opted for "additional training" as opposed to any real punishment.

"What's your take on it, Denise?" Benetti had asked.

"Sir, when Jess gave me the numbers, I was puzzled. So, I asked my chief legal NCO what he thought about it, and he explained that while it's obvious when a M-16 or other long gun has a magazine in, it's not obvious with handguns because the magazine is hidden inside the grip."

"But what about the disparity in punishments between the enlisted, NCOs, and the officers?" Benetti asked.

Miller had looked over at me, giving me the green light to answer.

"Yes, sir, that's troubling. By and large, soldiers receive Article Fifteens, and their punishments vary widely. Junior NCOs sometimes get letters of reprimand, but again their punishments vary widely.

The senior NCOs and officers seem to get a pass, sometimes with a local letter of reprimand or simply extra training."

"How do we fix it?" Benetti asked Miller.

"Sir, we don't," she answered. "In theory, you could reserve handling all negligent discharge cases to yourself, but the cure would likely be worse than the disease because everyone would freak out over having a three-star general passing judgment on their complacency and inattention to detail."

"The same subordinate commanders who now decide these cases would then forward them to you with their recommendations," I added. "Since each case must be decided on its own merits—to include the duty performance and rehab potential of the various offenders—you'd likely end up with a similar distribution of punishments."

"Different spanks for different ranks?" Benetti had asked, with a bit of skepticism in his voice.

"We do our best to keep the system honest," Miller had said, before I could answer. "That, in part, means letting the system work by allowing your subordinate commanders to use their own judgment to handle misconduct within their formations."

I cool down and shower, and the memory lingers like an unpaid bill. I'm still thinking about it on my walk to see General Lindsay. I knock on his open door, and he looks up from his screen. "Major Gilbert," he says, "it's time for us to work through the role Colonel Wolfe's command climate played in the run-up to the detainee killings."

The tension in the room grows as we dive into the heart of the matter—whether Colonel Wolfe is responsible for setting overly aggressive conditions that led to the battlefield executions. I take a deep breath, my mind focused on the events as they unfolded.

"Sir, there's no denying that Wolfe's approach set the stage for what transpired. The aggressive atmosphere he cultivated, the blurred lines between acceptable and unacceptable behavior, and his kill-them-all speech created an environment where overly aggressive actions weren't just accepted, they were the norm."

General Lindsay's brow furrows. "While I understand your perspective, Operation Judgment Day itself provides a powerful counterpoint. Scores of Iraqis were detained without incident, demonstrating a level of discipline that suggests controlled violence, not chaos."

I nod, acknowledging his point, yet determined to defend my case. "True, sir. But within those three days, there were moments that tested the soldiers' moral compasses. Situations that posed challenges, where the line between lawful and unlawful seemed awfully blurred. Look at Lieutenant Sullivan on Objective Gaslight. He ordered his men to shoot because he thought Wolfe's shoot-them-all order was in effect."

A thoughtful silence stretches before Lindsay speaks again. "And in that morally confusing situation, even when their lieutenant ordered them to shoot, the ground-force soldiers showed restraint. They refused to take life needlessly. Once on the scene, First Sergeant Durham took charge and prevented an attack on a building he suspected housed noncombatants."

"You're right. Some did hold back and disobeyed Sullivan's order."

General Lindsay holds my gaze. "Fleury and his men, they were the outliers. They took it upon themselves to step outside the boundaries of lawful killing."

"But, sir," I interject, "that was only after Durham questioned their request to dust off the detainees. That was the turning point. His rebuke reminded them to follow Wolfe's kill order."

Lindsay doesn't respond, and the room seems to hold its breath. As we unravel the choices made along the way, it is clear to me that the command climate drove choices and actions that converged to create a tragic narrative that will indelibly stain General Benetti's legacy.

Back at my office, I check in on my military justice team. They continue to grind away on reports of misconduct and command requests for legal advice. While I clear out my inbox, my computer dings, signaling an encrypted message from General Lindsay. I open the attachment and read his finalized findings and recommendations. His take on the facts with regard to Fleury and his men closely tracks my drafts. His findings related to their chain of command do not. My face tightens and I clench my jaw, realizing that Lindsay has watered down his findings against the leadership to the point of being unrecognizable.

As a prosecutor it's my job to hold those responsible for wrongdoing to account. That's how justice gets done. And yet, in the case of Colonel Wolfe it is disappearing like a puddle evaporating under the hot desert sun.

I dial the general and he picks up on the first ring. "Sir," I begin, my voice tinged with urgency.

"Major Gilbert," he answers, with a measured tone. "I was expecting your call."

"Sir," I start again, "why did you decide to let Colonel Wolfe off the hook for his role in the detainee deaths?"

"I believe that his actions, while not ideal, did not rise to the level of criminal."

"But sir," I say, with frustration gnawing at me, "what about his overly broad kill order? And the unit kill boards? And the trophy knives? The same knives he publicly presented to two troopers right before the operation. Doesn't all of it point to a commander who set conditions that were primed for war crimes? Shouldn't that type of recklessness warrant some form of accountability?"

"Jess, what happened during Operation Judgment Day is deeply troubling, but we must consider Wolfe's intent. Did he have the criminal intent to commit murder? Or did he have something else in his mind? I believe that it was the latter."

I pause, considering it. Mens rea, or criminal frame of mind, is fundamental to criminal law. In a case like this, it does feel murky. "Perhaps not murder," I concede, "but he was clearly derelict in his duty. His decisions undoubtedly contributed to the loss of innocent lives."

"There were casualties, and we shouldn't minimize the executions. However, we must also look at the broader context. I believe Colonel Wolfe's primary motivation was to save the lives of his own troops. Maybe it was at the expense of civilians caught in the crossfire, but he did not, at any point in time, order Fleury and his men to execute detainees. Fleury alone gave that order."

I frown, a knot of frustration tightening in my chest. Before I am able to gather my thoughts, Lindsay continues. "You raise valid points. The moral complexities of war are profound. And sometimes, commanders are called upon to make difficult decisions in the heat of battle."

"But sir, the order was not given in the heat of battle. It was premeditated."

"Okay, Judge, you are my criminal law expert. Assume you have the green light to prosecute Wolfe. Where do you go from there?"

The question hangs in the air as I take a moment to gather my thoughts. "Given the circumstances, I would likely start by focusing on violations of the law of war. I would also allege dereliction of duty and failure to follow rules of engagement."

"And murder, or accessory to murder? How does the law distinguish between lawful killings and battlefield murders?"

"It's just like any other crime. The government must prove each element of the charged offenses beyond a reasonable doubt. We also need to evaluate the means, motive, and opportunity. We would have to dig a little deeper to expose his true intent behind the killings. Was it a legal order with a legitimate military objective, or was it an illegal order that lacked a valid force-protection justification?"

"So, you believe Wolfe was an accessory to murder?"

"In my gut an accessory before and after the fact, but as a trial attorney I know it would be difficult to prove because a jury would struggle to find the requisite mens rea and might not link up the cause and effect of his kill order."

"And what about the trial itself? Wolfe would be entitled to a jury?"

"Yes, and by law all of the panel members would have to outrank him."

"And he would get a public trial?"

"Yes, that's guaranteed by the Sixth Amendment," I answer, my mind racing with the logistical challenges that would lie ahead. "Colonel Wolfe would also be entitled to a defense lawyer of his choice. High profile civilian attorneys might flock to take his case for all the free publicity they'd get for defending a war hero."

As I think it through, I map out the legal proceedings. My resolve isn't quite as firm as when I dialed the general's number. I sigh, realizing that deep down I'm glad that it's General Lindsay's call, because in the fog of war the lines between right and wrong blur. And when the fog clears, it can reveal a landscape so littered by ethical dilemmas, moral ambiguities, and after-the-fact justifications that nobody can find true north.

"We must also consider the broader context of the critical role Wolfe will play in the redeployment of his brigade," Lindsay says.

I know leading a brigade is no small feat, especially in Iraq. Colonel Wolfe is a class-A asshole, but his experience and expertise are assets, and if General Lindsay believes Wolfe's presence is crucial to ensuring the safe and successful return of his troops, who am I to disagree?

Lindsay fills the silence. "Jess, his leadership will be essential during redeployment. He knows his troops better than anyone. He understands the threats they will face, and his leadership will see them through this final leg of their deployment."

I understand his points, but don't like them. As a prosecutor, it's my duty to seek justice. As an Army officer, I must defer to my leaders and honor the bonds of loyalty that bind us together. I take another deep breath, grappling with conflicting emotions. The pursuit of justice is a noble endeavor, but so is the responsibility of command. Balancing the two—respecting the rule of law and deferring to the realities of military life—seems an impossible task.

"I understand," I reply, struggling to keep my voice steady. "Thank you, sir. I appreciate you taking the time to mentor me."

"Of course," he replies. "I value your commitment to justice."

I hang up, somehow with my respect for Lindsay intact. I realize that while our approaches differ, our goal is the same—to serve the United States and its interests to the best of our abilities. In this case, that means trusting General Lindsay, even if it means setting aside my own doubts and concerns.

CHAPTER 27

Jess
Baghdad, Iraq
27 August 2006

At its best, our investigation has been a roller coaster of accidental discoveries and epiphanies. At its worst, it's been a symphony of clashing agendas and dissonant loyalties. I feel like a tone-deaf composer trying to create a recognizable tune. The buck, however, will stop with Benetti. After reviewing, considering, and consolidating hundreds of pages of witness testimony, Lindsay finally completes his findings and recommendations. I deliver a signed copy to Colonel Miller in advance of Lindsay's brief to General Benetti.

"Hmm," Miller says as she turns a page, "the boss isn't going to like this."

"Which part?" I ask.

She shakes her head, "All of it."

That night, I can't sleep. General Lindsay's words linger and his findings echo, stirring a whirlwind of emotions. Where did his forgiving conclusions come from? He isn't a pushover. He's an understated and dedicated leader I deeply respect. Yet, he's human. Beneath his calm exterior, there must lie a man torn between competing loyalties. I ponder his complex web of allegiances to the United States of America, the Army, its mission, his fellow commanders, and the soldiers they lead. Does he feel an obligation to mentor Wolfe through his command? I know he feels a strong obligation to get the Raiders home safely. He stated as much in his recommendation, which would "minimize risk to the brigade by keeping Colonel Wolfe in command throughout the Raiders' redeployment."

I understand Lindsay's devotion to soldiers, their safety, and well-being. But he must also uphold the Army's values and ensure that justice is served. Then there's Lindsay's loyalty to his fellow commanders, like Wolfe. They share a bond forged through shared experiences, mutual respect, and the unspoken understanding of the burdens of command. But where should loyalty end and accountability begin? Perhaps General Lindsay's split loyalties are just a reflection of the inherent tensions within the military itself. Day to day there is a constant struggle to reconcile duty, honor, and justice in the face of an adversary who hides in the shadows amongst the civilian population.

As I do my best to empathize with General Lindsay, I can't help but wonder where my own loyalties lie. As a prosecutor my role is clear: investigate, charge, and prosecute lawbreakers. But as an Army officer, my role isn't quite as clear-cut. Do I really want a public trial of Wolfe if doing so discredits the Army, thwarts Benetti's efforts to win over the Iraqi population, and maybe endangers Wolfe's redeploying Raiders?

Baghdad, Iraq
28 August 2006

When I arrive at General Benetti's office, Lindsay and Miller are already there. They seem relaxed as they chat and sip their cups of coffee.

"Would you like a cup?" Major Brown asks me.

"No, thanks," I say, thinking it might aggravate the swarm of bees dancing in my belly.

Major Brown shows us in, and we quietly take our seats at the oversized conference table and wait for the general to join us. Benetti gets up from his desk and waves us all down before we have a chance to stand at attention. Benetti takes his seat beside Miller and across from Lindsay and me.

"Go ahead, David. I'm ready," Benetti says.

Lindsay begins, his voice steady and measured as he lays out his first finding—that Private Delgado's report about Colonel Wolfe taking ears was false. "Furthermore," he continues, "five of the Iraqis killed in action were lawful kills, within the bounds of the rules of engagement. However, three detainees were killed unlawfully."

A shiver runs down my spine as the gravity of Lindsay's words following "however" sink in. Unlawfully killed detainees—a war crime and a brutal betrayal of our military ethos. Lindsay's voice remains steady as he unravels the complex web of Wolfe's actions. "Sir, Colonel Wolfe failed to adequately communicate the rules of engagement for Operation Judgment Day to his Raiders. While he emphasized the need for deadly force, he did not condone illegal or wanton killing."

Even though I maintain a composed facade, a whirlwind of conflicting emotions churns. Benetti's brow furrows as he listens. I sense his doubts as his questioning gaze locks on Lindsay. Deep down, I share Benetti's doubts about letting the man behind the killings off the hook. The injustice of Fleury and his men being held solely responsible for the killings lingers in the room like a skunk's spray.

"Colonel Wolfe mistakenly believed that he had the authority to designate everyone at Objective Walter as a terrorist," Lindsay continues, his voice steady. "He overlooked the requirement to individually identify combatants when the means permit. Furthermore, his gross miscommunication about the scope of mandate to kill all military-aged males *may* have contributed to a chain of unfortunate events," Lindsay concludes, his stressing of the word *may* heavy with meaning.

Lindsay ends his briefing, and I'm rubble. Inside me, something crumbles. Is it my military pride as an officer, or is it my humanity that cracks? Wolfe, the blustering architect of this tragedy, is shielded while those who carried out his commands will face the consequences. It's a harsh collision of command, duty, and accountability that leaves me flattened by its unfairness.

CHAPTER 28

Jess
Baghdad, Iraq
28 August 2006

I lie awake, staring at the ceiling. Thoughts of Lindsay's findings and the upcoming trials swirl in my overheated mind. The rule of law is supposed to be clear and unwavering, but how can it truly exist when those in power put themselves above it? Fleury and his men will face grave consequences, yet Wolfe will remain safely above the fray. The hollow feeling of injustice gnaws at me, eating away at my professional pride.

My mind races, questioning whether military justice is nothing but self-serving propaganda. I turn over, trying to find comfort in the darkness, but my heretical thoughts persist. At its core, the rule of law should mean equality, fairness, accountability. Yet here I am, watching it all shrink in the face of hierarchy and power.

This isn't what I signed up for. I want to fight for what's right. But how? How do I reconcile my prosecutorial duty with the reality that justice is being unevenly distributed? My mind spins with possibilities, and deep down I know that I must find a way to make a difference. As I try to sleep, I console myself with the idea that change starts with those who dare to question and push back, and that's exactly what I intend to do.

★ ★ ★

Baghdad, Iraq
29 August 2006

I sit across from Colonel Miller, fidgeting. I desperately need to vent, or I might scream. "Ma'am," I start, trying unsuccessfully to keep my voice steady, "it's patently unfair that Fleury and his men will be held criminally liable while Wolfe and his staff will suffer no consequences."

Miller listens attentively. "I understand, Jess. It's frustrating when justice seems one-sided."

I nod, my words spilling out. "Right after the mission brief, Fleury questioned Wolfe's orders. Captain Foote shut him down. On the objective, Fleury requested air transport for the detainees and First Sergeant Durham second-guessed him. The atmosphere Wolfe created made everyone believe that their actions were justified. Yet only Fleury and his men will face murder charges."

"Yes," Miller says, leaning forward, "the chain of command should be held accountable, but the reality is far more complicated than your summary. Wolfe misapplied the air strike ROE to his troops on the ground. Giving Durham the benefit of the doubt, he may have only been seeking clarification. Neither Wolfe nor Durham told Fleury to kill prisoners."

"Wolfe's kill order was patently reckless. It set the stage for everything that happened afterward," I protest.

Miller sighs and taps her finger on the desk. "Prosecuting high-ranking officers is politically challenging, and prosecuting America's hero? No, it's too much."

I shake my head, feeling the weight of it. "Do you remember when we visited Courtroom 600 in Nuremberg?"

"It was such a privilege," Miller smiles. "Seeing where Justice Jackson stood and made his arguments about holding Nazi leaders responsible for their crimes against humanity."

"It was the birth of international criminal law. The trials established the Nuremberg Principles, making it clear that no person is above the law."

Miller nods, her expression thoughtful. "It also established that obedience to orders is never a defense," Miller says, leaning back in her chair and looking up at the ceiling. "The idea that high-ranking leaders far from the battlefields and concentration camps should be held accountable for sanctioning war crimes and orchestrating crimes against humanity was revolutionary."

"And the United States led the way in setting a precedent for fairness and accountability."

"True." Miller nods. "But as we sit here today, the United States remains one of the very few nations that has not signed the Rome Statute."

We sit in quiet contemplation, and then I say, "Rank should not shield anyone from criminal responsibility."

"You mean Wolfe?" Miller asks, raising an eyebrow.

"Yes! Colonel Wolfe is getting away with murder!" I shout, my anger boiling over.

Colonel Miller leans back in her chair. "Jess, I know it's frustrating, but we're damn lucky the ear allegation led to the truth about the detainee deaths." She pauses, letting me consider her words, and then continues evenly, "Otherwise, the Raiders' in-house fifteen-six would have spun the killings as Fleury and his men heroically preventing an escape."

"Still," I say, standing to go. "Wolfe encouraged this, and he'll walk free."

"It's the system. We must consider the second order effects of a public trial. What if Wolfe retained a celebrity lawyer, like F. Lee Bailey or Gerry Spence?" Miller sighs. "We advise and commanders decide," Miller says, looking away. "But I hear you. Keep pushing for justice, Jess. Your voice is important." I know she is trying to talk sense and soothe my wounded conscience, but frustration lingers. As I turn to leave, I remind myself that every step toward justice, no matter how small, matters.

That night, alone in my SEA-hut, I struggle with my conscience. I had hoped that my talk with Colonel Miller would help me sleep easier. To the contrary, I'm again staring at the ceiling. My mind is a tangle of thoughts about right and wrong, equal justice and the rule of law, and how it should all apply to Colonel Wolfe.

Thoughts about the rule of law keep swirling around and around in my mind. The Rome Statute and the International Criminal Court built upon the legacy of Nuremberg, yet the United States opts to stay outside of the Court's jurisdiction. We claim that we don't need to sign up for the ICC because our legal systems—such as the Uniform Code of Military Justice—already hold our home-grown war criminals accountable. But is that true? If the United States had signed on to the Rome Statute, would the ICC indict Wolfe? How would America react? I consider the implications. Would we respect the court's authority, or would we push back? I can't help wondering if our refusal to join is because we fear international oversight. Are we truly confident in our own justice system, or are we just protecting ourselves from outside scrutiny? I want to believe that my military justice system applies equally to all, but right now the reality is far from it.

It is hard to imagine the United States willingly handing Wolfe over for trial before an international court, but his actions should have consequences.

I toss and turn, grappling with whether the UCMJ truly offers the evenhanded accountability it promises. Are we doing enough to hold everyone to the same standard, or are we just giving it lip service and hiding behind our domestic laws to avoid international scrutiny? For the rule of law to mean something, it must apply equally to all. But here I lay, with a mandate to prosecute the trigger-pullers, but not the decision-makers.

I sigh, knowing my misgivings don't have easy solutions. Yet, I can't stop pining for a way to achieve justice for all. My worldview demands that I keep pushing, keep questioning, keep striving for a system that will live up to its propaganda.

Baghdad, Iraq
30 August 2006

Colonel Miller and I are summoned to the corps commander's office. We sit across from General Benetti. Our war-weary general fixes his gaze on us, his grave expression betraying disappointment over Lindsay's findings. I can't maintain my stoic lawyer's mask as I try to anticipate his questions and scramble to come up with alternative courses of action.

Benetti clears his throat and speaks, his voice resonating with authority. "Ladies, Colonel Wolfe's actions raise significant concerns. He willfully fostered an environment of excessive aggression within his ranks, and I believe his liberal interpretation of the rules of engagement paved the way for murder times three." He pauses, knowing his decision will impact not just Wolfe's career, but the lives of the thousands under his command. "The question before us now is how to best address the situation, while minimizing the impact on our deployed forces. Wolfe's division commander opposes relieving him due to their upcoming redeployment," Benetti says, bringing his fist up to cover his tight-lipped mouth. He lowers his hand and concludes, "During predeployment Wolfe fired his executive officer, and I can't ignore the risk relieving him might pose to the six thousand troops under his command."

Colonel Miller takes the cue to offer advice. "I propose you issue a formal reprimand. While Colonel Wolfe may have technically adhered to the rules of engagement, his conduct and its consequences speak to a dereliction of duty that cannot be ignored."

General Benetti nods, his expression contemplative. "Okay, but it must be airtight. It needs to link his questionable interpretation of the rules and the lack of clarity with his troops to the battlefield deaths of the detainees."

I nod in silent agreement.

"As you draft his reprimand," General Benetti continues, his tone firm, "ensure that it highlights Colonel Wolfe's failure to consider the second- and third-order effects that his actions played in this tragedy. His acts, omissions, and personal example cultivated a command climate where overly aggressive behavior was not only tolerated but rewarded."

Looking into the general's weary face, I am struck by the profound impact his daily decisions have on the lives of the 120,000 coalition forces entrusted to his care. Even though he addressed his comments to Miller, I feel a heavy sense of responsibility. I contemplate the delicate phrasing I'll need to craft to capture the essence of General Benetti's intent for Colonel Miller.

CHAPTER 29

Jess
Baghdad, Iraq
31 August 2006

The palace is deserted at the end of a long, frustrating night. I sit alone in the dimly lit JAG office, with the glow of my computer screen casting a soft light on my tired face. The weight of drafting the Big Bad's reprimand presses down. I pore over each word, striving to strike the perfect balance between accountability and fairness, as the sentences on my screen blur together.

Colonel Miller enters from the grand atrium, her presence a welcome distraction from the task at hand. "Hey, Jess," she greets me, her voice carrying a hint of exhaustion. "How's it going?"

I offer her a weary smile, rubbing my eyes. "I pulled an all-nighter working on Wolfe's reprimand."

Miller nods sympathetically. "It's tough, but we've got to get it right." She pulls a chair over from the next cubicle and sits beside me. I gesture toward my screen. "I've tried to capture the main points succinctly in one page. I want it to end Wolfe's career but must stay within the bounds of General Lindsay's forgiving assessment."

"Let me take a look," Miller says, leaning forward and adjusting the screen.

I wait anxiously as she reads. The seconds stretch into minutes as she meticulously analyzes each word, each phrase of my draft, which reads:

Subject: Letter of Reprimand

This memorandum memorializes serious concerns I have regarding your conduct and leadership as the commander of the 7th Brigade Combat Team. Your actions have created an atmosphere of hostility and reckless aggression toward the civilian population.

Specifically, you encouraged and rewarded violent acts, for example by tracking unit kills on boards and presenting trophy knives for confirmed kills. You creatively interpreted the rules of engagement and issued overly broad orders, such as directing the indiscriminate killing of individuals during Operation Judgment Day. Furthermore, you used fiery rhetoric to incite the soldiers under your command to engage in aggressive tactics, including the unnecessary use of force and the disregard for the lives of noncombatants.

Your reckless behavior set conditions where young and inexperienced soldiers were more likely to view the killing of noncombatants as acceptable, thus compromising the integrity and honor of your unit. Such actions are not only in violation of my intent but also undermine the principles of decency and respect for human life.

As a leader within our ranks, it is your duty to uphold the highest standards of professionalism and integrity. Your actions have fallen far short of these standards and have brought discredit upon yourself and the United States Army. It is my expectation that you take immediate steps to rectify your behavior.

I am considering whether to file this formal letter of reprimand in your Official Military Performance File. You have seven days from receipt of this memorandum to provide rebuttal matters for my consideration.

"You've done a great job, Jess," Miller says. "It captures exactly what General Benetti needs to convey."

I breathe a sigh of relief, grateful for her approval. "Thanks, ma'am."

Miller nods, her gaze drifting back to my screen. "I have a couple of small tweaks I'd like to make," she says, reaching for my keyboard. She makes the revisions and with each change, the reprimand takes on new depth and more clarity. "Perfect," she says. "I'll take it to General Benetti for his review. With any luck, he'll sign it, and we'll have Wolfe's career off the rails by the end of the day."

A sense of accomplishment glows within me. While the reprimand falls short of the public court-martial and prison term that Wolfe deserves, I am proud to be a small cog in the wheel of justice that will grind Wolfe's career into dust.

Baghdad, Iraq
01 September 2006

The early morning air is crisp and refreshing as I step out of my CHU to take an easy run around Victory Base. The sun peeks over the horizon, casting its warm glow across the barren landscape. I start jogging and the rhythmic pounding of my feet on the road fills the quiet morning. I follow a familiar path around the Al Faw Palace lake. The water sparkles in the early morning light, and I can't help but admire the tranquility of it. As I reach the end of my run and return to my hut, I'm filled with gratitude for the freedoms I enjoy, even in this war-torn land. But I'm also acutely aware of the challenges that still lie ahead, and the responsibility I have to shape a more just and equitable future.

I take a leisurely shower. Toweling dry, I pause to check the rash between my breasts. It's uncomfortable and seems like the "monkey butt" rash that combat soldiers complain about. I remember the guys joking about the rashes running from their tailbones to their belly buttons after their grueling road march from Kuwait to Baghdad. Because I flew directly into Baghdad, I didn't dare to ask questions about it. Now, I finally understand their dark humor. It's just one of those things everyone must deal with in this harsh environment. I apply ointment, hoping for some relief. I get dressed, thinking about how these irritations are only temporary. We put up with it because we must. It's a shared experience, bonding us to this hellish place. I grab a late lunch, head to the office, and check in with Colonel Miller. She asks me to sit.

"Has he seen it?" I ask.

"He loved it," she smiles. "And signed with no changes."

"Very nice," I say, holding my first out for a congratulatory bump.

Miller bumps, and her smile fades. "Okay, Jess, let's talk about trial sequencing. How do we approach the prosecutions?"

Damn, that was the world's shortest celebration. The new topic, of how to approach putting the trigger pullers in jail is difficult, because I'm still bothered by the disparity of treatment between Wolfe and his men.

Miller and I discuss trial strategies for what feels like hours. I lean forward, contemplating the options laid out by her. "I think we should start with Fleury. I know that normally we work up to the big fish, but he's already confessed. So, we have a solid case against him and if he elects to plead guilty, it will set a precedent for his men to do the same."

Miller nods. "That makes sense. And then we move on to Willowby and Gruber, building on the momentum from Fleury's conviction. With any luck, both will plead guilty as well."

I nod, feeling a glimmer of optimism. "Exactly, and then we can end with Taylor. He invoked and will be the wildcard. Trying him last should take the air out of his sails."

"Right, because once the others are convicted, General Benetti will grant them testimonial immunity and order them to testify against Taylor."

I go back to my cubicle to pore over the massive Raiders case file. The muted buzz of telephones and conversations create a steady hum in the background. I ponder the true nature of the military justice system. Does it promote good order and discipline in the ranks by delivering swift, harsh punishments? Or does it protect the rights of the accused by ensuring due process of law?

The answer is not a simple one. The military justice system serves two masters who are often difficult. There is a martial need for discipline and accountability within the ranks, ensuring that soldiers adhere to the rules and regulations. There is also a legal obligation to uphold the Constitutional rights of the accused, and to ensure that justice is served fairly and impartially.

As an officer on General Benetti's staff and a prosecutor representing the United States, I find myself caught in the tension between these competing objectives. How can I faithfully fulfill both obligations? That's a question that I grapple with every day. As a prosecutor, my role is to seek truth and justice, to hold individuals accountable for their actions, and ensure that the rule of law is upheld. But in doing so, I must navigate the military's unique justice system, knowing that the needs of the Army may complicate a case that would be clear-cut in the civilian world.

I see myself as a guardian of justice within the military system—a voice for victims, a champion for fairness, and a defender of the rule of law. I'm not happy that the little guys have been left holding the bag, but that doesn't excuse me from prosecuting their cases to the best of my ability.

A shadow falling across my desk startles me. I look up to see Major Brown, his rugged features softened by a friendly smile. "Hi, Jess," he says. "Mind if I steal you away for a bit?"

I raise an eyebrow. "It depends on what you're stealing me away for, Jimmy."

"Jimmy? Are we on a first name basis now?" he says, laughter in his eyes.

"Don't read anything into it, Major Brown," I reply in a strict monotone, with a hint of a smile.

He motions toward the door. "Lunch. Chow hall. Business only. You in?"

I close the file and give him a nod, curiosity piqued. "Sure, lead the way."

We make our way through the cafeteria-style food line and across the warehouse-sized tent, our footsteps clacking on the wood-plank floor. We settle in at a corner table and Brown's expression turns serious.

"Okay, here's the scoop," he begins, his tone measured. "This morning Colonel Wolfe came to Baghdad for his reprimand."

I lean in, curious as hell. "How did it go?"

Brown's eyes narrow and lips tighten. "I'll be honest, Gilbert. It was brutal. Benetti returned Wolfe's salute, then left him at the position of attention as he read the reprimand to him word for word."

I smile to myself, imagining it.

He nods. "Dereliction, failure, disgrace . . . It was all in there."

"I know," I say. "I drafted it."

Major Brown's eyebrows shoot up. "You did?"

I give Brown a rueful half smile. "Yeah, I did."

He shakes his head, clearly impressed. "Damn, Jess. You've got some guts." He pauses and his tone takes on a cautionary note.

"Listen, be careful. Wolfe made it clear that he's out for payback against any member of Benetti's staff who had a role in undermining him."

"He's gunning for us?" I think back to the tense interview in Tikrit. I will never forget the way Wolfe's eyes bored into mine as I read him his rights. If it hadn't been for Lindsay sitting there at the table, Wolfe would have lunged over the table and strangled me.

"Yep, he's on the warpath," Brown says, interrupting my grim thoughts. "Be vigilant, Jess. Watch your back."

I nod.

"I'm scheduled to take command of a battalion after I pin on," Brown says.

"Pinning on? Congrats on your promotion," I say. "Your battalion won't be with the Raiders—"

"No," Brown answers, "with a sister brigade."

"Good," I nod, standing to go. "Thanks for the heads-up, Brown."

Brown stands and claps me on the shoulder in a gesture of camaraderie. "Anytime."

As we head across the drawbridge and back into the Al Faw Palace, I'm acutely aware that the situation has changed, but I'm no shrinking violet and I feel I am ready for whatever lies ahead.

CHAPTER 30

Jess
Baghdad, Iraq
02 September 2006

I'm reviewing a stack of case files when a knock on the edge of my desk breaks my concentration. Startled, I jump and see Colonel Miller standing over me, her expression troubled. "Jess, we need to talk," she says.

I push aside my paperwork to give her my full attention as a knot forms in the pit of my stomach. "What's wrong, ma'am?"

She hesitates for a moment before she speaks. "It's Fleury," she says, her voice barely above a whisper. "He killed himself."

A wave of shock and disbelief washes over me. "What?" I whisper, unable to process it.

Miller nods solemnly, her eyes glistening with unshed tears. "I just got the call. They found him in a port-a-potty this morning. He leaned over his rifle barrel and shot himself."

"Are we sure?" I ask, unable to believe the news. Fleury didn't seem the type and now he's gone in the blink of an eye.

"He left a note, Jess," she says, her voice trembling. "He said . . . not to hold his men accountable for the killings. He claimed full responsibility, and said he ordered Taylor, Gruber, and Willowby to shoot the detainees."

I feel as if the ground has been ripped out from under me. What a waste! Was he overwhelmed by the guilt of killing detainees? Did he lack the strength to face the fact he was the one who invited his soldiers to join the club? Did he simply lose hope as he saw his unit scapegoat him? Or, was it the pressure of the cases I am preparing to bring against him and his men?

My mind pivots to legal issues that will surely arise from Fleury's death and note. "Ma'am," I begin, "the note is probably *Brady* material that we'll need to disclose to the defense."

"Yes," Miller says, furrowing her brow, "that's true, but the shooters will be barred from using Fleury's order as a defense. But in sentencing, they could use the note to show extenuation and mitigation."

I nod. "But what about Wolfe? Isn't he implicated by Fleury's note?"

A flicker of frustration crosses Miller's face. "Forget Wolfe," she mutters under her breath.

I blurt out, "No kidding, screw Wolfe!"

Miller shoots me a sharp look. "Jess, be professional."

"Yes, ma'am," I shrug. "I got carried away, but Wolfe's order and his refusal to own up to it is what really killed Fleury."

We talk through our options, trying to balance our legal strategy and ethical responsibilities. While disclosure under *US v. Brady* applies to criminal trials, and not to administrative matters like reprimands, we agree that it's better to give Wolfe a copy of the note, rather than risk him finding out later and making a big deal about it.

"We need to be transparent," Miller says, her voice firm. "Even if it means exposing a vulnerability."

"Yes, ma'am."

Miller's expression hardens. "Fleury's suicide is devastating, but we must adapt, press on, and continue to pursue justice."

The air is charged as Benetti, Miller, and I gather around the polished conference table in Benetti's office. I keep my gaze steady, my expression neutral, but my heart races. Miller and I have heard that Wolfe retained a slick New York City lawyer who has gone on the offensive.

General Benetti's stern countenance reveals nothing. He begins, "The good colonel has submitted a lengthy rebuttal, drafted by an Ivy League attorney. It raises some interesting points about Wolfe's battlefield decisions and the events that transpired under his command. It also threatens legal action against the US Army and the Department of Defense if I do not withdraw the reprimand."

My attention sharpens as my mind shifts into high gear.

"He contends that due to our ideological differences, my intention all along has been to destroy his career."

I steal a quick glance at Colonel Miller, her expression carefully neutral, her eyes unreadable. We've all had disagreements born from differing perspectives. But I never imagined a colonel would use those differences to attack the integrity of his three-star commanding general.

"Wolfe enumerates the intelligence that informed his decisions, presenting his interpretation of the rules of engagement as unimpeachable," Benetti continues. "He shifts the blame, suggesting that the criminal state of mind of Staff Sergeant Raymond Fleury was the proximate cause of the tragic events."

I fight to keep my emotions in check, even as the room seems to close in on us. Wolfe's words are a direct challenge not only to General Benetti's leadership, but to my commitment to justice and accountability.

"They do raise one valid question," the general continues. "If Wolfe wanted his Raiders to kill detainees, why would Sergeant Fleury and his men bother to conceal the true nature of their actions? Should Wolfe, in all fairness, be held accountable for their clearly criminal behavior?"

"Yes, sir," I blurt.

General Benetti's gaze settles on me, his eyes unyielding. Apparently, he's not in the mood for a pity party. While I admire Wolfe's argument for its shrewdness, I know that the truth lies between the lines of his slick rebuttal. I also know that pinning it all on Fleury is convenient, but pure nonsense.

"Wolfe also raises the question of command culture. He points to the Raiders who demonstrated restraint and highlights examples that General Lindsay brought to my attention in his report."

I do recall the instances where the Raiders displayed humanity and discretion amid violence and chaos. But they stand in stark contrast to the events that unfolded on Objective Walter. As we continue the discussion, my frustration with Wolfe's shameless scapegoating of Fleury simmers, threatening to boil over. Miller's attempts to rein me in only serve to fuel my anger.

"Sir," I interject, "please don't let Wolfe's lawyer get away with laying the entire blame on Fleury. It's not true and it's shameful to take advantage of his suicide that way."

Miller shoots me a cautionary glance, her brow furrowing in concern. "Jess, I understand your frustration, but please stay focused on the task at hand. Emotions won't help us navigate this situation."

I shake my head. "It's not about emotions, ma'am. It's about justice. Wolfe shouldn't get away with blaming it all on Fleury."

Miller sighs, her patience wearing thin. "I know, but we must be careful how we proceed. Focus on the facts and the evidence, not on the hyperbole."

I take a deep breath, hoping to calm the storm raging within me. "You're right and I'm sorry. It's hard to stay objective when someone is being unfairly targeted." Then a thought strikes like a bolt of lightning, and I can't hold back. "Wait a minute," I say, my voice rising with urgency. "Fleury's note—he said not to hold Taylor, Gruber, or Willowby accountable. He didn't mention Durham or Wolfe."

"You're right, Jess," Miller says, her eyes wide in realization.

"That's an important distinction." A surge of vindication momentarily sates my anger.

"Ladies," Benetti interjects, "thoroughly examine his rebuttal and get back to me tomorrow. Approach my response with caution and be sure to address each of Colonel Wolfe's claims thoughtfully and thoroughly. Please, no more loose ends."

Colonel Miller and I make our way through a maze of JAG cubicles back to her office. She takes a seat behind her desk, and I settle into a chair across from her. She takes her time closely reading the rebuttal and hands it to me. It reads:

> Subject: Rebuttal to Letter of Reprimand
>
> I am deeply disappointed by the baseless allegations made against me, and I respectfully request you withdraw the memorandum of reprimand you issued.
>
> The allegations are false, and I categorically deny any wrongdoing. Every unpopular war requires a scapegoat, and due to our ideological differences, it appears that you have made me yours.
>
> Your own investigation noted that the applicable rules of engagement were convoluted and difficult to interpret. However, I clearly had the authority as the on-scene commander to designate "groups, cells, and facilities belonging to terrorist groups" as lawful targets. I relied upon vetted intelligence to designate military-aged males on Objective Walter as hostile forces, but I never issued an order to engage noncombatants.
>
> The task of distinguishing combatants from noncombatants in asymmetric warfare, where terror groups actively try to blend into civilian populations, is exceedingly difficult. However, by approving my request for an artillery strike, both division and corps leadership concurred with my assessment that noncombatants would not be present on the objective.

The strike package was ultimately disapproved based upon a National Command Authority assessment that weapons of mass destruction might be buried at or near the objective.

The vast majority of soldiers under my command during Operation Judgment Day displayed remarkable discipline. The majority of encounters with noncombatants occurred without incident. Given the complexity and danger of the mission, the level of restraint displayed was commendable.

The true cause of the tragic and unnecessary loss of life on Objective Walter was the criminal state of mind of an individual soldier, Staff Sergeant Raymond Fleury, and he admitted as much in his suicide note.

I am deeply offended by your characterization of my actions as reckless and irresponsible. I have dedicated my life to serving my country, both in Panama and in Iraq, and I reject any insinuation that I have acted in anything but the best interests of the Army and the men under my command.

I request you withdraw your letter of reprimand immediately. In the spirit of transparency, it is my duty to inform you that my lawyer will initiate legal action against the Department of Defense if you do not withdraw it within seven days.

I look over at Miller with open-mouthed amazement. Colonel Wolfe's insubordinate rebuttal hangs between us like a slur staining the reputation of a man we both admire. Thankfully, the soft hum of the air conditioning provides a calming backdrop as we start to dissect the arguments outlined by Wolfe's clever attorney.

"It all seemed so black and white," I say.

"I believe that Wolfe intentionally blurred the line between permissible and unlawful actions, but the rules of engagement created a gray area, and must concede that Wolfe's interpretation could lead reasonable people to agree."

As we discuss the intricacies of military law, our conversation inevitably circles back to the critical question: *Who should be held accountable for the battlefield murders?* "Should we place the blame solely on the trigger pullers?" Miller muses, her voice tinged with frustration. "Or should the commanders who plan the missions also bear responsibility?"

I gather my thoughts and then answer based on my gut. "Accountability should extend to all levels, and commanders must consider the impact of their orders on their soldiers."

"So, as a practical matter, General Benetti should stick to his guns and put a formal, career-ending reprimand into Wolfe's official file."

I nod. "And all of them, from Major Jackson through First Sergeant Durham, should face similar consequences."

"What about Fleury's men, should the Army seek the death penalty?" Miller asks.

"Technically we could, but I have trouble with it," I say, my voice trailing off.

"The charge will be premeditated murder and their obedience to orders will not be a defense. So, we have to consider—"

"They're not Nazis, and certainly don't deserve to hang!" I blurt out.

"Calm down, Jess," Miller chides. "Under our rules, premeditated murder is still a capital offense. But let's not get the cart before the horse. Let's go back to Wolfe. That's more pressing. How should I advise General Benetti?"

"I don't know, ma'am," I shrug, still rattled about the possibility of seeking the death penalty.

"Well, Wolfe wasted his money," she says. "Because this is an administrative action and there is no standing to sue. I will ask the boss if, after considering Wolfe's rebuttal, he wants to withdraw the reprimand. If he asks about the threat of litigation, I'll tell him Wolfe hired a fool who either doesn't understand the law or is so full of himself that he thought he could bluff the United States Army."

CHAPTER 31

Jess
Baghdad, Iraq
03 September 2006

I'm far too busy to pay General Lindsay a social call, but I find the time because it's my last chance to say goodbye. I try to compose my thoughts as I walk over to his office. It's difficult to do because Fleury's suicide, Wolfe's rebuttal, and the pressure of the upcoming trials all weigh on my mind.

I knock on the frame of his open door and Lindsay looks up, a warm smile on his face. "Jess, come in," he greets me. "I'm glad you stopped by."

I return his smile, feeling a pang of sadness at the thought of our time together ending. "Sir, I just wanted to say thank you for everything. It's been an honor serving with you."

"The honor has been mine, Jess," he replies. "You're a bright officer, and I have no doubt you'll continue to do great things."

A silence settles over us and then our conversation turns somber. I begin tentatively, "Did you hear about Fleury?"

"Yes, I have," he says, his expression hardening. "You know, combat soldiers follow orders. Sometimes those orders cross ethical lines, but if following them will kill the enemy and save American lives, soldiers won't hesitate to follow them. But later when they have time to reflect, the guilt comes. Their conscience aches. The fact that they were ordered to kill does not wash the blood away. Nothing will."

We sit in silence. I learned early on that Lindsay doesn't need to fill silence with idle conversation. During our hectic investigation it was ideal because I needed every second to process, plan, and stay one step ahead of the Raiders and their divergent versions of events. Now, however, the silence is nearly unbearable.

"Did you hear about the suicide note?" I ask.

"He looked out for his men, right to the end."

"He did," I state quietly, my thoughts drifting to Fleury's sacrifice.

Lindsay and I share another moment of reflection, and I can't help but measure Fleury against Wolfe. Fleury's loyalty to his men stands in stark contrast to Wolfe's disloyalty to the same men. I push aside my negative thoughts to focus instead on the gratitude I feel for having served with General Lindsay. As I bid him a fond farewell, I steel myself to face the challenges ahead.

Lindsay nods. "You're a talented officer and lawyer. I hope our paths cross again."

"Thank you, sir," I say. "Good luck with your redeployment."

"Much appreciated," he responds. "Your determination to seek the truth was inspiring. Are you satisfied with the result?"

I pause, considering my answer. "Whether the final outcomes get us some measure of justice is still an open question."

"It's not easy," he agrees, "but Fleury's men must face the consequences for the choices they made."

I take a deep breath and then ask the questions that bothers me the most. "What about Colonel Wolfe? What about his choices, sir? What about his consequences?"

General Lindsay's expression tightens. "You mean the inequity of it, I assume?"

I nod.

"Wolfe may not face judgment from a general court-martial, but he will face career-ending consequences. The military justice system isn't perfect, but it does serve its purpose."

I frown and ask, "How so, sir?"

"While the unit's overly aggressive command climate may have made the killings more likely, Fleury and his men are the ones who crossed the line. They pulled the triggers and, as you so correctly pointed out, their obedience to Colonel Wolfe's order is not a defense. So, they will face prison and dishonorable discharges. Make no mistake, Wolfe will lose his career, but not in the public eye. The Army does not need to court-martial him to keep other commanders from making the same mistakes."

I try to accept his explanation about a system designed to maintain good order and discipline using different methods to achieve justice, but it's difficult for me to accept. "Yes, sir," I say, not convinced that justice should take a backseat to maintaining command authority.

Lindsay nods, acknowledging my reluctance to wholeheartedly accept his position. As we shake hands, I feel a strong mix of emotions. Respect for Lindsay. Disgust for Wolfe. Pity for Fleury and his men. On my walk back to the Al Faw palace, I contemplate the deadly choices and the bloody consequences that played out on Objective Walter. Although the path to justice is rarely a straight line, my moral compass is struggling to keep me on the jagged route I must now navigate without the benefit of General Lindsay's mentorship.

Tikrit, Iraq
15 September 2006

To lock things in before the Raiders redeploy en masse to Fort Campbell, I fly to Tikrit and represent the government at a joint pretrial hearing for Taylor, Willowby, and Gruber. All three elect to remain silent and decline to call witnesses. So, it only takes me a few hours to present an overview of the government's case. Two days later the hearing officer issues his report. In it, he finds probable cause to believe the three soldiers committed premeditated murder and recommends that the Army pursue the death penalty.

Baghdad, Iraq
18 September 2006

I sit silently across from Colonel Miller while she reads the hearing officer's report. "Great work, Jess," she says, laying it on her desk.

"There wasn't much to it," I say. "It was just a paper drill."

"Yes, but it rested upon the statements you and General Lindsay took during his investigation. This puts us in a strong position to negotiate deals. If the defense wants us to refer the cases noncapital, they need to plead guilty to premeditated murder. Of course, we'll have to check where General Benetti stands on the issue of capping their sentences at life with or without the possibility of parole."

"I'll reach out to the defense counsel and let them know they must request a trial before a judge alone, cooperate in companion cases, and sign stipulations of fact before we'll support any offer to plead."

"Right," Miller says, "and they must also promise not to raise compliance with Wolfe's Rules of Engagement at trial."

"I'm sorry, ma'am. I don't follow."

"Jess, we're operating from a position of power. We both know that obedience is never a defense. Let's lock it down and take the ROE off the table right away. That's the only way we can keep the defense from putting the Army on trial."

"While it is never a defense, ma'am, it may properly be considered as an extenuating circumstance or mitigating factor in sentencing."

"Either way, the defense may try to use it to distract, confuse, or mislead the court," Miller directs. "Tell the defense that taking the ROE off the table is part of the deal. That is not negotiable."

Fort Campbell, Kentucky
23 October 2006

Private First Class Charles Willowby and Specialist Jackson Gruber both enter into pretrial agreements with Lieutenant General Theodore Benetti. As part of their deals, they both tender written stipulations that the rules of engagement were not a factor in the murders.

Pursuant to his plea, the judge finds Willowby guilty of aggravated assault for shooting a grazing shot across the third detainee's head, and sentences Willowby to five years confinement. The next day, the same judge accepts Gruber's guilty plea for the murder of the second detainee, and hands down a twenty-year prison sentence.

In the quantum portion of their deals with the CG, Willowby had a sentence cap of three years and Gruber had a sentence cap of eighteen years. So, both soldiers benefit from their agreed-upon caps and receive the reduced sentences.

The judge is pleased with the outcomes, but it doesn't sit so well with me.

Willowby was damn lucky that his shot grazed, rather than killed, his detainee. And he was also damn lucky that I supported his plea offer despite its lenient sentencing cap. Gruber wasn't quite as lucky. His detainee died. I didn't support his offer to plea with a ten-year cap, because murder is murder and in Gruber's case it was premeditated. Still, it all seemed like such a tragic waste. A tragedy clearly set in motion by the Big Bad.

CHAPTER 32

Jess
Fort Campbell, Kentucky
10 January 2007

Specialist Taylor stands tall between his military defense counsel in Fort Campbell's small courtroom. In a clear, strong voice he pleads, "Not guilty, your honor," to the rail-thin judge presiding over the court-martial.

It's Taylor's right to plead not guilty and force the government to prove his guilt beyond a reasonable doubt, but his decision puzzles me. Sure, he will have a jury decide his case, rather than have a judge alone accepting his plea. But I will call Willowby and Gruber to prove my case. It takes me two long days to get in all the evidence necessary to prove my case. When the judge asks me to call my next witness, I respond with a firm, "The government rests, your honor."

The beady-eyed judge, the very same man who convicted and sentenced Willowby and Gruber late last year, asks the defense to call their first witness.

I glance over at Taylor, who hides his emotions behind a stoic mask. A defense counsel rises and says, "The defense calls Colonel Michael Wolfe."

Fear lurches in my gut just like when I read the Big Bad his rights back in Tikrit. That was on his turf. Now, even here on my turf, the fear still sits low in my stomach. Colonel Wolfe steps forward, his uniform laden with medals and insignia that reflect decades of distinguished service. He glances down and sneers as he passes inches from me.

I get up from my seat at the prosecution table and follow him to the witness stand. I keep my voice even as I direct him to raise his right hand and swear to tell the truth, the whole truth, and nothing but the truth. "Colonel Wolfe," I say, "will you please state your full name, rank, and unit of assignment for the record?"

As he locks eyes with me, I swear he is imagining how good it would feel to choke me to death. Instead, he states flatly, "Colonel Michael Wolfe. I command the Seventh Brigade."

"Your witness," I say to the defense and retreat to my seat.

"Colonel Wolfe," the defense counsel stands and asks, "were you present during the incident involving Staff Sergeant Fleury and his team's alleged mistreatment of detainees?"

Wolfe's eyes meet mine, and there's a flicker of something malicious there. He turns back to the defense counsel and says, "In accordance with the Fifth Amendment, I invoke my Constitutional right to remain silent."

A hushed murmur ripples through the courtroom.

I maintain my composure, but inside I'm rocked by Wolfe's invocation. The truth is ugly, but I assumed that a seasoned commander like Wolfe would stand firm, honor the values he swore to uphold, and testify.

The defense counsel presses and asks, "Did you order your men, including Specialist Taylor, to kill—"

The judge cuts off the defense counsel and turns to Colonel Wolfe. "You, sir, are permanently excused from this proceeding. You may return to duty."

Wolfe stands and strides out of the hushed courtroom. As he brushes past me, he says between gritted teeth, "Worthless fucking split-tail."

Heat rushes to my head. Why am I blushing? That arrogant son of a bitch just bullied me, and I'm the one who feels embarrassed?

I want to scream! I'm not surprised that Wolfe hates my guts—but hanging Taylor out to dry—it's unbelievable! Wolfe's loyalty to Taylor should far outweigh his selfish and pathetic desire to escape blame. Yet here he is, the Big Bad, invoking his right to remain silent and looking so damn smug about it too.

The defense asks for a delay, and the judge adjourns trial until after lunch. When we go back on the record, the defense calls their client to the stand. Specialist Taylor stands and calmly looks into the faces of the twelve panel members who will decide his fate. He steps up to the witness stand, turns, and looks at his wife and daughter sitting in the first row of the gallery, right behind his empty chair at the defense table.

I stand, approach, and swear him in. His righteous indignation is touched by a glimmer of fear. This is a pivotal moment; the one chance he has to tell the panel members his version of events.

The defense attorney begins by asking, "In your own words, can you please describe the events that took place on Objective Walter?"

Taylor's voice is steady, and his words are measured as he recounts the events that led up to the battlefield executions. He describes the tension, the chaos, and the difficult decisions made in the heat of the moment. He looks back at that fateful day with a somber honesty, revealing the dangers that he and his team faced. As he speaks, I notice that his testimony is resonating with the panel members. His account is not one full of bravado or excuses, but a candid retelling of the circumstances that led to the tragic outcome. His gaze shifts and connects with each member of the panel, as if imploring them to understand that the killings were not within his control.

I listen intently as Taylor paints a vivid picture of the harsh realities of war and the impossible decisions soldiers are forced to make. While the murders remain indefensible, his words give insight into the tangled web of duty, loyalty, and the demands of combat. The courtroom falls silent when his testimony concludes. The atmosphere is heavy with the horror of what he has revealed.

The judge asks me if I am ready to cross-examine Taylor. I stand and announce without hesitation, "The prosecution has no questions for the accused."

Yet another shocked murmur ripples through the courtroom. The judge's eyes bore into me, questioning my choice. I hold my ground because Taylor's testimony was an unflinching, honest account of what happened. So, there is no need for me to challenge it.

Specialist Taylor steps down from the stand, and pity wells inside me. While his actions were wrong, his testimony humanized him and the choices he made. I feel genuine sorrow for him, his wife, and his daughter, and once again I'm left wondering about the lines between empathy, accountability, and justice.

The panel deliberates for six hours. When they return to the courtroom, they convict Taylor for the one count of premeditated murder for the detainee he shot in the head. The judge then adjourns for the night, telling the panel members to return at 09:00 for the sentencing phase of trial.

Fort Campbell, Kentucky
11 January 2007

At 07:30 sharp, the defense attorneys and I meet privately with the judge in chambers. From the moment I first met him, I disliked the gaunt man and his bobbing Adam's apple. He never deployed but rose to the rank of full colonel based on his West Point degree and the Army's decision to send him to law school.

After exchanging brief pleasantries, he hands us a signed order. I read my copy silently. How can the judge sua sponte rule that the defense may not present evidence about Colonel Wolfe's kill order? How can he rule on this without first receiving a motion from me? I know that I could not ethically file such a motion because, if granted, it would suppress information that is clearly relevant to mitigate

Specialist Taylor's criminal state of mind when he killed the detainee.

I grip my pen tightly, trying to process the judge's out-of-nowhere order. Why doesn't anybody consider the damage the killings did to the soldiers who followed the kill order? Strangely, Fleury's death didn't call attention to it. Wolfe's silence also didn't change it. And now, the judge won't allow the defense to raise it as a mitigating factor in sentencing.

The ruling suppresses a crucial piece of information, and without it the truth will be hidden like a full moon behind dark clouds. I glance over at the lead defense counsel and his frustration mirrors mine.

"Your Honor," he says, "the defense respectfully objects."

I interject before the judge can answer. "The prosecution joins the defense's objection."

The judge turns his beady eyes on me, "Excuse me?"

"Sir, I don't think—"

"I don't care what you think," he snaps. "My ruling stands. Not one word about Colonel Wolfe or his alleged order, or I will hold the offending party in contempt."

It's maddening to see judicial power used so nakedly to obscure the truth. How am I supposed to ensure that justice is done, when the trial judge takes it upon himself to keep relevant evidence out of the courtroom? I lean back in my chair, running through my options. It's the court's duty to allow the defense to present its sentencing case, but the judge seems intent on protecting the Army's reputation, no matter the cost to Taylor.

The panel members are seated in the courtroom and ready to begin at 09:00 sharp. I stand and announce that the government will not call any sentencing witnesses. The judge glares at me in disapproval. He tells the defense to call their first witness.

They call First Sergeant Durham. He testifies to Taylor's outstanding military career and high rehabilitation potential. I have no follow-up questions for him. The defense then calls Mrs. Taylor to talk about her husband, their daughter, and the severe impact a prison sentence would have on their young family. I again have no questions. Finally, Taylor takes the stand. He takes responsibility for his actions, and requests leniency. The defense then rests.

The judge asks if I would like to call any rebuttal witnesses. A small part of me screams, *Call the Big Bad Wolfe*, but my better judgment prevails. I stand and answer stiffly, "No, sir."

The judge sends the panel to the deliberation room to discuss his sentencing instructions outside of their presence. He runs through a dozen standard instructions before announcing that the defense may not refer to Colonel Wolfe or mention his alleged kill order. He tells the bailiff to call the members, and once they're back in the jury box he turns to me. "Counsel, are you ready to present the government's sentencing argument?"

I take a deep breath and stand. "Your Honor, the prosecution waives its sentencing argument."

The panel members look surprised. The judge looks upset. But I hold my ground, because I can't in good conscience argue for a harsh sentence when I know that the full context of the killings has been hidden from the panel. I glance over at the defense team. Their surprise is palpable. Sitting down, I feel a mix of satisfaction and resignation. The system is flawed, but I am doing my best to level the playing field. As the proceedings continue, I remind myself why I'm here. Even when justice feels out of reach, I must keep pushing for what's right.

The defense argues that their client was a good and faithful soldier who, under the pressure of combat, lost his way. They argue that he has high rehabilitative potential and a young wife and daughter depending on him. The panel deliberates for two hours and sentences Taylor to ten years confinement and a dishonorable discharge.

CHAPTER 33

Jess
Baghdad, Iraq
13 January 2007

I have plenty of time to brood on my flights from Nashville back to Baghdad. But for the erroneous ear-taking allegation, the murders would have never come to light. A justice system that allows commanders to filter the information released and thereby hide the truth isn't very just. If Wolfe had been around to approve the unit's whitewashed investigation, Fleury and his men would have been portrayed by the Raiders as heroes. How many other incidents have been swept under the rug? It's maddening to think that truth can be so easily concealed and accountability can be so easily evaded. And in this case, when the truth finally did come out, the Army circled its wagons and protected the Big Bad, leaving his trigger-pullers on their own to face the consequences.

How can I work within a criminal justice system so deeply dedicated to protecting the Army and its reputation? I take a deep breath and remind myself why I've always been passionate about pursuing justice, wherever it takes me. I have a need to keep pushing, keep questioning, and keep demanding accountability.

As I cross Al Faw Palace's faux drawbridge, I catch a glimpse of

Saddam's killer carp lazily floating in the murky water. I take the marble steps up three flights, cross the busy JAG office, and join Colonel Miller in her corner office. It's late and I'm exhausted from my trip, but I need to back brief her on Taylor's case.

As I tell her about it, Colonel Wolfe's decision to invoke sticks in my throat. Was it driven by his views on duty and accountability? Or is he simply a coward who values his career above everything else? I think the latter and can't shake the disgust I feel toward a leader who abandoned his troops when they most needed him.

"Jess, this was an extremely challenging case," Colonel Miller begins, "and your emotions are running high. You need to take a step back and view it all with a more detached understanding of the big picture."

I nod, as my frustration simmers. "Yes, ma'am, but when Taylor needed Wolfe to be honest and take responsibility for the kill order, Wolfe abandoned him and took the Fifth."

Colonel Miller leans back in her chair and looks up at the ceiling. She lets out a breath and looks into my eyes. "Command is never black and white. Wolfe made a grievous error in his interpretation of the ROE, and he'll pay for it with his career. And I'm sure he'll struggle with the fallout long after he quietly retires."

I struggle to control my anger and say much too sharply, "Taylor doesn't get to retire quietly."

Colonel Miller shrugs. "Maybe Wolfe thought invoking might help Taylor's case?"

I wrinkle my nose and shake my head.

Miller continues, "By the way he invoked on the stand, the panel members might have inferred that Wolfe was partly to blame?"

"No, ma'am, I was there. It didn't come off that way."

"Maybe Wolfe hoped that the general would grant him testimonial immunity?"

I shake my head and look at Miller like she's lost her mind.

"Jess, there are nuances here that you are ignoring."

That, or the cowardly son of a bitch was just out to save his own skin, I think, but out of respect I refrain from saying it out loud to Miller. Instead, I say, "I just can't comprehend a leader giving an order and then abandoning his men."

Miller leans forward, her tone sympathetic. "As difficult as it is for you to accept Wolfe's disloyalty, you must respect his right to remain silent."

I nod, acknowledging the bottom line. While loyalty should be a two-way street, the Fifth Amendment is clear. As I leave Colonel Miller's office, I'm amazed at just how far short justice can fall.

Baghdad, Iraq
30 March 2007

I'm going blind reviewing case notes and drafting charges when my phone rings. I glance at the phone's small screen, and "Lt. Col. Brown" flashes. I answer, bracing myself for whatever news he might have from Fort Campbell.

"Major Gilbert," his voice crackles over the line, "it's been a while."

"Indeed it has, Lieutenant Colonel Brown," I reply, my tone neutral. "To what do I owe the pleasure of your call?"

"I thought you might want an update on Colonel Wolfe." My heart skips a beat at the mention of Wolfe. It's been a month since I saw him leave the courtroom. I push aside my emotions and focus on Brown's words. "I was in the grandstands last week when the Raiders assembled for their final formation under the Big Bad. It was a cold, rainy afternoon and Wolfe ran through all the standard stuff. He thanked them for their service, told them what a bunch of heroes they were, and wished his successor well."

I listen intently, the image of the Raiders standing in formation forming in my mind.

"Wolfe only choked up once, when he read the names of

the twelve Raiders killed in action. When the ceremony ended, thousands of rain-soaked Raiders lined up to shake Wolfe's hand."

The man who had no problem leaving Taylor swinging in the wind choked up for the lives lost under his command? It paints a complex picture, one that challenges my two-dimensional view of the Big Bad.

"But that's not all." Brown's voice pulls me back. "Wolfe claimed that the brigade that immediately preceded the Raiders lost three times as many soldiers."

I furrow my brow, absorbing the information. Those numbers raise some serious questions about the nature of the losses and the circumstances surrounding them. The truth is always more complex than mere statistics can convey.

"And while the Big Bad stood up there taking pride in his grim numbers," Brown says, "I noticed that they failed to account for Fleury and the noncombatants who died." He pauses and adds, "Anyway, General Benetti's reprimand worked. At the end of the ceremony, they announced Wolfe would retire."

"Thank goodness," I say. I thank Jimmy for the call and hang up. I'm left with a deep unease. In my mind, the pieces of the puzzle are still coming together, revealing an intricate tapestry of issues, loyalties, and repercussions. But at the heart of it, Wolfe primed Fleury and his men to kill and then left them to take the blame. The disloyalty and cowardice Wolfe displayed at Taylor's court-martial shocked me and lingers like heartburn. It stands as a reminder that our hardest choices are the ones that define us. Of his many sins, the betrayal of Taylor is the most unforgivable.

My thoughts turn away from Wolfe to Colonel Miller. Her loyalty to General Benetti is rock solid. She wholeheartedly believes in Benetti's vision and fully supports his strategies for stabilizing Iraq. Her unwavering support is evident in every decision she makes and every order she carries out. But could she extend that same level of loyalty to a commander like Wolfe, whose violence pushed the boundaries of law to its breaking point?

I am uncertain of the answer.

How would she handle receiving an ill-advised order, such as Wolfe's kill order? Denise Miller does not shy away from difficult decisions, but I can't help wondering where she would draw the line. Would she speak out and challenge her boss? Like Lindsay, Miller's loyalties are rooted in her deep sense of patriotism, duty, and honor, tempered by a strong instinct for what is right and what is wrong.

I contemplate the lofty, amorphous concept of the Rule of Law. Everyone says they support it, but what is it? It's defined as, "a set of principles, or ideals, for ensuring an orderly and just society." Okay, orderly and just is good, but based upon what principles? Ideally, shouldn't it stand for the idea that nobody is above the law? Don't we deserve a system of justice that's blind to rank and applies equally to everyone?

Suddenly, I realize that I'm less concerned about Lindsay and Miller and more concerned about me. Would my integrity survive mission planning with a commander like Wolfe? Would I have been swept up in his zealous drive to exterminate the enemy? Even after the fact, General Lindsay had a very hard time second-guessing Wolfe's expansive view of his battlefield authority as the on-scene commander.

"Don't worry," I tell myself. "You'll never have to make that call." But I'm not so sure and wonder if my rock-solid integrity isn't already cracked beyond repair.

Baghdad, Iraq
31 March 2007

The Big Bad's pride in his twelve-person KIA statistic occupies my mind all morning. What about the unit kill boards? What about men not counted in the twelve, like the detainees and Fleury? What about Willowby, Gruber, and Taylor sitting in jail? What about the soldiers who didn't fire warning shots and are haunted by the people they killed? What about those who shot center mass before the MAM could get his hands up above his ears? Will they ever forget the crack of the round just before it hit?

I open my email, fill in the Big Bad's address, and type:

> *Dear Colonel (Ret.) Wolfe:*
>
> *Congratulations on your retirement; it is very well-deserved. When you reflect on your career, I offer you some points to consider.*
>
> *Your men trusted you, and you failed them. You failed because you didn't trust them to distinguish between combatants and noncombatants. You willfully ignored your legal and moral obligation to respond proportionately to legitimate threats. Instead, you installed unit kill boards, banned warning shots, encouraged your soldiers to shoot center mass before people could "actively" surrender, and gave trophy knives to troops for their first kill.*
>
> *When you look in the mirror each morning, I'm confident you see the pleading eyes of the twenty-four men you lost in Panama and Iraq. I hope you also see the accusing eyes of the scores of innocent civilians who died because of your overly aggressive command climate and illegal orders. I hope you see the disappointed eyes of Willowby, Gruber, and Taylor. I hope you feel the sting of Fleury's suicide and that his ghost haunts your dreams as it haunts mine.*
>
> *You and I both know that you gave a kill order, and it set in motion events that led to battlefield executions. Hiding behind the Fifth Amendment shielded you from public*

scrutiny, but it can't shield you from two simple truths: you gave the order, and you abandoned the men who followed it.
  Sincerely yours,
  Major Jessica Gilbert

An hour later, the Big Bad responds. I pause and then delete it, because I don't care what he thinks.

Everyone judges the killings from where they stand. It's the quickest and easiest way to make sense of it. It's too overwhelming to consider all the causes and effects, and too painful to sort out the whole ugly mess. It's much easier to celebrate Wolfe as a hero or damn him as a cold-blooded killer. But just choosing a side misses the point, doesn't it? Orders were given. Orders were obeyed. Prisoners were killed. Constitutional rights were invoked. Raiders went to prison. Wolfe didn't. How can any of that sit right with anyone?

THE END

US ARMY ACRONYMS

15-6	An investigation conducted in accordance with Army Regulation 15-6
AAR	After-action review
AWOL	Absent without leave, a crime under military law
CHU	Containerized housing unit, a.k.a. SEA-hut
CID	Criminal Investigation Division
IED	Improvised explosive device
FOB	Forward Operating Base
FOBBIT	A play on "Hobbit" used to describe soldiers who never leave the FOB
IO	Investigating officer
MAM	Military-aged male
MEDEVAC	Medical evacuation
NCO	Noncommissioned Officer
NJP	Nonjudicial punishment (a.k.a. Article 15)
OPORD	Operations order
PAC	Personnel action center
PID	Positive identification

S-1	Adjutant who oversees the PAC at a battalion or brigade
S-2	Intelligence officer who oversees the 2-shop at a battalion or brigade
S-3	Operations officer who oversees the TOC at a battalion or brigade
SEA-hut	Southeast Asia Hut, a.k.a. CHU
SECDEF	Secretary of defense
SJA	Staff judge advocate
SOP	Standard operating procedure
TOC	Tactical operations center
UCMJ	Uniform Code of Military Justice, or military criminal law
WMD	Weapon of mass destruction

ABOUT THE AUTHOR

Lieutenant Colonel (Ret.) Brad Huestis served in the US Army as a paratrooper, artilleryman, and judge advocate. He is Airborne and Ranger qualified. Twice deployed, he received the NATO Medal and Bronze Star. He published *Ahab*, his award-winning debut novel about a wounded warrior recovering in Bavaria, in 2021.

https://www.koehlerbooks.com/writer/brad-huestis/

https://www.goodreads.com/author/show/21550058.Brad_Huestis

www.amazon.com/author/brad.huestis

IN PRAISE OF AHAB

Love *AHAB: A Hockey Story*, wonderful job!

    Bobby Orr, # 4

AHAB wonderfully captures how hockey in Germany differs from North America—with the outward passion of English Premier League soccer meeting the fervent loyalty of NCAA college football—and reminds us that it's the bond with the "boys in the room" that gives players the connections they'll never forget.

    Denny Wolfe, Senior Producer, ESPN Features Unit

Army veteran's hockey novel celebrates sports as rehab for wounded warriors.

    Seth Robson, *Stars & Stripes*

AHAB centers on teamwork and belonging—in life, the military and hockey—and what happens when some are left behind. The military themes and Bavarian settings are instantly recognizable and relatable, and you'll find yourself cheering for Will Foley as he battles through rehab to get back to his unit and onto the ice.

    Carolyn Warmbold, Editor and Author

Coming of age story? Check. Love interest? Check. Military connection? Check. Foreign setting? Check. Brad Huestis skillfully weaves a coming of age story that checks every box—throw in a good looking woman or two and some Oktoberfest bier, and it's close to perfect. A fun read with hidden depths that will stay with you long after you finish the last chapter.

 Genie Hughes, Berlin Brigade Judge Advocate

The story's Bavarian settings are vivid and unforgettable. A must read...

 MilitaryInGermany.com

Brad Huestis's debut novel is both charming and thought-provoking, combining the emotional freedom of play with the unflinching realities of life and the consequences of our actions. *AHAB* is a compelling story that goes beyond the subject of wartime and examines the human condition, showing we are capable of much more than we believe.

 Justin Herzog, author of *First Wave* and *Into the Void*

I recommend *AHAB* to lovers of the beautiful game of hockey and all lovers of fascinating fiction stories.

 OnlineBookClub.Org

ACKNOWLEDGMENTS

Without my wife's candid feedback and loving support, I'd be lost. Trusted friends and family also read and generously shared feedback on very rough drafts. Carolyn Warmbold, Bill Delehunt, Mariah St. John, Genie Hughes, Colonel (Ret.) Randy Swansiger, David Lindsay, and Bonnie Lindsay, all generously pointed me in the right direction.

I owe Colonel (Ret.) Denise Vowell and Colonel (Ret.) Mickey Miller special thanks for providing spot-on feedback. They were two of my favorite JAG Corp mentors and inspired the Colonel Denise Miller character. Lieutenant Colonel (Ret.) Alison Tulud, Michael Jetton, Dan Stone, Jim Neumiller, and Monica Lynch shared their valuable feedback on later drafts, and Kraig Hays generously proofread my final manuscript before I turned it over to the pros at Koehler Books.

John Koehler taught me the ins and outs of getting my manuscript from draft to market. His pocket guides to publishing and marketing are must-reads for aspiring authors. Becky Hilliker, Koehler's amazing executive editor took my storytelling and prose to the next level, and Danielle Koehler created a brilliant cover.

My heartfelt thanks now ends with you. I sincerely hope you enjoyed *The Big Bad*, because I sincerely enjoyed writing it and hope you stay tuned for my next novel—a heist thriller set in sunny Barcelona.

Brad Huestis
July 2025

www.ingramcontent.com/pod-product-compliance
Lightning Source LLC
LaVergne TN
LVHW041913070526
838199LV00051BA/2603